SHADOWS OF THE SOUL

ADALINE WINTERS

II

Copyright © 2022 by Adaline Winters

All rights reserved

No part of this book may be reproduced, stored in a retrieval system, or transmitted by any means, electronic, mechanical, photocopying, recording or otherwise without the express written permission from the author.

Cover design

by

Liberty Champion

IV

For my Dad,
You taught me that with patience and hard work I can achieve anything.

For my Mum,
You taught me to follow my dreams no matter my age.

Well done parents – you shaped a hardworking, stubborn, driven woman who is following her dreams and making them happen.

Chapter One

It's getting hot in here...

The handwritten letter clutched in my hand fluttered in the breeze, it having left a sour tang on the back of my tongue. If I let the paper go, the wind wouldn't relieve me of my burden. The elegant scrawl belied the nature of the words. My Grandmother was reminding me of my obligation to update her on the other factions. She was head of The Order—leader of the elementals, and I was uniquely positioned to provide intel on both the shifters and the vampires.

"Bear," Rebecca declared with a snap of her fingers.

I squinted at the burly man unfolding himself from the driver's seat of a sparkling new black truck. "Rhino," I countered.

"How obscure," Rebecca muttered.

"Final answer?" Maggie asked from her perch between us on the porch swing.

"Yes," Rebecca and I agreed.

'Guess the shifter' was our current game. Hudson Abbot, The Principal, leader of all American pack affiliated shape shifters, Terror of Tennessee, and bane of my life, had gleaned some of my secrets after we joined forces to stop the menace that was killing supernaturals. He'd taken it upon himself to keep a closer eye on me by moving into the converted stables on my property. Consequently, I'd gained a steady stream of random shifters traipsing across my land. Hudson had an unhealthy obsession with learning my secrets, along with his chief of security, Dangerous Dave. They dug and dug. So far they'd come back empty-handed, but one wrong move from me and my world would turn upside down.

Hudson was perceptive, analyzing, dangerous, and damn right annoying. He also kissed me like his life depended on it, and I was a heartbeat and hormone away from becoming a notch on his bedpost.

"You're both wrong. He's a mongoose," Maggie announced. Shifters could sense each other's animal - it was a pack hierarchy and survival thing. A fox didn't want to be challenging a lion.

I blinked. Mongoose shifter? That's new. Shifters were larger than their animal counterparts. How big would he be?

"You know, this could be avoided if you'd just sleep with him. Get it out of your system," Rebecca said, plucking imaginary lint off her dress.

"If it's inconvenient, why don't you sleep with him?" I snapped.

She lifted her nose in the air. "He's not interested in me. Hudson Abbot only has eyes for a certain fiery-haired, green-eyed elemental. He'd probably move back to pack territory before the weekend if you got naked and dirty with him."

I glanced at her. "I'm not having a one-night stand with a male who regards me with suspicion and contempt. Also, what are you saying? That I'm so boring in bed he'd run back to the shifter females before the sun had risen?"

"Don't be ridiculous. You can act bad in bed. Lay there like a sack of potatoes." She sighed and lifted her hands in the air. "All this passive aggressive flirting is making my hormones crazy."

"Still, it's not a good enough excuse. I will not sleep with someone to satiate your hormones."

"Spoil sport."

"Sex addict," I threw back.

Hudson exited the stables and glanced our way. His chocolate brown gaze collided with mine and a sinful smile played on his lips. He was tall, with strong thighs wrapped in blue jeans and a white shirt that bordered on needing a restraining order with how it was clinging to him. The breeze carried the scent of freshly cut grass mingled with a rich wild cedar that was purely Hudson. Ugh, now I was scenting him like a cat in heat.

I sighed and leaned back. "He has enough shifter honeys to keep him occupied. I'm simply a challenge. He doesn't want me, he wants to prove he could have me."

"So cynical," Rebecca murmured. She was right. I was cynical. Cynical kept you breathing. My last relationship ended in my torture and permanent maiming. It was bound to leave its psychic mark. Hudson knew my history, yet he pursued me all the same.

"Incoming," Maggie said before jumping up and running into the house. The front door slammed behind her. Maggie was a bobcat shifter who'd arrived to me alone, afraid, and abused. I'd offered her safety, a roof over her head, and food. In return, she helped to run my bed-and-breakfast home for the supernaturally inclined. Watching her emerge into a butterfly was worth it. But Hudson terrified her. It wasn't his fault, he'd outlawed the arranged marriage her father was forcing Maggie into; but while her mind had caught up, her heart hadn't.

I winced as he breached the ward, my magic pulsing around him, assessing his threat and allowing him through. No murderous thoughts from The Principal today, lucky me.

"You moved the ward boundary?" Rebecca asked.

"With us being the new popular shifter hangout, I had to, or suffer with permanent migraines."

"It's dangerous," she mused.

"It's necessary."

The wards used to outline my property, including the stables. Now they looped around the main house and gardens but excluded the main gate and stables, so the shifters were able to traipse back and forth as they pleased.

Hudson arrived at the edge of my wrap-around porch. The barrier was seven feet off the ground. He tensed and jumped clean over the white fence, landing lightly in front of me and Rebecca. I scrunched the letter in my hand tighter, folding the paper so it disappeared into my palm.

"Ladies," he drawled. His southern lilt was faint, but smooth like warm whisky. It made my insides melt, and my heart pitter patter a happy dance against my ribs. *We talked about this,* I reminded the useless organ. *He would tear you to tiny, tiny pieces after touching our soul.*

"Steps not good enough for you?" I asked, jerking my head toward the steps six feet away.

His lips twitched. "Steps are overrated. I took the most direct path to reach you."

I sighed. "Principal, what can I do for you?" See, I could be nice. My heart rolled its eyes and sulked.

"Can I borrow a whisk?" he asked, leaning back on the banister. It creaked, but held. Kudos to the solid workmanship, holding Hudson up was no mean feat. His ego doubled his weight.

"I'll get it," Rebecca said, rising to her feet and floating away in a swath of pale yellow cotton. She was ethereal, timeless, classic. Rebecca was a vampire princess and conducted herself in a regal manner that was bred, not learned.

"What does the Principal need a whisk for?" I wondered.

Hudson grinned. "Pancakes, would you like to come over for breakfast?"

I opened my mouth to decline. This was also a game. He came to ask for something, sugar, flour, a whisk— invited me for a meal and I politely declined the offer. The paper in my hand tripled in weight and I pressed my lips together. If I had breakfast, I could report back to my Grandmother and she would see I'd done my duty.

"I make fabulous pancakes. Blueberries are my speciality," he ventured, sensing my hesitation.

"Fine."

He blinked and folded his arms. "Fine?"

I gazed up at him, the sun haloed around his head in the cloudless sky. "Fine, I'm a sucker for blueberry pancakes, and if I come this once, you can leave me alone for a month."

He grinned. "A week at most and I'm sure we can upgrade 'fine' to 'exceptional.'"

I rolled my eyes. "Let it go." I'd once informed him the man who stole my heart would have to be exceptional—he'd been making a big deal out of it ever since.

Rebecca opened the front door and brandished a shiny metal whisk at Hudson. "Your whisk."

He plucked it from her fingers and smirked. "Tomorrow morning at seven?"

Rebecca's mouth fell open.

"Fine," I gritted out.

I'll survive breakfast. It was the smallest and quickest meal of the day. Get in, get out, and report back. Nothing to see here, Grandmother. My brain slow clapped at my cunning plan. Hudson turned and jumped over the fence again, landing with the feral grace only seen in cats.

"Breakfast is the most important meal of the day," he called out. "Prepare to savor it, Cora. Every single morsel will be an experience."

"Breakfast is a necessity, not an experience."

"Then you are doing it wrong. Breakfast with you will be entertaining."

"I'm not your entertainment."

"Of course not. But what follows should be."

I groaned and leaned back as he slunk away. We were doomed.

"You're eating with the Principal?" Rebecca mused. "Is that after a night of hot and sweaty kinky shifter sex, or is it a fuel up before a morning of hot and sweaty shifter kinky sex?"

"There will be no hot and sweaty, kinky, shifter sex."

"Okay, no kink," Rebecca agreed.

Help me, I'm surrounded by supernatural sex-starved addicts.

Maggie bounced out of the front door, her dark hair a wild tangle around her face. "You're letting him feed you? In his home?" she whispered.

Hudson threw me a glance over his shoulder, grinned his predatory smile, white, perfect teeth on display, and winked.

I frowned and narrowed my gaze. "Technically, it's my home. Why?"

Maggie shuffled on her sandals, the soles grazing the wooden floor as she glanced at Hudson. "Um, nothing."

Hudson whipped his shirt over his head with one hand and let it fall to the ground. He picked up an ax left buried in the tree stump, dropped a large piece of timber on it, and swung the ax. The wood split in two with a loud crack. The birds chattered in the trees. I wondered if they too were in awe of the specimen before us. His muscles bunched and tensed with the motion.

"Holy vampire ovaries, that man is a thirst trap," Rebecca mumbled.

"Why the hell is he chopping wood? It's not even cold," I pointed out.

"Does it matter?" she shot back.

"Umm, so they've grown again," Maggie said. She hooked a thumb over her shoulder. "Do you want to see?

I jumped to my feet and followed a twitchy Maggie with my vampire princess sidekick in tow. We trotted down the steps and around the outside of the house. We passed under some mighty magnolia trees whose leaves rustled in the breeze and entered the garden area reserved for the dead. Unmarked graves dotted the lawn, twenty-five in total. If you weren't part of a pack or vampire house, you were a loner. Loners didn't have access to consecrated ground, and were subsequently denied the rights of passage. I had lots of land, and a gift to help those loners pass on. During the final fight with Ric, the elemental, he'd revealed I'd not been simply giving the dead a place to rest. I'd been getting them a back door pass to heaven. After crossing Jennifer over, Ric's last victim, I ceased crossing over loners. Until I better understood the mechanics of my powers, I deemed messing with the Almighty's grand plan to be unwise. I didn't want to draw attention to myself or my activities.

We came to a stop under my largest magnolia tree, its branches draping over the ground casting a sweet heady fragrance in the surrounding air. Tom Wayfer was buried here. He should have been laid to rest in the Tupperware tub I'd gathered his exploded body into. But Maggie, in her teenage wisdom and thoughtfulness about recycling, had emptied him into the ground and covered his remains with soil. All creatures have residual magic. It's why we bury our dead in coffins and jars. If that magic fell into the wrong hands, it would be dangerous. White roses bloomed over the plot. They sprawled along the lawn and climbed up the trunk of the tree before weaving amongst the branches. The roses themselves weren't bad news.

"Didn't you cut these down a few days ago?" Rebecca asked.

"Yes."

"Should they be bleeding like that?" Maggie asked, leaning over to study the crimson droplets rolling over the snowy velvet petals.

"No."

Rebecca wrinkled her nose and stepped back. "What does it mean?"

My gaze darted over the flowers. "Nothing good," I answered. Magic skittered over the ground, the charge raising the hairs on my arms. The heavy scent of roses coated my mouth like fur. Someone had screwed with Tom's remains. Something unnatural lurked on my property, something that had corrupted a symbol of purity. Evil.

Chapter Two

Mushrooms are the devil's food.

It's a little known fact that shifters don't howl at the moon, and vampires can sunbathe. Both species had hearts that beat, and being bitten by either resulted in blood loss, but not a dramatic change of genetics. However, the rivalry between the two factions was on point. The only thing they hated more than each other was my faction, the elementals. We were considered an unstable, unpredictable, and unnatural race, despite our magic being rooted in the elements that surrounded the natural earth. Hudson told me it was because of our gifts. That they couldn't be sure what they were facing when going head to head with one of us. It was more fundamental than that. Elementals were embedded into normal society. They taught your children math, dispensed your medication, and advised the president on matters of security. We were everywhere. It wasn't our abilities the other factions didn't like, it was our influence.

Still, the shifters and vampires used our skill sets. Medical care proved one of the biggest issues for shifters. There were few doctors in the supernatural arena to see to their needs. I was trained and had the basic equipment to treat ninety percent of problems shifters faced, after all, their kind didn't get cancer or suffer with heart attacks. My side business brought in more revenue than the bed-and-breakfast that catered to lone supernaturals. As of two months ago, the pack had employed me to check into all shifter deaths. My gift, or curse, depending on how you viewed the world, meant I was uniquely qualified to do this. Being a psychic retro enabled me to view the last moments of someone's life.

Rebecca floated through the kitchen door, her nose wrinkling at the fried chicken on my fork. To my knowledge, she was the only vegetarian vampire in existence. It seemed unnatural.

"What is that smell?" she asked as she opened the refrigerator. The weird aroma hit me a second later. I dropped my fork.

"Maggie cooked," I explained.

Maggie could bake cookies. Any kind of cookies; double chocolate, lemon, oatmeal. She was an expert. Now take her out of that speciality and she could ruin toast.

Rebecca reached inside the fridge and took out a foil covered glass dish. She peered under the wrapping like she was checking for a bomb. "I think it's lasagna," she stated with a sigh of relief.

Maggie bounced into the room with a smile as big as the sun. "You found my mushroom lasagna. It's a new recipe."

I grabbed my fork and shoved the fried chicken in my mouth to hide my smirk. Rebecca eyed the dish with new found horror. "Thank you, I've already eaten."

"Nonsense, you can try a bite," Maggie said, snatching the dish and heading for the microwave.

"Remove the foil," Rebecca and I reminded her.

"Yes, yes, I'm not stupid," Maggie muttered, following our instructions and shoving the dish in the microwave. The front door creaked open and the familiar sound of expensive Italian leather slapped against the wooden floors. I got comfy, this should be good.

Sebastian rounded the kitchen door and blinked at the microwave. Too late now, she's seen you. Should have run when you smelled the mushrooms.

"Sebastian," Maggie said, grabbing some plates from the cupboard. "Perfect timing to try my new mushroom lasagna."

I'll hand it to the Vampire Prince of North America. He had a Vegas-worthy poker face. He slid into the chair across from me, his eyes burning holes into my head in accusation as Maggie presented him with a steaming plate of gray and pale cream slop. He armed himself with a fork and eyeballed the plate. Bella, or the White Furry Menace as I'd nicknamed her, flounced into the room with a mouse between her teeth. She dropped it on Sebastian's expensive loafers, turned, stuck her tail in the air and slunk out the room. Bella was a floozy. She offered males gifts. But me? Her shelter and caregiver? Nothing but haughty looks. Sebastian and Rebecca eyed her with jealousy. Being a cat excused you from sampling Maggie's culinary delights.

My plate of fried chicken disappeared and some of the bland slop appeared in front of me.

"It's better for you," Maggie said with her hands on her hips. "Everyone should aim to have at least two meat free meals a week."

Sebastian, myself, and Rebecca scooped a forkful and simultaneously deposited it in our mouths—one for all and all for one. I swallowed, and it came straight back into my mouth, my throat rebelling against the slimy taste. Like slugs slithering onto my tongue. Rebecca's delicate features twisted, and Sebastian chewed thoughtfully. I redoubled my efforts and won the argument with my body. It was heavy on the garlic, sloppy in texture, and the weird little crunchy bits tasted suspiciously like burnt parmesan.

"Could I have my chicken? I don't want it to go to waste," I asked.

Maggie huffed and held my plate hostage. "You don't like it?"

"I'm not a big lover of mushrooms."

"Me either," Sebastian said, jumping on my excuse and placing the fork on the plate.

Maggie turned to Rebecca. "And you?"

She tilted her head. "I like the concept, but it needs something."

Maggie swapped my plate, and I tucked into the chicken, devouring it before anyone got any bright ideas about stealing my food again.

"It's Monday," I stated. "What are you doing here?"

Sebastian blinked. "Can I not come to see my best friend without intentions?"

I arched a brow. Sebastian was beautiful. Everything screamed perfection from his manicured nails to his trimmed five o'clock shadow.

"She's having breakfast with Hudson tomorrow," Rebecca stated.

"Traitor," I mouthed.

She shrugged. "I'm living my nonexistent social life through you."

Sebastian's eyebrow twitched. "He invited you for breakfast?"

Maggie shot him a nervous look. "Yes," I answered.

"Alone?" Sebastian checked.

"I assume so."

"Is he cooking?"

"What is this? Twenty questions? Would you like me to film it for you?"

"Is. He. Cooking?"

"Yes, he borrowed a whisk. He's making pancakes."

"Blueberry," Rebecca commented.

I waved my fork at her. "What she said."

Sebastian leaned back in his chair with a huff. "He's playing hardball."

"He's playing with fire," I muttered. "But what's the problem?"

"Nothing," Sebastian said. "Just don't reciprocate the offer."

"Wasn't planning on it," I answered. The sooner it was over with, the sooner I could report to my grandmother, because I'd be damned if she was visiting me here. "But you still haven't explained why you are here."

Sebastian sighed. "The Princess of Italy is currently in residence."

Rebecca groaned. "Maria? She's beautiful, but a bitch."

Sebastian ran a hand down his face. "Every month it's someone new."

The king and queen of American vampires were busy hunting for a suitable bride for their son. Being my best friend, I often ran interference for Sebastian—appearing as his date for the obligatory monthly family meal. King Leon hated me. Queen Aira tolerated me. Fun times.

"So you're hiding?" I asked.

"I'm visiting my best friend, checking on her healing."

I rotated my ankle. It still ached, particularly at night. "I'm all good."

He nodded. I reached across the table and gave his arm a squeeze. "How long is she staying?"

He shrugged. "Until she gets a ring on her finger."

I pressed my lips together. "Perhaps you could have a long engagement?"

He glared at me. "The second my father sniffs weakness, I'll be at the altar faster than you can say honeymoon."

Rebecca hummed under her breath. "I'd offer to be your wife, but I'd cause more drama than a celebrity at a teenage party."

He shook his head. "No, it's time I addressed my responsibilities."

I grimaced in sympathy for Sebastian. "It's time?" I checked.

He nodded. "It's time."

Oh boy.

CHAPTER THREE

Heebie Jeebies.

We define insomnia as habitual sleeplessness. I yo-yoed between being an insomniac and a chronic sleeper. When I did sleep, not even the dead could wake me. Which was a good thing, as they were often the cause of my unconscious state.

Tonight, sleep eluded me. I threw my legs across the sheets, seeking the cool patches of cotton and concentrated on the luminous sheen of the full moon hung low in the cloudless sky. It was closer to the Earth tonight, a super moon that was a reminder we were both insignificant in the grand scheme of things and part of something wondrous. The heavy hum of power from the room on the other side of my apartment taunted me with my ignorance, my arrogance, and my stupidity.

Heaven. I had a direct line to Heaven. How many of the loners had I granted access to somewhere I shouldn't? How many had sins which weighed their souls and bound them for Hell?

I rolled onto my back and stared at the slowly rotating fan. The whirling set my teeth on edge. An unusual thrum of power rumbled through me. I huffed, swung my legs over the side, and pattered through my living room on bare feet. I drew the key from the chain hanging around my neck and chanted the spell to unlock the door. My hand paused on the cool metal handle before I pushed it open and faced my demons. A bitter note of deceit tinted the swirl of peace that encompassed me. I'd duped Heaven. I'd fed it at least one soul that wasn't worthy and possibly damned my own. Ignorance didn't equal innocence. The orb in the center of the room glowed an ethereal white. Wisps of pure energy caressed the ceiling and walls. I grabbed the infused oil from the side table and poured it around the orb in a circle while whispering the incantation meant to close portals. Bitter citrus and sage seeped into the air as the liquid settled in the burnt out crease left behind by my earlier attempts. I snagged the matches, lit one and dropped it onto the oil. Fire spun along the floor and intensified the sage, the orb shrank in on itself. I raised my voice and sunk more magic into every word that passed my lips as I commanded the portal to shut. My power sought the cracks and exploited them. It dug its claws into the portal and tightened the noose, drawing it closed.

"Para de lastimarme."

My head snapped to the right. A thin African American boy dressed in blue shorts and a white T-shirt too small for his body stood before me. He was seven years old at most. My heart shattered at the lost and pained look in his deep brown eyes. The orb flared and doubled in size, slipping through my net.

"Shit," I mumbled as the fiery oil burnt out and left another crisp ochre mark on my hardwood floors. The boy disappeared, leaving me alone with my road to Heaven wide open.

I stumbled through the door into the living room. "Harry," I hollered as I flopped on my sofa. My ghostly friend shot through the wall and hovered over my slumped body.

He peered down at me. "Are you well?"

I ran a hand through my long copper hair. "Do you still feel a pull to this house?"

He shook his head and clasped his hands behind his back. "No, not since you destroyed the soul stone. I stay because you need me, not because I'm compelled."

My head dropped on the pillow. "That's what I thought." So why was the ghost of a seven-year-old child hanging around my house? This was not good.

"Should I retrieve Miss Lexington?" Harry asked with a frown.

I huffed a laugh and slapped a hand over my forehead. "How would you do that?"

A deep frown marred Harry's features. He was still struggling with the drawbacks of being departed, mainly because I was the only person who could see and hear him.

"Don't worry," I reassured him. "I'm okay."

"Are you sure? It's time for breakfast. Perhaps some sustenance will recharge your batteries?"

A groan left my throat as I slammed my eyes closed. "Hudson, right." I had a pancake date with Terror of Tennessee.

"Ah, the first romantic stirrings of true love," Harry lamented. I peeked one eye open to catch him staring wistfully out the window, caught in some long ago memory of meeting his wife.

"The Principal isn't looking for my heart, he's only interested in my vagina."

"I think you underestimate the draw he has to you," Harry spluttered.

"No, I haven't. When The Terror of Tennessee wants to cook me breakfast, it's for one thing only and it's not to spend time with my sparkling personality."

"He's cooking you breakfast?"

"Yes."

"In his home?"

I sat bolt upright. "Yes."

"Alone?"

"Yes! Why does everyone keep asking me this?"

"No reason," Harry said as he darted through my wall and disappeared into the house somewhere. What the hell was I missing? Had I committed a shifter faux pas? Had I accepted an offer of marriage via pancakes? Just my luck.

I swept through my rear garden to check on the progress of the bleeding roses. I hadn't cut them, as I wasn't sure what magic they held. It was wise to leave them alone until I could figure out what was feeding them.

I halted next to the giant magnolia tree. The blooms had expanded overnight. Their crimson stained petals now spread over several grave plots and had invaded three more trees.

I stuck my hands on my hips and frowned. This wasn't just the residual magic left over from the unboxed remains, it was something more powerful. Someone was tampering with my property. They'd gotten around my boundary wards and crept into my personal sanctuary. My feet picked through the vines, my sneakers protecting me from their spikes. Stopping in the center, I spun in a circle.

"What wicked beastie are you?" I whispered. A literal interpretation would be blood magic. Good god, I hope it wasn't blood magic. The damn stuff gave me heebie jeebies. It was voodoo in the worst way, like what they portrayed in the movies, but worse, so much worse.

I sucked in a breath and bit my lip. Well, there was one way to test it. I bent and ran my finger over the bleeding bloom. The kid appeared in front of me, blood spurting from a broad gash across his throat. I grabbed my neck and fell to my knees. His soul deep terror and gut wrenching pain echoed in my body. I wasn't reliving his death in the strictest sense. My corporal body still stood in my garden amongst the murderous flowers, but I'd formed a connection to his tormented spirit and he was trying to pull me under with him.

"Stop," I cried out.

He flashed in and out of my swimming vision, coming closer with each new appearance. Blood splashed across his face, coated his cheeks, his nose, and saturated his chocolate brown hair. It defied gravity.

"Para de lastimarme, por favor," he whispered before disappearing, leaving me with the rising sun and the sinking feeling that something terrifying had come to White Castle.

Chapter Four

My heart for a blueberry pancake.

I'd converted the stables a few years ago. Long-term residents were lucrative and not generally problematic, unless Rebecca took a liking to them—then I had to hope they were single. In fact, the building had been transformed originally for the vampire princess, alas it wouldn't provide her with the hunting grounds for the number of sexual encounters she required. She preferred to swan around my bed-and-breakfast, picking off loner supernaturals for a night of passion. I hammered my fist on the navy wooden door.

A second later, it flew open. He would only be that quick if he'd been waiting for me.

My breath stuttered in my chest as I attempted to not ogle a freshly showered Hudson. Barefooted, with his shirt gaping open and still dripping hair, he looked like every red-blooded woman's wet dream. Don't drool. That would be embarrassing.

"Bad morning?" he asked, eyeing me from head to toe.

I frowned. "Why would you think that?"

He cocked his head to the side. "You have blood on your shoes."

I glanced at my white sneakers, finding dribbles of fresh blood staining them. "Huh, I'm afraid the story behind that is confidential."

"Really?"

"Really."

"So it's not from the massacred roses bleeding all over your lawn?"

My mouth popped open, then slammed closed. When in doubt, observe your right to the fifth amendment.

"That's okay, Cora. I can wait for your secrets."

"Good luck with that."

He smirked and retreated to usher me inside. I swiped at the side of my lips with the back of my hand. No drool. Outstanding—things were looking up.

"We're eating in the kitchen," he informed me as he crowded my back on the way down the hallway. Heat rolled off him in waves, sending little tingles of awareness along my spine.

The room opened up into a rustic kitchen, complete with exposed beams. I'd left some original paneling as features, including a two part stable door which separated the living area from the kitchen. He had the rear door propped open, allowing the early morning streaks of orange and gold to splatter across the tiled floor.

He indicated to the waist tall table set back into a nook with two stools. It was intimate. "Please, sit." He turned and started the gas ring before sliding a frying pan onto it. He moved through the kitchen with an efficiency that spoke of countless hours of experience. Somehow, I'd expected him to be pampered and waited on.

"You cook," I observed.

He glanced over his shoulder as he whisked a bowl of batter. "Breakfast would be a sad affair if I didn't."

I waved my hand. "I mean, you cook for yourself."

"I like to know what's going into my food."

"Is that because you're fussy?"

"No, it's because I'm the most powerful shapeshifter in existence." The batter hit the pan and sizzled, releasing a yummy savory smell.

"And that makes you a chef?"

"It makes me a target."

My heart sank. "Someone tried to poison you?"

"No."

I leaned forward and placed my chin in my hand. "You're a control freak."

"And I'm alive because of it," he said as he flipped a pancake. If my eyes drifted to his ass for a bit of shameless ogling, I couldn't be held responsible. There was something about a man comfortable enough in his own masculinity to cook.

"I'll add that to your list of skills."

He spun with a grin as he slid the pancake onto a plate and sprinkled blueberries onto it. "You keep a list on me?"

I blinked. How did he do that? Turn innocent words into an innuendo? He held up a glass bottle and quirked a brow at me. "Syrup?" Case in point.

"Always."

His smile hit epic proportions. Save me now. The Principal was flirting outrageously, and I was not immune. The encounter with the boy had left me starving—for food, not Hudson—perhaps both. Ugh, I needed to get out of here. Breakfast, then I'm out.

"How many would you like?" he asked.

I jerked back. "What?" Did he have a twin? I think I could only handle one. He was a lot of male. Maybe his twin wasn't as arrogant. And now I had twin Hudsons in my head.

He chuckled as he poured more batter into the frying pan. "Pancakes, Cora. Where was your mind at?"

Dangerous, dangerous places. "Um, five please."

He didn't blink. There were no smart comments about fitting it all in, no rebuke about my weight or size. He simply slapped three more pans on the cooker and multitasked pancake flipping like a pro. I was in deep shit. The more comfortable he made me feel, the more dangerous he became.

Dragging my eyes from Hudson, I inspected the personal touches dotted around the room. A stack of worn paperbacks sat on the shelf, alongside a few framed pictures of Hudson with various people. An apron hung on the hook next to the door and a vase of wildflowers sat central in the window. It was homey and unexpected, but also quiet. A minimum of two shifters occupied the stables in the months he'd been here.

He squirted some more syrup on the delicious stack and placed the plate in front of me. The copious blueberries toppled off the top. Hudson slid onto the stool opposite me with his own plate, his knees knocking against mine, making me tuck my feet under my chair. Don't want any accidental games of footsie.

I pulled free a forkful of fluffy pancakes and popped them into my mouth. Oh. My. God. The Terror of Tennessee slayed at pancakes. This was it. If I had to pick one food that I had to eat for the rest of my life, this was it. It was almost a shame to devour them. I tried slowing down, to savor the experience.

"Where did you learn to make pancakes?" I wondered between bites.

He chewed thoughtfully before swallowing. "Every Sunday, my mother would cook up an enormous stack of pancakes. It was like religion. No matter how many meals we'd missed together during the week, Sunday breakfast was non-negotiable. It was a time to share our week, our worries and our triumphs."

I knew next to nothing about Hudson's past. Not for lack of looking, it wasn't public knowledge and it didn't exist in any database. He was an enigma.

"My aunts saw the heart of a house as the kitchen, and the dining table the base of communications. Friday evening was our night. Aunt Liz would whip up a culinary experience and we would share our week. Even as a child, I was included." I glanced down to pull another scrumptious forkful into my mouth.

"Family is important to you."

I nodded. "Extremely. It isn't to you?"

He tilted his head. "The packs are my family. But also not."

"You don't have any blood relatives in the pack?"

"My parents are dead."

Way to go Cora. How to win friends and all that bullshit. "I'm sorry, I lost my mother too."

"And your father?" Oops. Damn cat was perceptive.

"Is lost, but I didn't lose him."

"That's awfully cryptic."

"He's cryptic. But also uninteresting. Did your parents lead any of the packs?"

He smirked. He knew I was redirecting, but was gentleman enough not to point it out. "No. My father could have, but he wasn't interested. He paid the ultimate price—his life."

I blinked up at him. "How?"

He sighed. "The old alpha died, and the three most powerful men fought over the position. My father, Christopher, was the strongest but didn't fight because he didn't want the position. He was happy to live out his life with my mother."

I sensed where this was going. "The new alpha didn't like that?"

"No. He murdered him and my mother while they slept. He was a coward."

"Why not you?"

He grimaced. "I was eleven. The pack takes a dim view of killing children. He was already risking the wrath of the pack by murdering my parents. Murdering me would have flipped their loyalties. He would have been dead before the week was out."

"So he let you live in the pack?"

"I left. I couldn't live under the rule of a cowardly tyrant."

"Did you join another pack?"

He shook his head. "No, not until I was ready to unite the packs. I drifted, I learned their rules, their weaknesses and their strengths. I put together the best parts of a pack and eradicated the archaic ways. Like the arranged marriage Maggie was bound to."

"Outlawing it doesn't mean they follow the rules."

He grinned. "No, but it means they meet swift punishment. For the most part, I leave the packs to run themselves, so long as they follow the basic rules. I only intervene if needed."

"Maggie's father missed the memo."

"He's got it now."

My eyes widened, and my fork paused. "You dealt with Maggie's father?"

His head tipped down so he could meet my gaze. "Their pack is under new management. I won't tolerate rape and abuse."

I studied his face. He'd really done it. He'd taken out Maggie's father and his sniveling abusive buddies. And he'd not once bragged or mentioned it to gain my trust.

"Thank you. I'll let her know. Perhaps it will help her heal."

"You've done a great job of that already."

I shrugged and chased some gooey blueberries around the plate before scooping them up and shoveling them in my mouth. The room fell silent, but electricity charged the air.

I glanced up to find Hudson's alpha stare fully locked on my lips. I swallowed. "What?"

"You have a little something," he said, tapping the corner of his mouth.

I thumbed the side of my mouth. Then sucked it clean. "Did I get it?"

Hudson sucked in a breath, making my eyes snap to him. He leaned over the tiny table and wrapped one hand behind my head. I stilled as my pulse skyrocketed. The cocky smirk dropped from his face as his breath feathered over my lips, making them tingle in awareness. His tongue flicked out and the tip licked the side of my mouth, which parted as a shudder rippled down my spine and my breath halted in my throat. Without releasing me, Hudson flew off his stool and rounded the table. His colossal body crowded me as he tugged on my hair to tilt my head back and wrapped his arm around my back, his palm engulfing my hip. He was a handsome guy. Strong, powerful, a hunter, a protector. Everything that made me feel female. Everything that made him dangerous. He held me like I was both precious and someone to ravish. It was intoxicating. This was why I'd avoided being alone with him. I didn't have the willpower to resist what he was offering, however fleeting his attention might be. It was still focused wholly on me at this moment, and when Hudson gave you his attention, you became the center of the universe.

His mouth descended on mine, his lips and teeth coaxing my mouth to open and let him in. He tasted of summer, sin, and sex. My hands dug into his hair and pulled at the strands. A rough growl rolled from his chest and up his throat, and I swallowed it with a moan. The power of making this beast growl for me was dizzying. Heat unfurled low in my stomach, and electric pulses of pleasure skimmed over my flesh. Wired tight with desire, a physical need stretched between us like an elastic band, the inevitability of us colliding in an explosion as clear as the Louisiana sky.

He broke away from my mouth and trailed his lips across my jaw to the sensitive part of my ear. My legs wrapped around his waist and drew him closer. He gripped my hips, lifted me, spun, and dropped me on the kitchen counter. His body leaned forward, pushing mine back as his hands swept underneath me. Utensils crashed to the floor as he pushed my t-shirt up and traced his fingers over my scars. I hid my imperfections, ashamed of the weakness they represented. I pushed my hands over his, attempting to cover them up.

"Don't," he growled. My hands stilled. "They are beautiful, you are beautiful inside and out, Cora." He leaned down and his lips followed the curve of each scar around my ribs. "Don't hide yourself from me. What I see is strength, beauty, and an extraordinary woman." He punctuated each word with a kiss on the raised gnarly flesh. A tear slid from my eye, down my temple and into my ear.

His tongue flicked out and embers of desire replaced shame. I sucked in a breath and arched my spine as he kissed the underside of my breast.

"I'm fighting the urge to flip you over my shoulder and have my way with you," he whispered.

I blinked. I couldn't do this. Could I? Perhaps, for a day, I could be Cora, and he could be Hudson. Not the elemental he despised and The Principal. Not Cora, the granddaughter of the leader of said hated elementals.

"I ca—" I started.

He grabbed my hands, pulled me up, shoved his shoulder under my stomach, and picked me up. I squeaked, which made him chuckle. My own personal caveman. He took three steps down the hall, when an intense, low, angry growl echoed from behind us. A tsunami of primitive wild magic splashed around us. My head shot up. A snowy wolf straddled the open doorway, her eyes ochre and piercing as they locked stares with me. Hudson spun and froze.

"Wendy, get out of my home," he stated. His tone was even, but brokered no room for argument. I tapped on his back, reminding him I was here. He pulled me so I slid down his body and landed with a huff. He gripped my arm and yanked me behind him.

I peered around his shoulder as the wolf took another step inside the home, defying the orders of her alpha—*the* alpha. What the hell was going on?

"Shift now," he snarled. His voice boomed with power that made my knees shake. Most creatures would sink to the floor, even humans. Good job I wasn't most creatures.

The wolf dropped to her haunches and pawed at her ears with a whimper. "Shift," he demanded.

A low whine which I felt in my jaw reverberated in the room. She shook her head and pitched forward, teeth gnashing toward us. Hudson lunged for her and gripped her around the neck, pinning her to the floor.

A figure blocked out the sun in the doorway, and the pack's chief of security emerged like the prince of shadows. He frowned at the scene, examined the chaos of utensils, then looked me up and down from head to foot. "Why do you have blood on your sneakers?"

"That's what you took from this situation?" My eyebrows rose, and I folded my arms while glancing at Hudson, who was wrestling a wolf to the ground.

Dangerous Dave ran a hand through his hair with a heavy sigh. "That's the third today."

Hudson's head snapped to him. "That makes fifteen."

"Fifteen what?" I asked.

"Wildies."

My jaw dropped. A wildie was a shifter who'd shed their humanity and along with it their mortal skin. They had given over to the wild animal that lay within them and were stuck in that form. A wildie was dangerous, unpredictable, and also rare. There were known reasons someone became a wildie; grief and trauma, to name a few, and more often than not, they needed to be killed before they slaughtered a town full of unsuspecting humans. I had only known of three wildies, ever. Fifteen was insane.

"The holding cells are full," Dave declared. "I clocked this one as she charged through town, heading directly for you." He nodded toward Hudson. "Like the others."

"We need somewhere to store Wendy."

They both looked at me. I held my hands up. "Why are you looking at me? I don't have any prison cells."

"A bed-and-breakfast, mortuary, doctor's office, and graveyard. It's hardly a stretch of the imagination," Dave said.

Wendy struggled beneath Hudson. "I don't have a prison, but I have meds to knock her out for a few hours while you figure it out."

Hudson's eyes narrowed. "Why would you have meds to knock out a shifter?" So I'm good enough to sleep with, but not trust. Glad we sorted that out.

I rolled my eyes as I edged around the room and moved past Dave. His hand snapped out and caught my arm. "Remove your hand," I gritted out.

A low growl curled around me. Dangerous, possessive, and powerful. I glanced over my shoulder, finding Hudson glaring at Dave. His shirt had torn on his biceps as his muscles bulged with power. He was seconds away from shifting.

"Let go of me," I whispered to Dave. His gaze darted between me and Hudson, a frown settling on his face. He released my arm, and I set off running toward my house.

It took me less than four minutes to retrieve the syringe, fill it with medication, and return to the stables to find Dave and Hudson locked in some kind of standoff I didn't understand. I snapped the lid off the syringe with my teeth and approached Wendy. Hudson held her still.

"What's in it?" he growled, his beast close to the surface. I steadied my gaze and stared into his eyes as they contracted into vertical slits. He was magnificent and utterly terrifying.

"Sedative, strong enough to knock out a shifter, but not harmful."

He scented the air like he was sniffing out my truth, then nodded once.

I pierced the needle into the scruff of Wendy's neck and plunged the medication into her. She whined, before going lax in Hudson's arms. He never took his eyes off me.

"Take her to the pack house. Put Shirley with Laura and Wendy on her own until we assess her."

I leaned back on my haunches. "You aren't killing them?" Wildies were always killed, it was pack law. They couldn't risk being exposed to the world.

He shook his head and stood. "These are settled, even-tempered shifters. They have no reason to turn into a wildie."

"Weird shit always happens around you," Dave commented as I stood.

"The weird shit only happens to me when you are around. I'd take a long hard look at yourself before pointing your paws at me."

I replaced the cap on the syringe and headed to the back door.

"Cora," Hudson said. "We aren't finished."

"Oh, but we are. I don't sleep with people that can't trust me."

I waltzed out of the stables and left a tiny piece of my heart in the stables. The Terror of Tennessee had snuck in when I wasn't looking and stolen it, but I wasn't hanging around to let him take any more. Damn blueberry pancakes.

Chapter Five

Here I go again... with a psycho stalker shifter. Wait, that's not how the song goes.

There were a thousand things more appealing than my current night time activity—speed dating with strangers. Was there a website where organizers get these ridiculous questions? Because nobody, not even Maggie, could come up with this nonsense. How will knowing what color best describes my personality narrow down my match? And if you could narrow down your personality to one color, surely you were boring as shit. The more pertinent question was: how can I get out of this? Perhaps a nice grisly murder would need my specific skill set. Rescued by homicide.

"Black," I stated to Seth, the weaselly wide-eyed twenty-year-old fox shifter. He swallowed and glanced around like the goth police would be here any second to rescue his twitchy ass. Too bad, Seth. The law enforcement here are sympathetic to the woman who can aid them in their more serious cases, namely death. Yes, I'm living up to my 'black' personality. Perhaps I'll have a chat with the dead next. With comedic timing, Harry floated into the room and stopped behind Seth with a perplexed expression. I took a sip of my fruity low alcohol wine. We wanted the guests relaxed, not drunk. This wasn't The Pit.

"In my day we courted a lady with escorted walks and flowers, not twenty questions wanting to know if you had three wishes from a genie what they would be?" Harry lamented. Oh, Harry, how I wish the dating scene was still that way.

A true gentleman of his time, Harry had been murdered in spectacular fashion by an elemental while hosting a 'Helping Vampires to Blend into Society' meeting in a church. Harry found his way to me and stuck around. Most of the dead didn't. They were happy to pass on to the next life. In fact, Harry was the first to refuse, claiming I needed his fatherly advice and guidance. My father was and always had been absent, so perhaps he had a point. Being raised by a brood of aunts, I possibly lacked in skills when it came to the opposite sex.

The buzzer sounded, and I flicked my wrist to check my watch, but I'd removed it with the encouragement of Maggie and Rebecca, swapping it out for an emerald bracelet which matched my dress. I'd definitely been here an hour, maybe more. I caught Maggie's eyes. She gave me a wave with a big smile plastered on her face. A sigh escaped me. I couldn't say no to that girl. The thirty males stood and rotated to the next female. Maggie's speed dating night for the supernatural community was a success. We'd needed to use the front reception rooms and the dining room to accommodate the party. It was good business sense. The next time they recommended somewhere to stay, we might be at the top of their list.

Rebecca quirked a brow from her perch across the room as a big guy with shoulder-length shaggy blond hair folded himself into the seat opposite her. She leaned around him. "Smile," she mouthed.

I rolled my eyes and redoubled my efforts to appear approachable.

"Damn, is that your sexy smile?" A familiar deep voice stated. "Because your vibe says you want to murder someone, not date them."

My eyes snapped to Hudson. "No, nope, not happening, move on," I commanded.

The chair creaked as he leaned back and made himself comfy. "Is this a habit?" he drawled, his southern lilting accent like warm whisky. "Attending speed dating events?"

I ground my jaw and crumpled the paper in my hand. "You tell me, you are here every time I am. Shifter honeys not chasing your tail or do you prefer it when they roll over and show their bellies?"

He grinned, making the hair on the nape of my neck prickle with awareness. All teeth. All beast. A slither of human. "None I'm interested in, I find myself drawn to red-headed little witches with a martyr complex and a bad attitude."

I leaned over the tiny table and crooked my index finger at him. He mirrored me. Hook, line, and sinker. "But I'm not interested in you," I breathed. His eyes dipped to my lips, and he smirked. Why me? Meghan and Kate get princes, Bella gets Edward, meanwhile I get lumbered with an arrogant psycho stalker shifter.

"Oh, Cora, if only that were true. Pick a man, any man, take him out on a date and prove to me how uninterested you are."

Harry frowned. "Persistent, isn't he?"

"I don't want any man."

Hudson tilted his head in a distinctly feline gesture. "Because you want me."

Perhaps if I'd given in the first time, he wouldn't have chased me. His beast might not perceive me as a challenge. The danger with Hudson wasn't that I didn't like him. He was a tall, handsome, dark drink of sexiness and he made me feel feminine, an almost impossible feat when I could flatten most males and break them into tiny pieces. There wasn't much to not like, and that was the problem. If I let him in, even for a minute, then I might fall, and my senses were screaming he wouldn't be there to catch me. He'd been living on my grounds for three months, calculating, assessing, plotting. Hudson had an entire country of shapeshifters to lead, yet his focus was on me.

Dangerous Dave chose that second to storm through the front door. His gaze narrowed on us, and Sheriff Robertson trailed after him. Oh boy, the pack's head of security and the town's sheriff meant one thing. There'd been a murder. Guilt gnawed at my mind for wishing for it not more than five minutes ago. The universe listened when I wished for murder, but ignored me when it came to Hudson. Typical. Sebastian trotted up the steps and entered the house behind them. The Vampire Prince of America had graced us with his presence. Now it was a party.

The buzzer sounded, and I shot to my feet. Hudson spun in his chair and eyeballed the newcomers. Dangerous Dave jerked his head at me to follow them outside. I hurried by Maggie with an apology and swept past the sheriff. Sebastian put his hand on my lower back and ushered me into the night. My arms wrapped around me as I shivered. Hudson, Dave, and the sheriff followed, the latter closing the front door behind him. The driveway was empty. No van, so no body.

"What's wrong?" I asked, spinning to face them.

"It's your Aunt Dayna. She's missing," Dave stated.

My brow furrowed as ice flooded my veins, my gut churning with worry. "How do you know?"

Dave darted his gaze away. "Aunt Liz called when she couldn't reach you, and asked me to look in on you." He and Aunt Liz were talking directly? Hmm.

"And why are you here?" I asked the Sheriff.

"I got a request to complete a welfare check on you from your aunts."

I put my hands on my hips and glanced at Sebastian.

"And you?"

He pinned Hudson with a look. "I'm here as your wingman."

Hudson folded his arms. "We agreed you would give her space, allow the effects of your blood to dissipate."

"You agreed with yourself," Sebastian shot back.

"Stop," I shouted. They fell into silence. "My aunt is missing. Why would I need a welfare check?"

Dave dug into his jeans pocket and produced his phone. He shoved it at me. "Because in the note left by the kidnapper, it demands you as the ransom item. Forty-eight hours, Cora, then they start shipping your aunt to you in pieces."

Chapter Six

Blood and Virgin Sacrifices.

It was four in the morning. The sun was threatening to turn night into day, and my reception room had emptied of supernatural singles and been replaced by the supernatural elite.

"Why would the kidnapper want you?" Dave asked.

I crossed my legs onto the sofa. "Easy. They heard I'm psychic and assumed I'm a precog, because most people do." My palm drifted over my stomach, the phantom ache persistent as I recalled the last time someone decided I could tell the future. That pain had been replaced by the sensation of Hudson's lips on my skin.

"How would they have found out?" The armchair creaked as Hudson leaned back. He followed my hand with a frown.

I shrugged. "These things have a habit of getting out. Three months ago, only my family and two friends had this knowledge. Now, that's expanded." I let the accusation hang in the air. Hudson and Dave stiffened.

"You're questioning our integrity?" Dave snarled. Oh boy, touchy subject. Cora Roberts, expert in diplomacy.

"I'm pointing out that a close circle of people knew for many years with no issues. Then the shifters stick their noses in my business and suddenly I'm being targeted."

Dave shot to his feet and pointed at me. "You're a hypocrite."

I cocked an unamused brow at him. "How?"

"I know–"

"Dave," Hudson snapped. "That's enough."

"No, please go on," I encouraged. "What do you know?"

Dave frowned and dropped his offending finger before running a hand through his hair. What had they figured out about me? The possibilities were endless. I wasn't exactly an open book.

Robert leaned forward, clasping his hands together and eyeing the two of us. "I think you should take a step away from Miss Roberts."

Dave, Hudson, and I snapped our heads toward the very human sheriff.

"Stay out of it," I barked. Then turned my glare on to Dave as I stood to my full height. My nose would brush his nipples, so it wasn't exactly impressive. "And you, stop making threats in my home. My hospitality is only holding out on account of our previous working relationship. I owe you nothing, not my time, not my home, not my food, and certainly not my secrets. If you have ferreted out a measly morsel of information about me, use it wisely. Because once you burn this bridge, there is no coming back."

Dave's mouth opened, closed, and opened again. Help, I'd broken Dangerous Dave.

Hudson tore his eyes away from Robert, who he'd been leveling with his full alpha stare.

"Boys, boys," Rebecca started with a twinkle in her eye. "She's the prettiest girl in town, and I'm sure you can behave like gentlemen while Cora decides if any of you are worth her time. But right now, we have an aunt to save and a nemesis to destroy."

Saved by the vampire princess sex addict. Also, she was the prettiest girl in town. A Nordic goddess with ice-blonde hair and blue eyes, Rebecca turned the heads of men and women, regardless of their preference.

Hudson leaned back in the armchair with a smirk of self satisfaction on his face. The idiot thought he had me in the bag. "You're right," he said. "Me and Cora will travel to Dayna's house and rescue her." Wait, what? He wanted to come with me? Probably hoping to score some brownie points.

"I'll go with Cora," Sebastian chimed in. "You stay here."

"And have you save her from death with your blood again?" Hudson snorted. "I don't think so."

Everyone's eyes were playing ping-pong with the two of them. Sebastian fisted his hands, the knuckles turning white. "It wasn't intentional."

"We are going into a dangerous situation. The people who took Dayna aren't looking for a tea party with Cora. Someone will get hurt."

"Which is exactly why I should be there. I can heal her."

"And I can protect her from getting hurt in the first place."

I rolled my eyes and glanced at Dave and Rebecca for help.

Rebecca looked like she was about to grab popcorn while Dave eyed me like I'd taken a shit in his cornflakes this morning.

"Hudson, you come with me," I decided. He grinned, full white teeth on display. "Don't get excited, princess. I can protect myself just fine, but I don't trust you with my house. Sebastian, stay here with Rebecca and guard the house. I don't like it when I'm called away."

Rebecca winced. The last time someone had lured me away, they had kidnapped Maggie.

"What about me?" Dave asked.

"You have enough on your plate with the pack," I said, referring to the wildies. His eyes tightened as he looked between me and Hudson.

"Wait, my Aunt Dayna is being held inside her own house?" I checked.

Hudson nodded once. "I think the point is to make it easy for you to find her. You are the ultimate prize, after all."

I rolled my eyes. "Sure. Let's go with that." It was more likely Aunt Dayna had put up such a fight they'd found it difficult to extract her from her home. Dayna's house was unusual. It was protective of Robert's women. The more I thought about it, the more it didn't sit right.

"We can take my car," Hudson said, rising to his feet. "It's a fourteen hour straight drive to your aunt's town."

I blinked. How did he know that? Ugh, never mind, I had bigger fish to fry than a nosy principal and his lapdog. "I have an errand to run first."

Hudson folded his arms, making me lament how I'd become jealous of a freaking shirt. "What errand?"

"I need to see a man about a spell."

"You're a witch. Can't you do it?"

I tossed a look over my shoulder. "This spell needs someone with a specific skill set. I could make it, but we don't have the time and it would be subpar."

"Okay, let's go," Hudson said, stepping after me out of the room.

I spun and slapped my palm onto his chest. "No, I go alone. I'll be back in about an hour."

"Cora."

"Hudson."

He covered my hand with his. "Someone kidnapped your aunt."

"I know."

He sighed like it took extra effort to deal with my dumb ass. "Someone who wants you. They could already have people waiting for an opportunity to take you. They could hide on the borders of your property."

I ground my jaw. I hadn't thought of that. "Fine," I gritted out. "Hope you like the water, kitty."

His face dropped, and I considered it a win.

There was a distinct odor around the Rockhard and Lenson pharmacy. It wasn't unpleasant and had a herby undertone that was no doubt a result of the concoctions they brewed. The two men dispensed drugs to humans during the day, but by night they were elementals specializing in potions. Supernaturals from across the country sought them out.

Lucky for me, they'd settled in White Castle. Despite the early hour, the air was humid and sticky, unnaturally so for October.

"We are going to see the Scientists?" Hudson checked. "Aren't they booked months in advance?" Like me, they'd earned their nickname from their unique skill set. There wasn't a potion they couldn't brew.

"Not for family."

"You're related to The Scientists?"

"Not all family are blood relations, Principal, sometimes there are those you choose."

The front of the shop was in darkness, so I moved around the building and knocked three times on the window as I passed it. The door swung open, revealing a heavyset man who indulged in the finer things in life. His gray eyes widened behind his thick-rimmed glasses.

"Cora," he bellowed, yanking me into his arms and hugging me tight. "I haven't seen you since that nasty business with the gangrene on my–"

"Rockhard," I interrupted. Unfortunate name. "Meet Hudson."

I was released, and Rockhard stared over my shoulder. "Oh my, girl, he is delicious with an extra helping of lick."

"Who is it?" Lenson shouted.

"Cora and her new boy toy."

"Ooh, let me see."

Lenson came hurrying down the hallway, wiping his hands on the neon pink apron. He was the opposite of Rockhard, all narrow lines and slim build. His receding hair had opened up on the top in recent years. He was still handsome though, and Rockhard also thought so. I'd never witnessed two people more in love.

They eyeballed Hudson. "Good for you, Cora," Lenson said.

I shook my head. "He's my, umm, tenant?"

"That's what you kids are calling it now?" Rockhard muttered.

"How's your grandmother?" Lenson asked.

It took all of my concentration to keep my posture easy and not curse him. The last thing I needed was for Hudson to join the dots and realize my grandmother ruled the species he despised. "She's good, thank you."

"How was that last batch of nulling bombs?"

I squeezed my eyes closed for a split second and calculated the chances of Hudson missing that red flag. Perhaps a hole would open up and I'd fall straight into the pits of hell. Yes, that seemed far more likely.

Time for your big girl panties, Cora. The devil wasn't coming to rescue you today. I cast a glance at Hudson. A tiny frown was etched on to his features as he tried to put the pieces together. Good luck, buddy, I'm not sure I even know the fabric of my being. Not completely.

I shoved past Rockhard into the back of the store. Rows and rows of bottles and containers lined the walls of the room. A stone table with various lab equipment sat proudly in the center. "I need something," I said when we'd all gotten inside and shut the door.

"How did you meet?" Rockhard asked.

I groaned. "I don't have time for this. We aren't having sex, but I do need a few potions from you."

"Shame," Rockhard muttered.

Lenson leaned against the table and crossed his ankles. "What do you need?"

I relaxed my shoulders. "A detector spell."

Rockhard's eyebrows climbed into his hairline. "For elementals?"

This was the tricky part. "Broader. For everything. I'll also need a neutralizer potion, and lastly, a telepathy charm."

Lenson squinted at me. "What the hell have you gotten yourself into?"

I folded my arms. "Someone has kidnapped my aunt."

Rockhard jerked. "Stella?"

I shook my head. "No, Dayna." He had a soft spot for my Aunt Stella going back some years and an incident nobody would tell me about.

"And you suspect foul play?" Lenson guessed.

I shrugged. "Something feels ... off."

"Always trust your gut, kid," Rockhard said with a twirl of his hand. "Follow me. Will your friend be coming?"

I glanced at Hudson. He narrowed his eyes. I sighed. "Looks like it."

We followed the owners down the hallway, then a narrow set of stairs to what would be the basement. We rounded a corner and descended again.

I could feel Hudson's unease behind me. "Doing alright back there, big guy?"

"I'm fine."

I chuckled as the giant underground atrium came into view. Water sloshed against our feet as Lenson and Rockhard waded into the enormous pool. Several caves made up the room, each filled with waist high liquid that was lit blue from underneath by enchantments. I climbed into the warm pool after them and started across to the next cave. I glanced over my shoulder, finding Hudson still on the edge. "Come on, is the big bad kitty cat afraid of the water?" I taunted.

"This is why you changed into a tank and shorts?" he asked.

I shrugged. "That and a cocktail dress was a little over the top for a rescue mission."

His jaw ticked, then he dived headfirst into the water and swam straight past me to the opposite side of the pool before climbing out and shaking his head.

"Showoff," I muttered, following him and descending into the next pool. We found Lenson and Rockhard muttering to themselves three caves in. They moved through the water, grabbing various items from the nooks and crannies on the cave walls and popping them on a round table raised above the water.

"Why the water?" Hudson asked from beside me.

"They make potions. Dangerous potions and spells that, if they spilled or leaked, could have disastrous consequences. A lot of the spells they weave are also volatile and go wrong. The water acts as a neutralizer. It's enchanted to absorb any magic."

"Clever," Hudson mumbled.

"Let's talk about payment, boys," I said.

Rockhard waved his hand at me. "I want to hear the story of how you met."

"As payment?"

He nodded. Why me?

"And I want you to share your intentions," Lenson declared, pointing at Hudson.

"What happened to blood and virgin sacrifices?" I muttered.

Hudson chuckled. "Are you trying to tell me something?"

My cheeks flamed. "Absolutely not. I may not be experienced and entertain a different lover in my bed every night of the week, but I'm no virgin. I prefer my sex to be meaningful. Sex takes work, effort to understand what turns someone on. Multiple orgasms and satisfaction don't happen instantly." I snapped my fingers.

Tiny sparks of amusement glinted in his eyes as he studied me. "We shall see."

"There will be no seeing!"

"Awww, our little Cora is all grown up," Rockhard commented, leaning on Lenson. "I'm so proud. Will it be a summer wedding?" He wiped a fake tear from his eye.

"Keep weeping, there will be no wedding. Hudson is here because he can't keep his nosy ass out of my business."

"I'm here because your ass can't stay out of trouble."

Lenson glanced over his shoulder at me with a smile. "Embrace the good, Cora, keep it close. Treat it like the rare find it is."

"I'm only rare while my panties are still on. Afterwards, I'll fade into a trail of conquests."

"This again," Hudson groaned.

"I'm sorry, does my self-respect offend you?"

He gripped my arm and spun me in the water to face him. "The fact you think me so shallow offends me."

I scoffed. "Really? Tell me, how many women have you bedded?"

He tilted his head and pursed his lips. "Including one-night stands?"

My eyes went wide as he confirmed in one question exactly my suspicions. "No, let's go with relationships that lasted over a week."

He gritted his teeth. "Twelve."

I slow blinked and willed him to see the mismatch we made. "Twelve," I repeated.

He ran his hands through his hair. "Ask me how many women I've chased. How many women I have pursued?"

"It's irrelevant."

"It's absolutely relevant. You push me to be better, to think beyond my own views. You challenge me in a way I've never known. I want to be a better man because of you. Don't stop this before we have a chance."

"And when the next young, perky thing bats her eyelashes at you?"

He jerked back. "I would never cheat."

"No, but I'd be sidelined for that younger model. I can't live like that."

"So you do want a proposal."

I shook my head. "No."

"Let me get this straight. You won't be with a man because you don't know if it will be forever, but you won't give them the chance to give you forever?"

I nodded even as my heart shriveled around the edges at his assessment of me. "That about sums it up."

"Then what will it take?"

I shrugged. "Extraordinary. Nothing less."

"You should have sex," Rockhard interjected.

"No!" I shouted. Why is this the solution people come up with?

"Yes!" Lenson agreed.

I threw my hands up in the air. "There shall be no sex."

"I'd make it good for you," Hudson said. "You'd enjoy it, I promise."

Cocky, self-assured, jerk. I growled into the cave. It echoed, making it sound more badass than what I could manage alone.

Hudson smirked. "Cute."

I'd give him cute. I rotated my hand, gathering my magic. The water surrounding us answered my call, and a whirlpool formed around my legs. "No magic," Lenson shouted. "Cora!"

I huffed and pressed my lips together before releasing my power. The water swished and lapped at the walls. Lenson handed me the three items I'd requested, one in a small glass vial, one in a silk bag, and one in an orb which would detonate on contact with the correct spell.

"Thank you," I gritted out before tucking them into my coat pockets.

"Teach those kidnappers the consequences of messing with a Roberts woman."

I waded through the water, my thighs aching at the resistance, before hurrying outside into the street.

I took three steps then rounded on Hudson and slammed my hands into his chest, pushing him up against the wall.

"One day soon, we are going to have this out," I told him. "You will realize I'm not a little girl you can push around and seduce. Then you can get your rocks off with your shifter honeys and leave me the hell alone."

He blinked, then shook his head, a small smile tilting up his perfect lips as amusement danced in his eyes. He was toying with me. Again.

"Let me tell you what's going to happen. You will fight me, because you need me to prove to you I'm worthy. We will dance around each other, while the chemistry continues to build. I'm okay with that, because when we finally get together, we will explode. I will deliver on extraordinary, not because I'm a better man than most, but because I'm determined and persistent." He leaned down, his lips skimmed my ear. "When you come to my bed, you won't want to leave. I can take everything you have to give, Cora, and match you. I won't break, and I won't hurt you. Because of that fact, I intrigue you. Have you ever truly let go?"

I jerked back, my lips grazing his. His eyes flared with need and a wild hunger I could get lost in. His hands gripped my hips, and he tugged me against him. Danger, danger, someone send in a bucket of cold water—ASAP. A growl erupted from the entrance to the alley.

I turned and spied a tawny wolf, hackles raised and teeth on display. "Again?" I wondered.

Hudson sighed, let go of me, and tucked me behind him. I should be offended, but I was letting him deal with his pack. I had enough responsibilities.

"Frank, shift," Hudson growled low. Full of command. Frank snarled in response.

I peeked around him. Frank wasn't listening. "Would you like me to get some sedative?" I'd stored several vials in the trunk. Just in case.

Hudson reached for Frank and grappled him to the ground. "You're carrying it with you now?"

"Do you want it or not?"

"Yes," he gritted out.

I sighed and sidestepped the two of them. Cora Roberts—tamer of the Terror of Tennessee.

Chapter Seven

Hearts and the horizontal tango.

"One hour," I warned as we pulled up outside of my Summer Grove house. "Then I'll be leaving without you."

"Noted," Hudson answered as I slammed the car door closed.

"And I'm driving."

He scoffed, shook his head, and peeled out of my driveway with an unconscious wolf shifter in the trunk. My front door swung open revealing Dangerous Dave. I trotted up the stairs and into the house. He scented the air and quirked a brow at me.

"Nothing happened," I snapped. I'm sure Hudson's smell was all over me. Damn cat was scent marking me.

"Cora," a familiar voice called from somewhere deep in the house. I reversed my steps on the stairs and popped my head around the corner as Aunt Liz stepped out from the kitchen while drying her hands on a floral dishtowel. "Kitchen, now."

She glanced at Dave. I darted my gaze between them, before I mirrored his expression from moments ago. Dave smirked and waltzed out of the house. The door snicked closed.

"Coward," I muttered as I made my way to the kitchen. Aunt Liz pulled off a power suit and an apron like no other. I slid on to a chair. "I didn't know you were coming."

She tossed me a glance over her shoulder. "My sister has been kidnapped, and the culprit is demanding my niece in exchange. I know you, Cora, you'll have some half-baked plan which involves you turning yourself over to these evil people."

I opened my mouth to deny it. She tsked. "Dave already informed me. You think it's a solid plan. But it isn't. You've no idea who, how many, or what you are facing."

"We can't leave her there," I stated.

Aunt Liz huffed. "Really, Cora, you should know better. Dayna can handle herself." She turned, slid an omelet onto a plate and put it in front of me. My stomach rumbled. How long had it been since the pancakes? "Don't you think it's odd?" she continued.

"That she's being held in her house? Definitely."

"What does that tell us?"

"That she wants me there. If Dayna wanted them out, she would have them out. That house of hers wouldn't allow anything in unless she permitted it."

Aunt Liz nodded. "Agreed. So for whatever reason, she wants you to meet these kidnappers—while they're alive."

I spooned the last of the omelet into my mouth before digging around in my pockets. I placed the three items on the table. "Nulling potion, detection spell, and telepathy charm."

"That should work," she said, examining the items. "What's the telepathy charm for?"

"Hudson is accompanying me, and it will be handy to have silent communication. I've no idea what we are walking into, and while he's the biggest, baddest shifter, he's not aware of our ways or what dangers we might be facing. He's used to dealing with problems with brute strength."

"You'll have to both wear it before you leave."

I pressed my lips together. I hadn't told His Suspiciousness about my plan to link our minds yet. He already acted as if I was the mastermind behind a secret plot to sedate shifters.

Aunt Liz frowned and leaned back in her chair. She hit me with the Roberts' hard assed stare. "You haven't told him."

"Yet."

She took a deep breath, like I was testing her patience. Lucky her, she didn't have Hudson on her ass every second. That would test the patience of a saint. I grimaced. Her eyes softened, and she leaned over the table, taking my hands. "At some point, Cora, you will need to take a chance on a man to trust your heart to."

I blinked back the sudden tears. "How do you decide who is safe?"

She tilted her head. "You can't. It will feel like jumping off a cliff and not knowing what awaits you at the bottom. It could be sharp, jagged rocks that will smash your body to pieces."

"Exactly."

"Then again, he could catch you and take you flying high above the clouds."

"What if it's both? What if he takes me flying, then drops me from a height? I won't survive."

She squeezed my hand. "That's the thrill of falling in love. But if you don't take that leap, you'll forever wonder what could have been. Don't waste away an old woman without knowing love, at least once."

I nodded as Rebecca swept into the room. She smiled at me, no doubt having heard all of our conversation. "Are we saying yes to the Terror of Tennessee?"

I squeezed my eyes closed. "I don't know."

"Better than a no," Rebecca replied.

"Ask yourself this, Cora," Aunt Liz said. "If he was after one thing, why would he have rebuffed all other advances from numerous females? Why would he move himself off pack grounds and onto yours? Why would he wait this long for a quick roll in the sack? And why would he cook for you, the first woman ever, a meal in private? The answer is easy, Cora, shifters only protect and provide for their mates."

"Plus, you accepted the meal," Rebecca tagged on.

"So?"

"It's like admitting you trust him to care for you, a proposal of intentions."

"But nobody knows," I whispered.

"Everyone knows," Aunt Liz said. "The packs, your grandmother, even Karen at The Pit."

My mouth fell open. Mates were family, cherished, and forever. Hudson's mate would be the only thing above the pack in his life. There's no way he was this stupid. They would never accept an elemental as their principal's mate. He would be expected to find a nice feline female and make furry babies. I couldn't give him that. As far as he was aware, mating with me might make me powerless. The Roberts woman's curse meant if we married a stronger male, they could take our power for themselves. It's why I had a bouquet of aunts and no uncles. However, no man could take my power. I wasn't built the same way as other elementals. My magic came from a different source. But he couldn't know that. Could he? What if—no. Don't imagine yourself in a future with him. Happy, loved, safe—damn it. Now that image was planted in my mind.

Aunt Liz smiled. "You imagined your future as Mrs. Abbot."

I glared at her. "The curse," I muttered.

Aunt Liz waved her hand. "Would he take your power? As his mate, it would leave you defenseless, something that would go against the bond."

I felt my objections withering away along with my resolve, because one thing I was sure about Hudson Abbot is that he was strong enough in his own right and too proud to take an ounce of power from me.

"I'm so screwed," I confessed.

Aunt Liz chuckled as she grabbed my plate and took it to the sink to rinse. My aunt didn't chuckle. It wasn't her style. I frowned as she hummed a tune and shared a look with Rebecca. A smile played on Rebecca's lips.

"Wait," I stated, standing and rushing over to Aunt Liz. I grabbed her arm, spun her toward me and studied her closely. Wild hair, red slightly swollen lips, a flush on her neck. Like a beard rash. I blinked. Who…

I snapped my fingers. "You are doing the horizontal tango with Dangerous Dave."

Her eyes went wide and darted to the door. "Shush."

"No tango yet, only the prelude," Rebecca informed me.

"Now who's been holding out on the shifter?"

She rolled her eyes. "You have to make them work for it a little. No point in being easy."

"Are you sure you can handle him?"

"Darling, the more pertinent question is, can he handle me?" She winked then waltzed out of the room, leaving me with disturbing images of my straight-laced aunt.

"Everyone is having sex but me," Rebecca pouted.

"You have plenty of sex. Perhaps what you need is a more meaningful connection."

"All my connections are meaningful."

"For a night."

"I can't limit myself. It would be selfish to males everywhere. An experience with me is like therapy."

"That's the most twisted logic I have ever heard for avoiding a relationship."

"But it's still logic."

Save me now.

Armed with my haul from Rockhard and Lenson, plus a bag of spare clothing, some throwing knives, and a picnic from Aunt Liz, I flung open the front door in time to see Hudson jumping out of his SUV.

He looked me up and down and quirked a brow.

"What?" I snapped as he grabbed the bag from my hand and threw it in the rear of the car.

He shook his head. "Are we auditioning for a modern version of Xena? Or maybe an exotic dancer? Do we need to make a stop at Randy Rogers?"

Randy Rogers was the seedy stripper bar in the next town. I'm pretty sure nothing was made of natural materials, including the strippers.

"We are wearing leathers for protection."

"Nothing can protect you from me when you look like that."

I huffed. "They are a natural repellant for many spells, plus they prevent scrapes and scratches."

"Again, I can't make any promises."

"You're impossible."

He grinned and opened the passenger door. I ignored him and rounded the car before jumping into the driver's seat. He chuckled as he climbed in next to me. "We can take the driving in shifts."

I reached under the chair, lifted the handle and rolled it forward. Then I pumped it so my head popped over the steering wheel. Damn Neanderthal.

I dug in my pocket and pulled the silk pouch Lenson and Rockhard had given me. I handed it to Hudson, who took it from me like he was handling a bomb. "What is it?"

"Telepathy charm," I answered. "Open it."

He tugged on the ribbon and tipped the contents out. Two dime-sized discs of rose quartz fell onto his palm, each held by a piece of brown leather string.

"I wear one, and you wear the other. It needs to be touching your skin. In about eight hours, it will enable us to read each other's thoughts. A handy tool when we are walking into an unknown situation with an anonymous threat."

He rolled the quartz between his fingers. "You want me to put this on?"

"It didn't come in different colors."

"You trust me enough to be in your mind?"

"You won't be in my mind. You will hear my thoughts, and I yours. There's a difference."

I reached out to grab my half. He batted my hand away before dropping one on his lap and opening the other. "Turn around."

I met his eyes. It was a move toward the trust I accused him of never having. I spun in my seat and lifted my pony tail. His thumb skimmed the jumping pulse in my neck as he settled the charm against my throat before tying it. I sucked in a breath and spun back, finding him tucking his own charm under his shirt.

Hudson turned on the radio. Classic rock music blasted into the car before he dialed it down and lounged in his seat. I side-eyed him. His head had fallen back and his eyes were closed. He looked peaceful. I sped up and covered the next few hours of driving in silence. Aunt Dayna lived on the outskirts of a backward town. It was miles from any airport, so car was the easiest and quickest way to reach her. Luckily, most of the journey was on the main roads. Only the last hour would be a tough drive. The atmosphere changed at some point, making me check on Hudson. His heated stare was directed at my face. My gaze darted back to the road.

"It wouldn't work," I started. "Me and you. It would never work."

"Why?"

"You need a furry queen to sit by your side. Two things I'm not."

He sighed. "You are dooming our relationship before it even starts."

"I'm being logical to avoid any heartbreak and pain."

"Thirty years."

I glanced at him. "What?"

"That's how long the pack has had my full attention. I mediate, enforce, and make decisions they can't. Under my leadership, the packs became unified in a system to make us strong, less vulnerable. I put us on the supernatural powerhouse map."

"I know your resume. What's your point?"

"My point is, they can suck it up or get out. I have given them everything—my time, my family, my protection. They will accept whomever I choose as my mate. That is final."

"Can you guarantee your people wouldn't attempt to take my life?"

"No. Can you say the same for me?"

I snapped my head toward him. He grabbed the steering wheel and kept it steady. "Why would anyone try to murder you for being with me?"

"You tell me."

"No one would care," I gritted out, turning back to the road and batting his hand away.

He hummed in his throat like he didn't believe me. "So now we've got rid of that obstacle. What's stopping you?" he asked.

"You don't trust me."

"Trust is earned."

"I'll rephrase. You are suspicious of everything I do."

"I'm cautious. That's not a crime."

"No, but let me sum up our brief but colorful history."

"Please do."

"First, I've had a professional working relationship with your head of security for years. I helped to uncover the perpetrator behind unexplained shifter deaths and took them down alongside you."

"One of your kind was killing them to get to you."

"That should make you trust me more, not less. If I'm willing to give up an elemental, then you should realize that I am not governed by the shackles of my species, but by my morals."

Silence coated the car, the heavy oppression of his thoughts pressing down upon us. Had I won an argument with Hudson? Perhaps. So that meant I'd proved I'm trustworthy and therefore it shouldn't be an obstacle to our relationship. Wait, I'd removed an obstacle, opening up the path for us to be together. I glanced at him. He had a smug smile plastered on his face. Damn it. How do I keep backing myself into a corner again and again with this man?

"I don't appreciate being played for a fool," I ground out.

"I'm simply getting you to realize that you are arguing with yourself. I trust you. You have yet to trust me, that's the issue. I will not use you. I won't hurt you or advertise your abilities. Whatever happened in your past, he wasn't your mate."

"Neither are you."

"Yet."

I rolled my eyes. "About that. You tricked me and then put an ad out, declaring your intentions to everyone."

He chuckled. "You're off the market. People need to know."

I squeezed the wheel tighter. "You have no right."

"You are judging me by human standards. I'm not human, Cora. Shapeshifters are dominant. They assert what they want with no apologies. We don't take without asking, but we don't hang around on the sidelines waiting for the green light, either."

"I…" The temperature dropped, making our breaths puff out in white clouds before our faces. A fog descended in front of the car, making me ease off the accelerator. Sleet slapped against the windscreen in a white heavy sheet. I shivered, thankful for the warmer leathers I'd chosen. I glanced up at the rapidly darkening sky. "What on earth is happening?"

"Cora!" Hudson shouted, grabbing the steering wheel and jerking it to the left. A terrible screeching sound echoed through the car, then we were airborne and spinning. I looked over at Hudson. He unclipped his seatbelt and lurched out of his seat toward me. He pressed on my button, releasing me from my restraint, and then we were barreling through the car door as he cocooned me with his body. We hit the ground and my teeth jolted, catching my tongue. Coppery warm blood exploded in my mouth as we rolled. My heart pounded so loud I could hear it pulsing in my ears.

We stopped with me laying on top of Hudson, his arms wrapped around me in a punishing grip. "Are you alive?" I wondered.

He laughed like his breathing was a certainty. "I smell your blood. Where are you hurt?"

"I bit my tongue."

"Should I kiss it better?"

I slapped his chest and pushed, standing up and dusting my pants down with my hands. He leapt to his feet and glanced at the thick fog surrounding us.

"What did I hit?" I wondered. Oh god, please don't let me have hit a car and hurt someone.

"Bear shifter."

On cue, an almighty roar split the air. I froze. Instinct kept me locked in place.

Hudson snarled. "You didn't hit them hard enough."

"What if it's like the others? A wildie for no reason?"

His pupils had turned vertical as he scanned the thick fog. "Then we try not to kill it, but if it's a choice between us or it, we win. Clear?"

"Crystal."

A shadow lurked in the fog, the distance distorted by the sleet and swirling wisps of mist. Another joined it. Then another. I took a step away. "Hudson, I don't think there's one."

He stepped back with me. "Agreed."

"Do we fight or run?" I asked. It didn't sit right, slaughtering innocent shifters who seemed to be caught up with something unknown.

"Run, at least until we get out of this fog, so I can see them coming."

We turned and sprinted. "Wait," I called out. "My bag, I need it."

"You'll have to sacrifice your fresh panties."

"The stuff Rockhard and Lenson made is vital."

Hudson mumbled a string of colorful curses and changed direction. "Keep running," he shouted.

I took off running, the thump of multiple feet growing closer behind me. My arms pumped and legs burned as I pushed myself faster. The familiar ache ran the length of my spine as my monster threatened to escape and protect me.

Red-hot pain sliced my calf, making me cry out, but I didn't turn back. The extra seconds would cost me my life. A low growl came behind me. Hudson's arm wrapped around my stomach. He slammed my bag into my hands and in a smooth move, he shifted to his giant tiger form and I was suddenly riding on his back. He loped faster and faster as the distance between us and the beasts increased.

I clutched his fur and leaned against his neck. The icy sleet whipped my hair, pulling it free from my ponytail. I glanced behind us, finding nothing but thick fog. How did he know where he was going? Even cats can't see through fog. Freakish fog that appeared out of nowhere.

An enormous howl of anger erupted from every direction. My head snapped forward. The fog condensed into furious heavy clouds outlined with a carmine hue. A face formed and stretched, lightning flashing behind it as it reached twenty feet. It opened its mouth wide and terrifying and descended toward us. Hudson darted to the left to avoid being eaten by the cloud monster. My heart thudded in my chest as it gained ground and chased us. I gripped Hudson's fur tighter with one hand, throwing my free hand out and yanking at the moisture in the surrounding fog before forming it into a water ball and blasting it at the horrifying face. The eerie features shattered into the mist. "That was creepy," I muttered.

Hudson huffed through his nose. My guess was he was laughing. He zig-zagged a path, no doubt confusing our scent trail. The howls grew distant.

Hudson slowed, then halted. He bent down, and I got the hint and slid off his back. The cold pierced me now I was away from his fevered body.

He transformed, leaving a gloriously naked Hudson in front of me. I blinked, but refused to turn away and blush. "What now?"

A howl laced with anger and despair echoed around us, coming from every direction.

"In here," he said, leaning down. He yanked open a door on the ground and flung it open. A storm shelter. Lightning struck the ground, mere yards away from where we stood. Hudson grabbed my arm, flung me over his shoulder, and jumped. The door clanged closed, plunging us into pitch black as we fell. I yelped at the jostle of his shoulder in my belly as he landed. He pulled me off him and grabbed my hips.

"Stay here while I find a light," he muttered.

The howling wind and sleet battered against the door above my head. Rumbles of thunder and lightning hammered into the ground, causing a tremble in the earth surrounding us. I swallowed and tried to find my bearings as the darkness gave me a dizzy sensation.

A small wall light encased in a cage blinked on next to me. I spun and found myself in an underground bunker. The entire space couldn't be larger than my bedroom, but it held a double bed, bookcase, kitchenette, and a two person sofa. A high shelf edged the room, stuffed full of various teddies and dolls. A flowery curtain separated the next area. I assumed it was the bathroom.

"There's not enough room to swing a cat in here."

Hudson flashed me a grin. "You could try, but I might class it as foreplay. I'm partial to tail rubbing."

"In your dreams."

"Every night."

I took two steps and dropped the bag on the bed. Hissing at the pain slicing up my calf, I looked over my shoulder.

Blood seeped down my pants leg and was pooling on the floor.

"Damn it."

"Get on the bed, let me see." Hudson motioned with his hand and started opening cupboards, his naked butt tightening as he bent. Lord, save me now. He was so damn masculine and pretty. I followed his instructions and flopped face first onto the bed. A puff of washing powder wafted from the sheets. At least they were clean.

Hudson clanged around the tiny kitchen. "You'd think they'd have a bowl," he muttered.

"Try under the bed," I said into the pillow.

The bed moved. "How did you know?"

"Space is at a premium. It's where I'd store stuff."

"There's spare male clothes under here, too." More's the pity.

Water splashed against metal. Then the bed dipped, and he was touching my leg. I hissed as the material pulled against my wound, making me clutch the comforter.

"Sorry," he said. He was gentle as he prodded. "It's a deep claw mark. The wolf caught you. It might scar."

"I'm alive," I stated, turning my head to the side to look at him. "Scars don't matter. Beauty doesn't matter. Don't pity me."

His hand paused, and he met my eyes. "You are beautiful inside and out. Your scars are the marks of a survivor. I don't pity you. I admire you." My heart gave a little pitter-patter of happiness. He wasn't just handsome, he was smooth and disarming. He looked back at my leg. "But this will take time to heal."

"My bag. The pink plastic pot." He unzipped my bag and rummaged through it, emptying various items onto the bed.

"Got it."

"Rub it on the wound. I'm going to want to hit you. But it will speed up the healing and kill any infection."

He unscrewed the lid and sniffed the contents. "Smells like ass."

"But it works."

He placed the pot next to my head and frowned at my leg. "These pants need to come off."

"No one ever told you cheesy chat up lines don't work?"

His lips curled. "I don't need chat up lines. But these will need to come off if I'm going to cover the wound."

I groaned and pressed my forehead into the comforter. He was right. But stripping to my panties in front of the Terror of Tennessee seemed like a bad idea, even if he was rocking the naturalist life. Shifters didn't find an issue in their nudity.

"Fine," I gritted out and lifted my stomach. The wound on my calf stung every time I moved. I wasn't standing again. My hands popped open the button and slid the zipper. I wiggled my hips and peeled them down my body. Half way over my butt I got stuck. I either stood and risked hurting myself or asked for help. I tensed and prepared myself for the agony.

A firm hand pushed on my spine. "Stay down, I'll help."

I rolled my eyes. Not that he could see, but the sentiment was the same. His warm hands curved around my hip bones and he pulled. "As much as I appreciate seeing your ass in leather," he grumbled, "it's a nightmare to get off."

"It's not meant for easy access."

"Then you shouldn't look so damn sexy in it."

He tugged harder. I cried out as the leather tore into shreds and I was relieved of my pants.

He grabbed the pot and slathered it onto my wound. Tears bloomed in my eyes and I clenched my jaw to keep from crying out. It burned like a bitch. But by morning I would walk without a hobble, and in a week, the scar would look like the injury happened months ago. Of course, that wasn't all down to the healing balm.

"Breathe," Hudson murmured.

"I know how to goddamn breathe, you overgrown house cat."

He chuckled. "I see being injured makes you tetchy."

"No, I'm as happy as a pig in shit while it feels like you are holding a naked flame to my skin."

"All done," he said, rising from the bed. I glared at his back as he put the balm on the drainer and washed his hands in the sink. He darted into the bathroom with a handful of clothing and returned dressed in distressed jeans and a checked flannel shirt. My eyelids drooped and my vision got blurry. My heart jumped in my chest. The balm forced sleep. I was about to pass out. Sleep was the best healer, but I couldn't sleep now, not with him here. I'd be vulnerable. I dragged my head from the comforter and flopped down again.

He glanced at me over his shoulder. "Sleep, Cora. You are safe."

Chapter Eight

The ghosts of the past can't hurt you.

Daylight streamed through my apartment window as I checked my watch. Neil would be here soon. I glanced at myself in the mirror one last time. It was date night, and I was dressed to kill. Tonight I would reveal all of my secrets to the shifter that had stolen my heart. The doorbell sounded.

I hurried to the front door, my heels clacking on the tiled floor. I threw it open to find two strangers on my doorstep.

"Cora Roberts?" a thick and burly dude with a shaved head asked.

I tilted my head. "Who wants to know?"

"That's her," the smaller guy muttered. He flung something in my face and a sharp pain exploded across my left temple. The world spun, *and I blinked awake to find myself in a chair. I jerked my limbs. Correction, I was tied to a chair. Big and burly stood in front of me.*

"Good. You're awake," he stated, stepping out of my line of sight. Neil coughed and gasped as the smaller guy punched him in the chest. He was also tied to a chair.

"What's happening?"

"It's simple, you give us the winning lottery numbers for this weekend, and we let you and your boyfriend go," the bigger dude stated.

I stared in horror. "I can't read the future, only the past."

I grasped for my power, heat bloomed in my chest. Tendrils of magic stirred, then dissipated. I glanced down finding a large bloodstone laying against my chest secured with a crude piece of string around my neck. They'd blocked my power. I was a sitting duck. My beast raised her head. No, I couldn't let her out. Not now, not ever.

"I don't believe you," the burly guy answered.

Neil spat blood onto the floor. "Give them what they want, Cor."

"I can't."

He shook his head. It morphed and changed as I watched Neil transform before me in horror. I closed my eyes and trembled. The world twisted again. My wrists ached as I looked up, finding them shackled by metal cuffs to the ceiling. My toes barely touching the floor. I shivered from the cold, my clothing long gone.

"Last chance, Cor," Neil said as a cruel grin split his lips. He slapped the studded leather belt in his hands in warning.

I let out a sob. "I cannot tell you the future, no matter how much you beat me."

He sighed and let the loop of the belt free, the end dragging on the floor. "We shall see."

The first lash caught my stomach. The flesh tore and blood spilled out. I sucked in a breath and braced myself. The second caught the underside of my breasts and I screamed as fire flashed across my body and sweat trickled down my spine and face. My voice broke with each subsequent wound. My heart shattered at the sadistic pleasure marring Neil's face.

"Cora," a voice shouted. I looked around the darkness seeking the masculine timber that was familiar.

Neil grabbed my hair and yanked. "There's no escape, Cora. I'll stop hurting you when you give me what I want."

I leaned forward and bit his cheek. He snarled and smacked my face, which whipped to the side.

"Cora! For fuck's sake, wake up."

I struggled in the chains and cursed Neil, his heritage, his existence, and the rest of his life. I hoped he burned in Hell for eternity.

"Please, Cora, open your eyes."

I followed the voice. And found myself staring into hazel eyes that were tight with concern. "That's what happened? If he wasn't already dead, I'd kill him myself," Hudson gritted out as he cradled me closer to his chest. I sucked in a breath and clutched my stomach. The phantom pain made my insides ache. My gaze darted around the low lit room. We were on the bed, in the storm shelter. We were on the bed.

"It's okay," he reassured me. "I'm not going to let anyone hurt you."

I didn't think. I twisted in his arms and straddled his lap before grabbing his face and fusing his lips with mine. It was frenzied, hot, and delicious. I needed him to chase away my nightmares, to restore my faith in relationships, and to make me feel protected.

He dragged his lips away from mine. I growled and tried to reconnect. "Wait, you're upset, emotional. I don't want you to regret it. To not know who you are sleeping with."

"I need you."

He grabbed my hips and tugged me closer before burying his face in my shoulder. I ran my fingers through his hair. Damn, cats have soft hair. He lifted his head. His eyes were lit from within as his cat peered out at me. "Say my name," he growled. "Convince me you know who you are with."

I kissed his jaw, nipping at the flesh. "I'm Cora, and you are the infuriating Hudson, who has been chasing me for months." His steel length grew beneath me. "And now you've caught me. What are you going to do?" I challenged.

He looked into my eyes. Studying my expression, weighing up my demons and deciding if they were worth it. I pulled back, away from him, from the judgment in his gaze. He flipped us and pinned my hands over my head before settling between my legs. "You are worth it."

"You heard that?" Oh shit. The telepathy potion had kicked in.

He grinned as I caught his thought of 'that's right, baby, all your secrets are mine now.' I had to will myself not to think of the things which would make him slaughter me on the spot.

He skimmed his nose along my throat before coming up to my lips. They parted as electricity sizzled between us. His lips descended upon mine with a ferocious kiss—dominating, wild, and devastating. I drowned in everything Hudson. His scent, his taste, his touch—everything set me on fire until I was sure we'd burn the world down at our feet. My chains slipped, my true form yanking to be free. It wanted to preen in his presence. He moved down my body, gliding his hands up my t-shirt and pulling it over my head before unsnapping the front clasp of my bra and releasing my breasts. He leaned back to peer down at me, his gaze memorizing every curve and every flaw of my body.

'You are so fucking beautiful. It hurts to look at you,' his inner voice rasped.

I shot up and yanked at his shirt. The buttons popped and flew around the room. I pulled my legs out from under him and wrapped myself around him like a koala. One hand folded around his neck, keeping his lips locked with mine while the other was between us as I opened his jeans. My hand found his hard length. Oh. My. God. Yes.

A rumble of approval came from his chest at my thoughts. He tore my panties from my body, and his fingers skimmed along my sensitive flesh. I gasped and ground down, wanting him inside me. I didn't have the patience for foreplay. A deep ache had settled inside me, and it was begging to be filled.

"I got you," he growled before pushing me back on the bed and untangling my legs from his waist. He descended upon me, his hot lips exploring my neck, then my breasts. He grazed his teeth over my nipple, making my breasts swell and ache.

"Don't tease," I panted.

He grinned at me before leaving a blazing trail down my stomach. He nestled his shoulders between my legs, stretching them wide before throwing them up and over his back. Finally, he gave me a long lick that left no part of me unexplored. My head tipped back as I panted through the pleasure he was making me feel.

Just a little more pressure. His hands pinned my hips to the bed as he followed my thoughts and found the precise way to make me scream. My hands gripped his hair and he growled, causing the most amazing vibrations. My climax slammed into me like a freight train. He left me for a second, his jeans hitting the floor.

"Shit," he muttered.

I tipped my head up. "What's wrong?"

"Condom?"

I pointed at my bag. "Side pocket."

He arched a brow and dug around in my bag before pulling out a fresh box of condoms. Okay, so maybe, just maybe, I had bought a packet recently. Margret at the checkout had made a show of twisting the box and eyeballing the description before handing them to me. The perks of living in a small town. A foil packet rustled, then he climbed back onto the bed, grabbed my thighs and yanked me up to straddle his lap. His hand threaded into my hair and he pulled me in to kiss me senseless. A second later he pushed inside of me. I gasped at the stretch, sparks of pain mingling with pleasure. He grabbed my ass and urged me down further. Everything inside me clenched with need.

"Fuck," he muttered against my lips, before increasing the pace. Every single thrust built my need, our mouths barely parted as we devoured each other. I couldn't get enough as my nails raked down his back, causing him to growl into my mouth.

I needed a little more friction. He reached between us and his thumb brushed over my sensitive flesh. I arched my back and exploded around him. A ripple of pleasure shot down my spine, my body preparing to realign to make room for my beast I kept shackled. He collapsed on top of me, and with a deafening roar, found his own release.

He rolled to my left, then pulled me against his body. As the seconds passed, our breathing settled. I'd fucked up.

Perhaps he hadn't noticed my last thoughts? Cora Roberts - Master of Optimism.

He clutched me tighter. "You are safe with me."

I squeezed my eyes tighter as my heart constricted. I wanted to believe him, to take that step off the cliff and be caught. I wanted the passion that blazed in his eyes to fill my life, the love that he offered to fill my every day with happiness. I wanted a partner, someone to enjoy the good times, and to stand by my side through the hard times. And now that he had exposed me to what it would be like, I no longer wanted it, I needed it. He waited in silence as my thoughts ran away from me. They whirled with the prospect of that life, to end the loneliness. But the threat he posed by being that close to me, to invading my life, to making me depend on him—could I take that risk?

"I–"

"Don't," he cut me off. "Don't catastrophize our relationship. I haven't given you any reason for the doubts you have. You have your secrets, and when you are ready to share, I'm here to listen. Until then, I am that partner you hope for."

A tear slipped free and dripped down my cheek and onto his chest. His hand dug into my hair and pulled it back to stare into my eyes. "Trust me enough to take the risk, Cora. I won't go looking for your secrets. We both have things we need to discuss when we are ready, but relationships don't happen overnight. They call it falling in love, because that's exactly what it is. A fall, but I will be here to catch you. Give us a chance."

I looked in his eyes, that were still glazed with pleasure as silence stretched between us while my heart and mind warred. The world continued turning, but everything else fell away, leaving only us. "Okay."

"Okay?"

I nodded. "Okay."

He pulled me up and kissed me with a gentleness I didn't think he had in him. It was a promise to treat me this way, with tenderness and respect. He sealed my fate in that moment, as I had never felt more protected, safe, and at home than when I was in his arms, surrounded by the promise of a future filled with hope.

Chapter Nine

We are family.

We emerged into a different world than when we left. The storm shelter sat a hundred yards from an abandoned dilapidated cream farmhouse with several crumbling barns located amongst some sad trees that clung to existence by a thread. I'd ditched my ruined leather pants for the spare pair of leggings in my bag. My tank top and jacket had survived our adventure. The clear and bright cerulean blue sky lay in sharp contrast to the grassy landscape covered in white roses stained with crimson. The same roses that were growing on my property. These weren't planted, they'd rained down and scattered along the floor, but the petals were glowing with life. Not one wilted bloom in sight.

Hudson scanned the distance as we walked, his thoughts clear as the sun, even if he wasn't projecting them into my mind. I stayed quiet, letting him draw his own conclusions. Speaking at this point would incite his suspicious beast.

We'd trekked over a mile before the questions began. "Do you have any idea why the same creepy roses that are growing in your graveyard are here?"

"Blood magic."

"I'd figured the wildies were focused on me. That it was part of some idiotic plot to take me out."

I swallowed, because while the timing had been suspect, I had thought the same thing. Clearly, we were both incorrect. "Me too."

"But all of this is linked. The roses, the wildies, your aunt's kidnapping."

"It appears that way."

"The question is why would the perpetrators of the kidnapping be trying to prevent you from reaching your aunt, when that's exactly what they have requested from you?"

"That is not so clear. Maybe it's you they were trying to take out."

"Hmm, perhaps."

My mind disconnected from the future it had imagined. Not even twenty-four hours had passed, and he was going to leave me. Not that I could blame him, I carried more secrets than the Pentagon. His hand engulfed mine, and he pulled me to a stop. I spun to face him, his hazel eyes burning with promises of passion and partnership.

"I am not a naïve man, Cora. I understand and acknowledge that strange shit happens around you, and I walked into that with my eyes wide open. I am not frightened by the danger that seems to stalk your every move." He gathered me in his arms and planted a kiss on my lips that stole my breath and made tingles draw down my spine and into my core.

He drew back, but kept me wrapped in his arms. "Besides, life was getting too boring."

I snorted. "Never a dull moment with me. That I can promise."

He grinned and grabbed my hand before dragging me along with him. A breeze, which smelled of the earth, spun around us, lifting the roses from the floor. It felt like the universe was giving me the green light to a future with Hudson at my side.

Hope—that's what was whispering through my mind. Hope and excitement. My heart threw itself a party. Hudson represented everything light, and it was like taking my first breath of fresh air after living in the city smog.

"How do we stop the telepathy?" Hudson asked as we walked in the direction he swore the car was in. Intuition told me it was the opposite way, but who was I to argue with the nose of a shifter?

"We remove the necklaces," I answered.

"It's not as intrusive as I thought."

"Exactly. You need to be directing your thoughts, or be completely unguarded."

He pointed ahead of us. "There."

The car wasn't just wrecked, it was upside down in a ditch by the side of the road and looked like it had been the loser in a monster truck rally. "Damn, we are at least three hours' drive away from Aunt Dayna's, we can't walk."

The tell-tale hum of an engine foretold the car that rounded the corner ahead of us. "Here comes the cavalry," Hudson said.

"What did you do?"

"I called for backup while you were sleeping."

A shiny black Cadillac Escalade pulled to our side and stopped. Hudson opened the rear door, and I peered inside. Oh wonderful. Here comes Dangerous Dave—we were saved. I sighed and jumped in the back of the car. Hudson shut the door and got in next to Dave.

"What the fuck happened?" he asked, gazing at the overturned car amongst the bloodied roses.

"A bunch of crazy shifters ran us off the road and chased us into an underground bunker with an entity in a storm, and then when we emerged in the morning it had rained white roses covered in blood," I summarized, leaving out the naked limbo part. Dave arched a brow at me and shot me his hard assed stare. Ha, nice try, far scarier creatures than you schooled me. I opted for a change of subject. "I thought you'd be too busy with my Aunt Liz for a rescue mission."

"She was called away. Something about a political spat involving the Order's leader and the United Kingdom's missing vampire princess." He cast a glance over his shoulder at me. Wonderful, my grandmother was in a pissing contest with Rebecca's parents—again. His nostrils flared, and he glanced between me and Hudson. "Seems like I'm not the only one who's been busy."

I rolled my eyes because, of course he could smell what we had been up to. "We are grownups, unless Hudson has to clear all his conquests with you prior to the deed?"

"Only the dangerous ones," Dave muttered before turning around and setting off. "There are snacks in the cooler next to you, courtesy of Liz."

"Ooh, Aunt Liz makes the best snacks." I popped the lid of the cooler and plucked out the note from the top.

Cora,

For the love of my ovaries, please tell me you took advantage of your trapped in a tight space situation with the Principal. If not, you lose your female card—I revoke it on behalf of all women everywhere.

Love, Rebecca
P.S. I hope you are safe.

I scoffed and dug around in the cooler for less judgmental food. I grabbed a turkey salad sandwich and handed it over the seat to Hudson. "Here."

He took it. "You're sharing?"

"Don't read anything into it, big guy. It's not a proposal or an acceptance of one."

"For now."

"Did I miss something?" Dave asked, as if he didn't already know. Perhaps he assumed I was a passing fancy, the flavor of the month.

Stop, Hudson said in my mind. *The doubts, the worries, stop.*

I stuffed a sandwich in my mouth to focus on anything else. The healing balm had done most of the work, but it was still draining on my body and I needed all my strength to face whoever held Aunt Dayna. Which meant food and rest, so I fell asleep full on sandwiches and Maggie's lemon cookies.

The sun had dipped low in the sky, casting a peachy glow across the grassy land surrounding my aunt's ranch-style house. There were no signs of life, not in the house or outside.

"You notice anything strange?" I asked the two shifters that surrounded me.

"Other than the three of us hiding out in a bush?" Dave answered.

Hudson glanced around. "There's no noise. No birds, no insects, nothing is moving."

"What does it mean?" Dave asked.

"Nothing good," I answered. "The things that repel nature are intrinsically evil. They are born that way, no good exists within them, so the natural world shies away from their presence in a bid for self-preservation, because where true evil resides, death and destruction will follow."

"You get that out of a fortune cookie?" Dave asked.

I pressed my lips together. I'd worked with Dave long enough to know he was attempting to relax me with humor in a tense situation that was undoubtedly about to get worse.

"What's the plan?" Hudson asked.

"The plan?" I said, rising to be in full view of the house and any nasties that lurked in there. "The plan is to walk in and take my aunt. You guys stay here. I'll holler if I need you." I tapped my head to make sure Hudson understood the hollering would be mental.

"For the record, I hate this plan," Hudson said.

"Noted, but in the absence of divine intervention," I glanced at the sky, nope, "this is our only option."

"We could storm the castle, all three of us," Dave suggested.

"And risk my aunt's life? Do you like your testicles attached? Because Liz will fry them for lunch if she hears that. Also, the house won't allow any harm to come to me."

"Is it sentient?" Dave asked.

I glanced down at him. "Think of this house as a dragon, and the Roberts women as the treasure chest that it guards."

"Interesting," Dave said, eyeballing the house with new-found curiosity. Built in the 1960s, Dayna's house was a sprawling single story home, complete with open plan living space and an immense garden. But the magic that seeped into the building came from the land they had built it on. We suspected a coven of elementals had once used the wooded area to perform powerful rituals, and consequently to bury their dead, back when witches were being persecuted by idiotic power-tripping human men. Elementals weren't witches, but we were the fuel behind the fear of the unknown that led to many innocent women being murdered.

"I'm perfectly safe unless the devil himself has come to collect me."

"Is that a possibility?" Dave asked.

I huffed. "Demons don't walk this earth."

"As far as you know."

Oh, I knew—too well. Insider knowledge.

Having this control over Dangerous Dave could be a blessing. My Aunt Liz was scary, and he was trying to be in her good books. I stepped out of the safety of our recon bush and took sure strides toward the house.

Don't die. I just got you, Hudson projected into my mind.

Don't worry, Principal, I just got you too and I'm nowhere near finished.

I don't plan on being finished—ever.

My face didn't betray the happiness that comment made me feel. But my insides were doing the best happy dance anyone had ever seen. Hudson didn't only want me in his bed. He wanted me by his side, leading the pack. I swallowed the lump in my throat. I didn't want that responsibility. The pack would be a problem. I wasn't stupid. Just because he said it would be fine, didn't make it true. There would be protesters, resistance, challengers.

The curtains twitched in the living room window. *Head back in the game, Cora. Rescue your aunt, then devise a plan to win over the pack which doesn't involve fighting half of them to prove you are worthy.* Being with me had its disadvantages beyond our different species. There were things that hunted me, things that would bring a world of trouble to Hudson's doorstep if they scented my true heritage.

The front door swung open, revealing a dark and gloomy hallway. That wasn't ominous at all. No one was there to greet me. It could be the house welcoming me, but I didn't feel the presence that normally enveloped me like a warm hug, which meant the house was hiding its nature. *Hmm, what are you up to?*

I stepped over the threshold, and a sense of utter dread consumed me. My knees wobbled, but I straightened my spine and stalked inside, the front door slamming closed behind me. I swung a left through the archway, finding the sunken living area empty of anything living or dead. I edged around the room and passed through the kitchen. A soft glow drew me toward the dining room. My shoulders tensed with the unknown situation I was walking into. I felt the reassuring weight of the nulling potion in my pocket and strode through the open door.

My gaze snagged on the ominous being occupying the chair at the end of the table. Dressed in a smart suit with one leg thrown over his knee, to anyone else he might appear to be a charming man, with sharp cheekbones and ebony hair cut into a fashionable short style. He exuded power and instilled an awareness in your molecules that recognized the predator in the room. To me, however, he was family.

"Shit," I muttered. "What are the odds?"

"Indeed, take a seat, Cora. We have much to discuss."

And just like that, on an early October evening, I found myself seated opposite the devil himself. Perhaps I should play the lottery today?

Chapter Ten

Whomever said 'better the devil you know' clearly did not know the actual devil.

"I'm honored, Lucifer, but there's no need for the pomp and circumstance. You could have phoned for a catch up or made a house call."

That better be a sarcastic nickname for the nasty you are facing, Cora Roberts, Hudson pushed into my mind. Oh shit. Of course he could hear me all the way out here, and now I had the pack's suspicious head of security and the Terror of Tennessee listening to my secrets. I considered ripping the necklace off.

Don't you dare, I will come barreling into that house before the clasp breaks.

Lucifer's glacial blue eyes bored into mine. "You have been successful at warding yourself from me, from my kind. It proved impossible to even locate your general area. Kudos to you, Cora, I'm impressed with your resourcefulness, but that meant I needed to be creative to get your attention. And with no lover to speak of, I took the next best thing—your family."

"She better not be hurt."

He cocked his head to the side. "Or else?"

He wasn't threatening me. He was curious. Would I let my beast out of the box to save my aunt? "I am here alone, as you requested. You can let her go."

He smiled. It wasn't pleasant; it was terrifying, speaking of pain and promised violence. "Bring her in," he demanded. Two people entered through the back door, each with an arm around the waist of my aunt. She sagged between them as her feet trailed on the floor. She acted the part well, but my aunt was far from incapacitated. The King of Hell should know better than to underestimate a Roberts woman.

They dropped Dayna on the window seat. The guy to the left built like a beanpole with straw hair turned and folded his arms, while the auburn-haired stout woman to the right sat next to Dayna and turned to me and Lucifer.

"Your demons are wearing the locals," I stated. "You went to the trouble of possession. What gives?"

He flicked a hand in their direction, dismissing them. "They did a little recon for me, picked out the best aunt to get your attention."

I snorted. "Most vulnerable you mean."

"I don't get my hands dirty unless I need to." Oh, don't I know it? The fate of the human souls who resided in those bodies wasn't certain. The demons could slaughter the soul on their way out, or they could simply leave. Few demons bothered visiting Earth, because of the enormous surge of power needed for a successful possession. If they messed up, they might end up stuck in purgatory. Given the rarity of possession, most supernaturals believed demons couldn't even walk the Earth. Some doubted their existence altogether, and that's the way Lucifer liked it. How could you defend against an evil you never knew existed? I knew better. I'd experienced firsthand the horrors Hell produced.

"You wanted me, and here I am. Now what?"

"I want access to your naughty little back door."

That better not be a metaphor, Hudson growled in my mind.

Ew, gross.

"I don't know what you're talking about," I stated. He couldn't know. I'd only figured out my personal alternate dimension was a doorway to heaven a few months ago.

"You owe me. Don't play coy, Cora. Feigning innocence doesn't suit you," Lucifer stated with a slow smirk. He totally knew. Fuck.

I glanced at Dayna. She winked at me from underneath the tangle of her hair. "I don't want to discuss this in front of anyone."

His gaze flickered to Dayna. "Your family don't know?"

My jaw popped with tension, and I shook my head. He steepled his hands together and arched a brow. "I see." He snapped his fingers. Magic burst around us and coated my skin. A silencing bubble formed around myself and Lucifer, excluding the others.

"How, exactly, do I owe you?" I asked.

"You have been a naughty niece."

I rolled my eyes and caught Dayna's wide-eyed stare—if only they understood the half of it. "Your point?"

"My point is, you've been stealing souls that by all rights belong to me."

I pressed my lips together. "I didn't realize until recently."

"Ignorance isn't innocence."

"Agreed, but I didn't deliberately set out to deprive you."

"No, but now you owe me."

"It's not like I can pop in and retrieve the souls."

"Fickle creatures, angels. Self-righteous beings with an inflated sense of self-worth. It wouldn't harm them to have a shake up." I resisted pointing out that he too was an angel. A fallen one, but still at heart an angel. Not that he had a heart.

"Indeed, but that shake up would cost me my life."

Lucifer tilted his head to the side as if considering whether my life was worth the rebellion.

"I'm not going in," I reiterated, in case his evil brain had missed the memo.

He waved his hand. "Fine, but you still owe me."

Ugh, being in debt to the devil wasn't a fun position to be in. "What do you want?"

"If you won't go in, then give me access."

I leaned back in my chair, the hairs on my arms standing on end. What he was asking for would defy the natural order. It would upend the world as we know it. "Why?"

He spread his hands out in front of him. "I want visiting rights to my father, my brethren. I want to go home, Cora. Surely you can understand that?"

I arched a brow. I was no fool. Lucifer had the opportunity to go home anytime he wanted. God would not bar him from heaven so long as he lived by the divine principles. The first would be to do no harm to humans. If he was truly repentant, he would be welcomed back into His grace. Lucifer wanted to use the back door because no one would ever let his arrogant, unrepentant, self-absorbed ass in the front. But why? For what purpose?

"Your father is looking for you," he said. My gaze snapped to him as genuine fear ran its icy fingers down my spine.

"You're lying."

"Your warding is effective, that's how you've eluded him for so long, but don't think he won't use your weakness for family against you."

"Like you."

He bobbed his head, then leaned in closer. "I can protect you."

My chest tightened. There were too many loose ends flying around in the wind. All my father needed to do was pull on one to make me unravel. I unpacked my carefully crafted contingency plans in my mind, searching for the most workable one. I needed to leave Maggie and Rebecca running the guest house. Sebastian could help. Hudson—damn, Hudson wouldn't let me go easily. I'd have to break up with him before we'd even begun. Dave would question Aunt Liz, who wouldn't give up my secrets, not even the ones she knew. Then they would break up. Hudson would be unhappy. He would look for me. *Kill him,* the insidious voice whispered in my mind. Death was a constant entity that stalked my thoughts and guided my actions, but right now, it wasn't the answer. I squashed it.

"Before you pack up your life and run, know there are thousands of people looking for you. The second you use a credit card, register your pretty face on a CCTV camera, use a passport or driving license, he will know."

Shit, shit, shit. I needed to go to ground. But I couldn't protect myself the same way at any other location. I'd pooled all my time and effort into making Summer Grove House impenetrable.

"The best thing you can do is take my offer of help in exchange for the access you already owe me," Lucifer pushed.

"It's a good deal, Cora. You're family, so I have a soft spot for you."

I rolled my eyes. He had a soft spot for one thing alone, his own agenda. I happened to fit it. If I stayed, I'd be putting everyone I love in danger. I rubbed my temples. "I need to run."

"I can hide you." Uh, huh, sure. Satan says, 'come hide in my lair, I'll keep you safe'. He must think I'm an idiot.

The surrounding bubble contracted as magic sizzled in the air. And things were about to get a whole lot worse, because while Lucifer had been keeping everyone from hearing us, he'd also cut off my link to Hudson.

"More secrets, Cora? Ah, your shifter male approaches."

Lucifer's glacial eyes flared red for a split second. The door bursts open, and a prehistoric nightmare thundered in. Aunt Dayna shot to her feet and raised her hands. The house flared to life, bolstering her magic as she slammed air into Lucifer. He sailed out of his chair, his back hitting the wall with a thump. Hudson's jaws snapped in his direction, going for Lucifer's throat.

"No," I roared, launching myself between Lucifer and Hudson.

Move, he shouted in my mind. I shook my head just as Lucifer's lackeys came running into the room, and they'd brought reinforcements. A group of six men covered in black robes raised their arms and chanted in Latin. Not good. I grabbed Dayna's hand and yanked on Hudson's tail to get his attention.

"We need to leave now."

Dayna pulled me toward the door.

Why? Hudson's gravelly voice echoed in my mind.

"Because in thirty seconds this entire house is about to move dimensions, having a new zip code in Hell."

He threatened you, and I can rip off their heads in half that time. Problem solved.

"But I'm okay. Come on, big boy, you should know me better than that. The King of Hell isn't enough to tear me away from you," I shouted.

Hudson grunted and ran after me and Dayna as we fled through the door. Dave's SUV skidded to a halt outside the house. I threw the door open, stuffed Dayna in the front passenger seat, then dived into the rear. Hudson changed mid leap and slammed the door closed as he slid in beside me.

"Drive!" Hudson growled. I glanced out the rear window as we sped away. Lucifer stood on the porch, glancing between me and Hudson as a slow smile tipped his lips up. Dammit, me and my big mouth.

The house hummed with power, and an explosion spun the car 360 degrees. Dave righted his course and stuck his foot down. The house lit up from within, then folded in on itself, hopping from our dimension to Lucifer's.

"It will be back," Dayna called out from the front.

"The demon?" Dave asked.

She turned to face him. "No, the house, silly, it gets homesick without me."

"Somehow, I'm finding these conversations less and less weird."

I chuckled. "You've been hanging out with me too long, Dave."

"Still fucking weird," Hudson ground out as he hit me with his hard alpha stare and pushed the next thoughts into my mind. *I'm waiting for you to explain why you protected Lucifer fucking Morningstar.*

Get comfy, Hudson, because that's one secret I'm not ready to share with you.

You are making it impossible.

I warned you, you said you'd be patient. Breaking your promise already?

That was before.

Before what?

Before you sat and had a conversation with the devil like you were old friends, before you stepped between us and protected the most evil being known to humanity.

The devil isn't evil. He's complicated. The souls he's responsible for are evil. Do you think God would put someone in charge of Hell who was malevolent? Lucifer made a mistake he's being punished for, but remember, he is still an angel.

And now you sympathize with the devil. I feel like I don't know you at all. Your secrets run so deep they make it impossible to protect you—even from yourself.

I blinked back the tears. Perhaps my Hudson issue would resolve itself before we reached home. He'd move off my property and leave me in peace. Alone, but in peace. That peace didn't look as appealing as it had twenty-four hours ago.

I don't need protection. I'm more than capable of handling my own enemies.

I'm worried you don't recognize your enemies, even when they call themselves Lucifer and threaten your family.

Then leave.

He huffed a laugh, causing Dave and Dayna to glance behind them.

I might be angry with you, Cora. But you won't get rid of me that easily.

He yanked at the chain and broke the necklace before depositing it onto my lap. "This has run its course."

I stared at the slender chain, feeling a sense of doom at his words. Perhaps we had run our course? What was the alternative? That he kept pushing until I broke and spilled my secrets? He thought being on first-name terms with Satan was bad? His head would explode if knew the truth.

Warm hands cupped my cheeks, and Hudson pulled my face toward his. "Stop it," he warned. "Stop catastrophizing. No secrets will chase me away, Cora. But I am allowed to be frustrated in the meantime."

"What did I miss?" Dayna said, peering at us.

"They fucked," Dave answered.

"We are mated," Hudson declared.

"We are seeing how things go," I corrected.

"Ooh, are we going to get a show?" Dayna asked.

"What the hell? Why would you think that?"

"Well, your lover is holding your head like it's a precious diamond and he's naked."

"No show," I gritted out.

"Prude."

I didn't take my eyes from Hudson's. He was everything that made me weak, and that made him dangerous. I decided then and there that I didn't care. I'd been living a half life. I wasn't happy. I was existing, but I wasn't happy. I needed more. I needed him. And now that I'd had him, I wasn't sure I could ever give him up.

Chapter Eleven

What you do under the influence of the full moon is your business.

Five hours and two naps later, we pulled into a classic diner complete with a black and white tiled floor, red vinyl booths, and rotating ceiling fans that did nothing but move the stifling air around us. The carnivores were hungry and demanded a combo of meat and grease that increased my cholesterol by being in the same room.

"What can I get you?" Marla, a slender teenager rocking platinum pigtails, asked.

Aunt Dayna scooped her wild honey blonde hair off her shoulders and tucked it into her flower power headscarf. "Garden burger with fries, and a chocolate shake," she said.

"Same," I added.

"Triple bacon cheeseburger, extra fries, a portion of onion rings, and a chocolate shake," Hudson said.

"Same," Dave said.

Marla gave Hudson a weird glance before sauntering off.

We'd grabbed some clothing for Hudson from a tiny town market, but our choices were limited, meaning he was wearing a lemon T-shirt, two sizes too small for his wide chest, and a pair of khaki shorts which rode up too far. To finish the ensemble, he'd stuffed his feet into navy and white striped boat shoes.

Dave pinned Dayna with his suspicious attention. "What happened?" he asked the second we were alone.

She sighed and swept her hair out of her face. "They ambushed me. Lucifer and his demons caught me in the herb garden out back. I never saw them coming. They didn't trigger any warning system because they simply stepped through the dimension, not over my wards."

"But you could have prevented them from getting in the house," I pointed out.

She grimaced. "He threatened to go find one of my sisters if I didn't cooperate. I thought with Cora coming, she'd have backup and we'd have a greater chance of learning what he wants with no bloodshed."

I pressed my lips together and frowned. "We are weaker apart. Perhaps it's time to regroup."

"Do you know what he wants?" Dave asked, switching his attention to me.

"What all self-absorbed overlords want. Power."

"And what has that got to do with you?" Dave pushed.

I cast a glance at the three curious supernaturals surrounding me. "He believes my gifts would give him access to more power."

"Your retro gift?"

I stared at the cutlery on the table. "It's linked to it, yes."

"What aren't you telling us?"

"That's enough," Hudson intervened before the conversation descended into a fight. "She's been through enough. I'm sure if there is something important to share, Cora will do that."

Dave huffed, leaned back, and folded his arms. "Help me understand how you know Lucifer."

Thin ice, Cora. Tread carefully. "He's had dealings with my family before."

Dayna didn't even blink at my side. "That's right," she said. I was lying, kind of, and she backed me up. That was family for you. Dave narrowed his eyes on Dayna as Marla appeared with four plates stacked up her arms. She slid the giant burgers to the men, then the less offensive ones to me and Dayna. Dave and Hudson tucked into theirs before I'd even picked up my fork. Saved by cow corpse.

Hudson proved to be a comfy pillow as the carbohydrates hit my system and I passed out for the rest of the journey.

"Cora," Hudson whispered in my ear. "Wake up, we're home."

I jerked awake and swiped my lips with the back of my hand. Damn it. We weren't at the drool on each other stage of our relationship.

Hudson chuckled. "You can drool on me anytime."

I said that out loud? *Get your head together, Cora.* I stretched my arms as Dave stopped the car. The front door swung open and our welcoming committee appeared consisting of two vampires, one shifter, and a ghost. It was a regular supernatural hangout.

My door popped open and Hudson offered me his hand. I took it and slipped out of the back seat and onto the ground.

"Ooh, what did I miss?" Rebecca asked with a gleam in her eye as she swept toward us in a puff of white tulle. Guess we were rocking the vampire princess look today.

Sebastian frowned at my hand in Hudson's. "Yes, what did we miss?"

I waved at Dayna, trying to redirect their attention. "We rescued Dayna and she's okay."

Sebastian folded his arms. "Clearly, but tell us something that's not obvious."

"They're mated," Dave announced.

"We are not mated."

"As good as," Hudson said.

"If she says you're not mated, then you're not mated," Sebastian ground out.

I arched a brow at my best friend. What was his problem?

Hudson moved closer to me so his chest was brushing against my back. He narrowed his eyes at Sebastian. "You are going to need to find another woman to placate your parents with. Cora is officially off the market and everyone will know. You can no longer use her."

"I am not using her," Sebastian snapped.

"Really?"

I rolled my eyes. "Stop it," I said to them both. "I am not a piece of meat to be fought over."

"Correct, because I've already licked and claimed you—everywhere," Hudson responded. My cheeks flamed. He spun me around, then cupped my face in his hands and dropped a panty-melting kiss onto my lips that made everything female in me sit up in awareness. We could forgo the judgment and skip to the good part, I thought. He grinned like he'd heard me.

"I need to check in with the pack. Stay out of trouble until I get back," Hudson stated.

I blinked. "I don't get into trouble. It's all of you involving me in your supernatural drama that lands me in trouble. My life was peaceful before I met you."

"Somehow I doubt that."

"Do you remember the day you phoned me because of Roberto and Julia?" Dave started. "They'd decided to experiment and things got a little wild. So wild they called a doctor who couldn't get access to—"

"Yes, that's enough, Dave."

"Or how about the time Beatrice shifted mid-labor, and you called me to come and persuade her to turn back?"

"Both examples of shifter situations, proving my point that I am dragged into supernatural shenanigans, not welcoming them." My lips tilted up in a wicked smile. "Which brings me to the night the pack's head of security called me to assess a bunch of tripping wolves in a club that caters to a particular brand of sexual activity."

"I was responding to a call from a friend," Dave growled.

Rebecca sniggered as I nodded. "Sure, while dressed in leather trousers and carrying a whip around as an accessory?"

"I'd confiscated it from a couple."

"Does Aunt Liz know what you like to do under the glow of the full moon? She's a bit of a prude my aunt, you might scare her off."

This time, it was Dave's turn to grin wickedly. "She may act like a prude, Cora, but she knows what I like under the full moon, half moon, or no damn moon."

"Ew."

"As enlightening as this was," Hudson began, "we need to check in on the pack." He turned, grabbed Dave by the arm and pulled him toward the stables. I glared at his retreating back. That's right, leave me to the wolves. Well, I mean, he was technically taking the wolf with him.

I sighed and spun to face the firing squad. "I have no intention of dissecting my relationship status on the stoop. It's uncouth."

Sebastian snorted. "Uncouth was sucking face with the Principal in view of your family and friends."

I glared at him and refused to blush. "If I wanted to have wild monkey sex on the lawn in the middle of the day, there isn't a damn thing you could do about it."

"I'll be there waiting," Hudson shouted over his shoulder.

"It might scare off the guests," Sebastian mused.

Rebecca smiled. "Or attract them."

"They would be the wrong sort of guests," I pointed out. "The point being, I'm not discussing my love life out here."

Rebecca clapped her hands. "Okay, that settles it, all vampires, shifters, and elementals inside. Maggie, put the kettle on. Cora needs tea and cake in order to spill the beans."

Harry peered at me as we climbed the steps. "You are positively glowing, Miss. Roberts. I approve."

At least someone did.

CHAPTER TWELVE

Early morning calls.

If White Castle was the epicenter of the Supernatural elite, then Summer Grove House had unwittingly become the unofficial headquarters. Six months ago, my home was a blip on the map frequented by the Vampire Prince of North America only because he was my best friend. Ghosts came and went quickly as they moved on, and I was a small town doctor with a speciality in the deceased. Today, the Principal—leader of the shapeshifters—lived next door, my vampire bestie was here more often than not, and I had a ghost in residence that refused to move on to his afterlife. Meanwhile, my previously absent grandmother was now sniffing around my life and attempting to direct it in order to further her political power. To top it off, Lucifer had come topside to force me to let him into Heaven. I had no delusions. I hadn't come out of that confrontation unscathed by chance. Lucifer had let me walk. Why was the pertinent question. And was everything—the roses, the wildies, Lucifer's presence —connected? Holy shit.

I shot up from my bed, threw my dressing gown on and zoomed down the stairs. The house was quiet. Where the hell was everyone when I was having an epiphany? I glanced out the window. The moon hung high in the sky and cast a gloomy glow over my lawn. The clock chimed a cheery tune and then bonged, once, twice, three times. Right, everyone was asleep, silly me. Even the dead disappeared at this time of night. Where to, I didn't know, but Harry was regularly absent when my insomniac ass was whizzing around the house like a kid hyped on sugar. Ooh, cookies. Maggie baked oatmeal and chocolate chip. My feet moved toward the kitchen. I caught myself half way and cursed. I needed to speak to someone who could tell me I was putting together two and two and coming up with five. I needed reassurance. I needed Hudson. I was out the door and halfway across the lawn when I felt it.

An insidious entity was creeping along the border of my home, testing the wards, feeling out weak points. It was weighing up the consequences of breaching the barrier.

I stepped on something sharp and hissed as it sliced open the sensitive sole on my foot. The roses, having extended beyond the graveyard, were now covering my front lawn. Something was feeding them, something with power. I continued my trek to the stables, my bloodied sole seeping into the ground. The network of vines shimmered with magic as they devoured the power in my blood. That wasn't good. I picked up speed, jogging the final few yards before hammering my fist on Hudson's door. The hairs on my nape stood to attention, sending a shiver of awareness down my spine. I glanced over my shoulder. The boy was back. His mouth was moving, shouts and screams falling silent in the night air. He was terrified, but he'd been silenced. My guess would be he'd been magically bound as they murdered him so no one would hear his pleas for mercy. There was something perverse about not allowing someone to vocalize their dying thoughts. He flickered out of sight, then back, but closer. His arm reached out toward me as he clutched his neck and blood poured through his fingers and onto his face, again defying gravity.

I edged back and leaned my back against the door, trying to create the biggest distance between me and the boy. He flickered out again, then was off the lawn and on the gravel leading up to the stables. My heart thudded in my chest in a crazy rhythm. Few things supernatural scared me, but right now, facing the spirit of an unknown child who'd been murdered in a grizzly manner, I was terrified. Something wasn't right, it didn't feel right, it felt unnatural—and death was natural. Even when someone met a violent sudden end, the death was genuine. It still involved the soul leaving the body and starting anew in whichever afterlife awaited them. Their bodies broke down and once more became part of the natural order. But this was wrong. I could feel it in my bones.

The boy drew closer. I tried to meld with the door. Perhaps Hudson was still at the pack? I glanced at the main house. At a sprint, it would take me less than thirty seconds to get back. With bloodied feet and a thorny landscape, I'd be lucky to make it in a minute. I contemplated screaming. Rebecca would hear me and come darting out the same way I had, resulting in her feet being torn to shreds.

He inched closer, so close I could see the popped blood vessels in the boy's eyes. What had they done to this poor boy?

The solid wall at my back gave out, and I fell backward. I flailed my arms, trying to maintain balance. Strong arms caught me and I stared up into Hudson's warm hazel eyes. He grinned at me. "Falling for me?"

I glanced out the door, finding the boy almost upon us. "Shut the door," I yelled.

Hudson's head snapped to the outside. Then with the hand he wasn't busy using to hold me up like a swooning fairy princess, he slammed it closed. Something hammered against the wood. He grasped me and moved backward, taking us deeper into the house.

"It can't get in," I muttered. "The extra wards around my house are also set around the stables."

Up to a few months ago, any damn spirit could enter, so long as it wasn't malevolent. But I'd updated the wards, allowing only those I invited into my home. The boy got in the first time because my magic invited him to reveal himself. But he wouldn't be getting in again. The shutters on the windows banged like we were in the grip of a storm. Wind howled like a raging beast circling the building.

"You sure about that?" Hudson growled. If he'd been in cat form, his hackles would have been up. Something smashed in the kitchen. We dashed in there, finding the glass from the door in pieces on the floor.

"Pretty sure." I bit my lip. "Unless…"

"Cora?"

"Unless it's not a ghost in the traditional sense," I murmured. "But then it wouldn't have gotten past my first wards. Only those whose bodies are on my property can breach that, or those I invite."

"You sure you don't have the body of a young boy tucked away somewhere?" Hudson grabbed a tablecloth and swept the glass on the floor to one side.

I blinked in surprise. "How did you know it was a boy?"

"I saw him."

My lips pressed together. This was bad, so very, very bad. If the spirit was breaking through so that people who normally couldn't see them suddenly could, it meant the magic was strong, that the purpose was malevolent, and it would be damn hard to stop whatever was coming for us. The wind ceased, the world seemed to right itself and the crickets chirped outside once more alongside the early wakening birds.

"Did you stand on the glass?" Hudson said, coming to stand in front of me.

I glanced down. Blood pooled from under my feet onto the white tiles.

"No, it was the vines outside."

"What possessed you to come running over at three a.m. barefooted and scantily dressed?"

I drew my gaping dressing gown across my body and tightened the belt. "I needed someone to talk to."

His eyes softened as he swept me up bridal-style and strode toward the master bedroom. "What are you doing? This is no time for kinky fuckery."

He snorted as he laid me down on the bed. "While I'm interested in your kinky fuckery thoughts, right now, I need to clean up your feet. Stay here."

He stalked out of the room into the adjoining bathroom and returned seconds later with a stack of white towels and wet flannels. He lifted my legs, sank onto the edge of the bed, then laid them across his lap before swiping my left foot with the warm flannel. I hissed but didn't move, allowing him to clean me up. I'd forgotten what it felt like to be cared for, and it was more seductive than his naked body. Okay, maybe not more, but as bad, because it solidified another little hook that linked my heart to his.

He dropped the now bloodied towels to the floor and began massaging my calf. I groaned and dropped my head back on his pillow. He chuckled in pure male satisfaction. I didn't care. It felt freaking wonderful. "What did you need to talk about?"

My eyelids drooped and I yawned. "I think Lucifer's plan was always to let me go," I mumbled. Damn, that was good. He switched to my other leg, easing up a little as it was still tender from my tangle with the shifter from a few days ago.

"Why would he do that?"

I wiggled my shoulders, sinking into his pillows. They smelled of him, woodsy, sensual, male. "To follow me, and find out where I live."

"Why would the devil want to know where you live?"

I sighed. "To get access to my house and, by extension, my power."

"Your retro gift is tied to the house?"

"No, my other power, the door in my room."

His fingers paused. "What's in your room, Cora?"

"Home," I mumbled, then the lights went out, and I drifted into the most glorious, dreamless sleep.

CHAPTER THIRTEEN

Unlucky for some.

For the second time in as many nights, I woke in the arms of a prehistoric shifter while in a strange bed. I peeked through one eyelid. Not just in his arms, I was draped across his chest with my leg thrown over his. His hand caressed my bare back in a soothing rhythm. I'd also lost my clothes overnight, but now it meant my bits were pressed against his hip, separated only by a thin piece of cotton. Sunlight streamed through the trees outside the window, casting a dappled pattern along our bodies. It would be easy to think this was our life. Perhaps one day it could be. As it stood, the Principal had rogue wildies, and I had the devil plus whatever had killed and sent the boy my way.

"I wish we could stay like this," I whispered.

His hand drifted up my spine and tangled in my hair, before tugging my head back. "We take the moments where we can find them. If we wait for them to be handed to us, our lives will have already passed."

I climbed up his body and straddled his waist. My hands landed on either side of his head, and my hair formed a glossy red curtain around us.

"What are you doing?" he asked as his eyes slanted. His cat was eyeballing me, ready to play whatever game I was offering.

"Taking the moment," I said before dropping a kiss on his lips and along his jaw. His hands shot to my ass and drew me against him. He groaned as I nipped and licked my way down his neck and over his collarbone.

"As much as I want to also take the moment," Dave drawled from behind me, "specifically, to scour my eyes with bleach, your presence is required back at the house."

Hudson grabbed the sheet and yanked it over us as I buried my head in his shoulder. "Don't you knock?" I muttered.

"The back door was open."

"Smashed open, Dave."

"Same difference. We aren't big on personal boundaries."

"I'm aware."

"Are you coming?"

I turned my head and pierced the wolf shifter with my gaze. "Are you going to give me some privacy so I don't have to flash my ass at you?"

"Again," Hudson snarled. "Leave before I decide to handle your behavior."

Dave raised his hands in the air and backed out of the room. "So you're aware, your Aunt Liz is on her way back."

I groaned at the thought of explaining myself and Hudson to her. Then again, people in glass houses shouldn't throw stones. She was shacking up with the second most powerful shifter in North America.

"He's gone," Hudson said. I lifted my head and met his hazel eyes, which were laughing at me. "We can continue this tonight."

"Tonight, sure, maybe."

He arched a brow. "Got a hot date?"

"Nope, got a growing house of aunts, a spirit problem, and the foliage has turned deadly. Tonight might be quiet, but recent events suggest not."

I climbed off Hudson with one last look at his magnificent body. "Hey, Cora," he said, leaning forward.

"Yes?" I asked, hunting in dismay for my clothes to only find my robe. Walk of shame it was. Rebecca would be in her element.

"Where's home? And why does the devil want access?"

Icy fear coated my veins as I blinked at the knot in my robe and tried to pull my thoughts together. I had two options: I could lie or declare it to be top secret information. I spun to face him.

"Home is complicated. Technically, you are on the grounds of my home right now. However, I've had homes in different towns, and originate from somewhere else. So really, I'd need the context."

"What did you mean last night?"

Last night? What the hell did I say last night? "Last night I came to tell you I think Lucifer did what he did in order to follow us back to my house and geographically know where I live."

"Why?"

I shrugged, aiming for causal nonchalance. He narrowed his gaze. Too damn observant. I had to fall for a crazy, suspicious asshole who was capable of sniffing out a lie three miles away. At this rate, Hudson would uncover all my secrets before the week was out. I wanted to trust him, but I'd been taught and conditioned that those who knew my secrets would murder me for them.

"This is one of those things that requires that trust we are building," I answered honestly. "I won't lie to you, but I also won't lay myself bare."

"I see."

He got off the bed and pulled his jeans on. A little part of my soul fractured at the hurt look in his eyes. I reached out a hand and touched his shoulder. I expected a rebuttal. He spun, grabbed my hand, and yanked me into his arms. My breath burst from my lungs at the contact.

"Do you understand what being a mate means?" he growled low.

"Family, partnership, protection."

He nodded and tucked a strand of my hair behind my ear. "Protection against all others, you would be my priority.

Whatever secrets haunt your soul, you can trust me to take care of you, to keep you safe. Without all the information, and with the devil on your trail, I can't do my job as your mate."

"We aren't mated."

He clasped my hand and pushed it over his heart. It thudded, sure and steady. I gazed up into his cat eyes. "My animal has accepted you, it knows. And whatever you are hiding inside you, also knows." I bristled as he continued. "Our human sides need a second to catch up, but when they do, we will be mated. In the meantime, try to tell me everything you can so I can protect you."

"I have told you everything I can, anything more would endanger you."

His lips tipped up. "I can take care of myself."

"As can I, Principal. If you are looking for a damsel in distress to hide away in your castle, I'm not the woman for you. I won't apologize for being capable, and I won't make myself less to make you feel comfortable in your masculinity."

A deep laugh rumbled from him. "And you have no idea how attractive that makes you. I lead the shifters of the North American packs. I offer them protection and safety, but my mate needs to stand strong at my side, and hold her own, not cower when trouble comes knocking. I stopped underestimating you the day you stood on the porch in cut-off jeans with the sun shining through your copper hair like fire and declared yourself as the undertaker. Only a fool would attempt to contain your power, Cora, and I'm no fool."

He sealed the promise of acceptance with a kiss, hooking another tether from my heart to his. I was screwed. So utterly and completely screwed. And in this moment, I couldn't bring myself to care one iota.

Chapter Fourteen

The safe word is pineapples.

"Prepare yourselves," Dave shouted as we made our way through the stables.

"If you and my Aunt Liz are naked, then no amount of preparation will save me from the trauma."

"She's not here yet," he said as I opened the front door and came to a halt. The breath left my lungs as I took in the incredible sight before me. Roses encased my home like a floral wrapper. White bloodied blooms blanketed the windows, the doorway, even the roof, and had tripled in size. Vines wrapped around the porch railing and draped over the swing chair. It was awesome, and utterly terrifying.

"They grew," I whispered.

"Understatement of the year," Hudson muttered as he swept me up in his arms and walked across the garden.

"We discussed this," I stated, batting his arm. "No damsel in distress routine."

He quirked a brow at me. "You have no shoes on, and mine won't fit you. Your feet just healed."

I glanced down at the thorny rose-covered lawn, comprehension dawning has to what had powered the roses evolution. "My blood."

"Was all over the lawn," Dave stated.

My head whipped to him, he side-eyed me. "How did you know?"

He tapped the side of his nose. "I've scented your blood enough times to identify it."

"And you say I'm creepy."

Dave remained stoic and continued. "The real question is, why the fuck are the roses bleeding your blood?"

A shudder made my body tremble in Hudson's arms. "They must have absorbed it."

"I stand by my previous statement. Weird shit sticks to you like glue," Dave mumbled.

We approached the porch, finding a gaggle of supernaturals eyeballing the macabre floristry with wide-eyed fascination.

Hudson let me down the second we hit the wooden steps leading up to the deck. Rebecca turned around and swept a cool stare up and down my state of dress. "Walk of shame?"

Called it. "Not really. I'm on my property."

"Dear god, please don't talk about wild monkey sex on the lawn again," Dayna groaned.

"I interrupted the wild monkey sex," Dave said. "On account of the escalating murderous floral arrangements."

"Not a sentence you hear every day," Maggie said. Huh, she'd stuck around long enough to have a conversation while Hudson was here. That was progress.

"Do we know why they grew?" Rebecca asked.

"My guess is it's something to do with Cora's blood being all over the lawn," Dave aptly pointed out.

Everyone turned to me. I sighed and marched inside. "Again, not a discussion for the garden." They followed and took their typical seats in the parlor. Except Hudson, who picked me up and deposited me next to him on the sofa. I guess I should be thankful he hadn't plonked me on his knee.

"I'll make tea," Maggie said, rushing off to the kitchen. She still stuck around long enough to talk to the shifters, small steps and all that.

Harry floated through the wall and came to a stop directly in front of me. "Miss Roberts, we have a problem."

I smiled at his understatement of the year. "What are you smiling about?" Dave asked. "Nothing here seems funny."

"I'm smiling at the irony of my aunt arriving and giving me a lecture on my choice of bedmate, which I'll let her get out in full before I remind her of her current suitor's faction." Although she'd pushed me toward him, perhaps it wouldn't be a lecture.

Dave huffed, and I patted myself on the back at a job well done in redirection.

"I need you to come with me," Harry pressed.

I wanted to shout, "Damn it, Harry, I know the house is experiencing a scene out of 'The Day of the Triffids'. But I wasn't about to advertise I could see the dead. Hudson had figured it out, and by extension, Dave knew. Rebecca was also clued in, because my room was above hers and she could hear me talking to them. I came clean soon after she moved in. It was that or claim insanity. However, Maggie and my aunts were in the dark, and that was the way I wanted to keep things.

"First order of business," I started.

"Cora," Harry huffed. "Do not ignore me. Nothing could be more important."

"Lucifer," I finished.

Harry's face went three shades paler than it had before, and that was saying something. Death wasn't great for the pallor.

"You win," he sighed. "I'll wait."

"What about him?" Dayna asked as Maggie reentered the room with a round tray of cups and a teapot. We eyeballed the tray, each of us ready to intervene should she find trouble between the door and the coffee table. A ball of white fur shot between her legs. Maggie spun and lifted the tray in the air. Everyone exploded out of their seats. Rebecca reached her first and, like a circus act, caught each of the china pieces without damage.

"Damn cat," Maggie muttered as I flopped back on to the sofa, Hudson following. Rebecca placed the tray on the table and smirked as Bella stuck her tail in the air and slinked over to Dave. She wrapped her tail around his legs before trotting over and giving Hudson the same treatment. A loud meow was directed at me.

I folded my arms. "Go find your own food and your own man."

She meowed again. I rolled my eyes and glanced at Maggie. "Would you feed her, please?"

"Sure, come on, Bella," she said. Bella hissed in her direction but followed all the same as she exited the room and went to the kitchen.

The external wards clanged, and a familiar power swept through my senses. I'd changed them to not detect shifters, but everything else was still registering. The door flew open and the vampire prince graced us with his suited and booted presence.

"Who died?" I asked.

Sebastian fixed his favorite tie. "No one." He grinned. "Yet. But the day is still young." He glanced at my proximity to Hudson and pointedly at my empty chair. I waved a hand at it. He smirked and folded himself into my chair. It was the comfiest.

"What did I miss?" he asked, helping himself to a cup of tea.

"Nothing. Cora was about to explain why Lucifer is targeting her," Rebecca said.

"Did we already deal with the queen of hearts style overgrown garden situation?"

Harry lifted his hand and opened his mouth. I shook my head at Sebastian and also in response to my ghostly friend.

"Back to Lucifer," I started.

"Who invited you?" Hudson growled at Sebastian.

My eyes rolled so hard, they did a 360 and checked out the state of my brain. "I did," Rebecca said, glaring at Hudson. "He's been her friend longer than she's been in your bed."

Sebastian took a sip of his tea and smiled. It wasn't friendly. It was his calculating smile that made me want to slap the information out of him.

"And in the interest of political treaties," Sebastian said, "I think it best that I represent my faction on all matters that concern the wellbeing of the supernatural community."

Hudson narrowed his gaze, folded his arms, and leaned back next to me. I slid my gaze between them. What treaties? What had I missed? Ugh.

"Proceed, Cora, before they burn each other into the ground," Dave said, his predatory gaze tracked on Sebastian.

"Lucifer kidnapped Dayna, demanded my attention, then put up a piss poor fight when we rescued her. He let us go."

Silence coated the room as everyone struggled to connect the dots I was hinting at. I'd have to draw them a map to navigate my mind. "He couldn't locate me, so he drew me out, made some overtures about needing my power, but ultimately let me go."

Hudson put it together first. "He followed you home."

I nodded. "What about the blood magic?" Dave asked.

"The roses are the result of a gathering of power."

"Is it connected?" Hudson asked.

"It would be foolish to think otherwise."

"Miss Roberts, I must insist on speaking with you," Harry said, standing in the middle of the coffee table. I ignored him as best as I could.

Rebecca tapped her fingernail against the edge of the china cup. "The roses are bleeding your blood, Cora."

"I stepped on them when going to see Hudson this morning."

"Bloody bootie call?" Sebastian snarked.

"So your blood powered the roses to grow from a small mess on the lawn, to covering the entire house and tripling the size of the flowers?" Dave asked.

"They'd already expanded last night. My blood added gasoline to the fire."

Dave's gaze bored into my skull. He was analyzing what I'd said and probably finding crater-sized plot holes. When under the gaze of Dangerous Dave, deflect onto something more significant than that which you are trying to hide. Or at least make out it's more significant.

"There's a boy," I said. "Blood magic needs a catalyst. It's violent, and almost always involves the sacrifice of innocence. In some cultures, they believe we are born with a certain amount of power, whether it be for luck, fertility, health, or monetary gain. As we live our life, that power wanes because we use it up. Therefore, people who use blood magic often use children as the trigger. The more powerful the initial catalyst, the quicker the spell will gain traction to achieve the wielder's will."

"And you think the boy is the spirit of the victim they sacrificed?" Sebastian asked.

"Yes."

"How can you be sure?" Hudson added.

I swallowed the lump of fear. "It's the manner of his sacrifice. His throat was slit, but the blood spilled in the reverse direction, falling over his face."

Rebecca frowned, and Maggie gasped while slapping a hand over her mouth.

"They hung him upside down first," Hudson figured out.

"No blood wastage, and it avoids tracking down the victim's front, which may be seen as tainted."

Maggie ran out of the room, her hand still over her mouth. I couldn't coddle her. Living with me wasn't always a walk in the park. Hudson's offer to move to pack lands would be safer for her.

"How can you see him?" Dayna asked.

I glanced at Hudson. He came to my rescue. "We both saw him last night. The magic is powerful enough to breach the barrier between the spirit and the living."

"Crap, that's not good," Dayna said.

Rebecca glanced at me. "So you think Lucifer lured you to Dayna's and followed you home, but his voodoo priest knew exactly where to place his sacrifice in order to gather the power? But this started before your trip to Dayna's."

My mouth opened, then snapped closed. "That disproves your theory," Dave stated.

I ran a hand through my hair and pressed my lips together. "Then what the hell is Lucifer playing at?"

"I don't know," Dayna said. "When was the last time you boosted your wards?"

"A month, maybe six weeks."

She stood and ran her hands down her dress. "Until we figure this out, we need to protect you and that starts with wards. I'll go see to them now."

"Thank you," I muttered, staring at the floor. I thought I had this figured out.

"Miss Roberts, if you are quite finished, I need you to follow me to your rooms immediately," Harry shouted.

I blinked up at him. A glare of pure white light surrounded him, not just any light, heavenly light. Oh shit.

I jumped up. Hudson made to follow me as I rushed toward the stairs. "I'll be down after a shower and a change of clothes," I shouted. Hudson grabbed my arm. I planted a kiss on his lips. "Guard the house while I get cleaned up."

He nodded, and a tendril of guilt threaded its way through my body. I was using his instinct to protect against him. Harry shot past me, Hudson released my arm and I hauled ass up the flights of stairs to my rooms.

I flung open the door and came skidding to a halt. The door to my secret room, the one with a portal to heaven, was straining outwards.

I fumbled for the key around my neck, stuck it in the door, muttered the spell, and threw it open. The scent of lemons overpowered my senses and blinding light engulfed the room. The expanding portal was twice the size it had been a few days ago. Heaven had set up residence in my former dining room.

"Holy shit," I breathed.

"This is what I was trying to tell you," Harry shouted. I glanced over my shoulder, seeing him on the other side of the room. He was avoiding the light. One touch and he'd be living his best afterlife.

I ran my fingertips along the glowing strands. They wrapped around my hand in a gentle caress. "You should have shouted louder."

"Does anyone ever tell you you're stubborn?"

"Constantly, perhaps we need a secret word."

"Like a safe word?"

I pulled my hand back and spun to face Harry. He either had an excellent poker face or he was clueless. "Sure. You pick."

"Pineapples," he stated, as I closed the door with some effort.

"Pineapples?"

"It's not a word used in everyday conversation, but not so obscure as to raise eyebrows."

He was missing the point. Nobody else could hear him, so no eyebrows would rise from anything he said. "Fine, pineapples it is." I swept past him into my bedroom. "And Harry?"

"Yes?"

"Stay away from the light until you are ready to join the afterlife."

He blanched. "Yes, Miss Roberts. Or is it soon to be Mrs. Abbott? I love a good wedding. I clean up well in a tailored suit."

Cora Roberts—entertainer of all: alive, dead, and everything in between.

CHAPTER FIFTEEN

People with standards have enemies.

Hindsight is a wonderful thing. Unfortunately, I wasn't blessed this way. My gifts lay in the past, specifically the departed. Which is why when I waltzed down the stairs in a pale green strappy summer dress and sandals, I walked straight into the kitchen, predicting food in my future and what I got was a scene that would forever be burned into my brain.

"Put my aunt down," I growled at Dave.

He stopped trying to suck the life out of Aunt Liz who he had pinned against the wall and looked over his shoulder. "Hypocrite," he muttered.

"How am I a hypocrite?"

He stepped away from my Aunt Liz and rounded on me. "Only this morning I caught you dry humping Hudson."

"In the bedroom! Have some decorum, Dave, get a room. You are in a guest house, it's not exactly hard."

Aunt Liz smirked as she went around Dave and snatched the kettle off the stove. She filled it with water, then popped it on the heat. "Tea?" she asked.

I folded my arms. "Tea will not fix the trauma."

"Tea and cookies?"

I huffed and plonked my ass in the chair. I was acting like a needy child who was playing off her parents when they got a new partner.

"You drive a hard bargain. How were the negotiations?"

She opened the cupboard which held the dry goods, like pasta, then closed it. Next, she opened the pan cupboard. Hmm, it seems my aunt was more fazed by Dave than she was letting on. I glanced at him, finding a big frown marring his forehead. "Top left next to the stove," I said. She opened the correct cupboard and retrieved the tea bags and jar of cookies.

"The negotiations?" I prompted. Perhaps she didn't want to speak in front of Dave.

She spun around. "They were productive. Everything is fine."

I tilted my head. Rebecca's parents had been locked in a battle with The Order for years. We were harboring a royal deserter. They wanted their princess back, and we didn't feel the need to bow to British Vampire royalty. My grandmother took great pleasure in having a bargaining chip over them. My only worry was the day she decided to cash in and feed Rebecca to the wolves, because I would never allow them to take her against her will.

"So are they backing down?"

My aunt nodded as she fumbled around the kitchen, looking for cups. She swiveled to Dave and held a cup out. "Tea?"

He scowled like she'd offended him. "No, Liz, I don't drink tea."

She chuckled. "Of course. I was teasing."

My eyebrows attempted to climb off my face. Aunt Liz was teasing? Was the world ending? I checked out the window for apocalyptic weather or flying pigs. Nope, neither. Whatever Dave had done, I didn't like it.

Dave shifted his gaze to me. "I need to leave. Walk me out, Cora."

"I'll return for my cookies," I declared as I stood. "Make sure Rebecca doesn't eat them all."

Aunt Liz did a toodle-oo wave at us as we exited the kitchen. Dave herded me toward the back door, and I blinked at the sudden onslaught of sunshine. Hudson sat on the steps, hands clasped in front of him as he gazed across the gardens. He'd also showered and changed. His damp hair was curled along the nape of his neck, and was in sharp contrast to the white shirt he'd paired with dark jeans and scuffed boots.

"What's up?" I asked as soon as Dave closed the back door.

He put a finger to his lips and pointed at Dayna, who was on the edge of the house reinforcing the wards. She murmured something, then turned toward us and jogged up the steps. She threw a bag of dust in the air. The magic shimmered around us, and the world fell silent outside of our little bubble.

"Something's up with Liz," Dave said as he scratched the back of his head.

"Yes—you."

Dayna sniggered as Hudson stood. "He means she is acting unusual."

"She seems a little scatterbrained. That could be the lack of oxygen from Dave's tongue being shoved down her throat."

"It was a test," Dave stated. "She would have never let me do that in a public area. She's a private woman, Cora, who should be mortified that her niece found her in a compromising position. Instead, she's forgetting where everything lives in your kitchen, the one she's cooked multiple gourmet meals in."

"Perhaps you are underestimating your prowess," I ventured.

Dayna scowled at me and parked her hands on her hips. "While I'm not doubting Dave's mad skills, my sister doesn't go doolally over dick."

"So, what do you think it is?" I asked.

Dave's nose twitched. "She smells funny."

Now he mentioned it, her normal lavender soapy smell was absent. I didn't detect anything unusual, though. For all we knew, she'd run out of her usual body wash and we were having a secret meeting about it.

"Keep an eye on her," Hudson said as he wrapped an arm around my back and drew me to his side. "We have some pack business to take care of. Call me if anything weird happens."

I smirked. "Anything weird? That's a broad spectrum of problems that regularly occur at Summer Grove House."

Rebecca burst through the back door. "Hate to break up your not so discreet secret meeting, but we have a problem."

I smirked at Hudson. "Should I call now, or wait until you've left?"

"No need, this is shifter related, and they are here with Norbert."

We ran after Rebecca through the house and down the stairs to my makeshift lab and surgery. Rebecca held open the door. "I'll keep an eye on Liz," she whispered. I nodded and stepped into the room.

The pack's doctor was a squat man with pale blue eyes, graying bushy hair, and matching eyebrows. He was the only official pack medic that boasted a medical degree. He also made a mean homemade loaf with honey.

Today he didn't come bearing baked goods. He had in each hand a bear cub held by the scruff of their necks. They growled and snarled as he pinned them on my examination table. These were the bear cubs I'd delivered a few months ago.

He nodded at Hudson. "Principal." Then he looked at me, back at Hudson, and finally back at me. "Consort royal."

I froze. Hudson laughed. Dave looked smug. Awesome.

"No, you are mistaken," I stated as I moved toward Norbert.

He tilted his head as he gazed between me and Hudson like he could see an invisible thread between us. "If you say so."

I almost growled. He was deferring to me as the royal consort, second only to Hudson. This was the beginning of the end. I was not mate material, definitely not consort royal material. The shapeshifters didn't utilize the royal hierarchy in the strictest sense. Hudson's kids wouldn't automatically ascend to the throne, but while he was The Principal, he was for all intents and purposes their king. Which meant Hudson's mate would automatically be afforded the title of consort royal. It pushed me into a limelight I couldn't afford.

"Stop, breathe," Hudson said, stepping between me and everyone else. He cupped my face and tilted it toward him. "One step at a time. Don't fret about the pack."

"For what it's worth, I think you'll make an excellent consort royal," Norbert said.

"That's yet to be determined," Dave muttered.

And there we had it. Another shifter would be accepted based on their heritage. I would be tested, questioned, challenged. My peaceful future was already in the wind. Hudson claimed I was worth it, which meant so was he.

I stepped around him and glared at the black fur balls. "What's wrong with them?"

"Frank," Norbert nodded to the cub in his left hand. "And Fred, have been stuck in their animal form for three days."

I winced. Child wildies were unheard of. This was unnatural.

"They escaped their parents earlier this morning. They were tracked through town and caught on the road coming down to your property."

I risked a look at Hudson. Was he about to throw me under the bus?

"They are drawn to me," he stated.

Dave blinked. That was a wild reaction for Mr. Stoic. He knew he was protecting me. "We don't have anywhere left to store these two. I'm scared the adults would tear them to pieces."

"There's a bigger problem," Hudson said as he bent down to get eye level with the cubs. Frank lashed out, nearly catching Hudson in the eye. Damn, the kid was fast.

"What's that?" I asked.

He looked at me over his shoulder. "Shifters under the age of one rarely survive being a wildie."

"I didn't think kids went wildie?"

"It happens, but within a few weeks, they burn themselves out and end up dead. The conflict is too much for their bodies and young minds."

I gazed at the two innocent cubs and decided to stop hiding behind Hudson. That wasn't the actions of a consort royal. "What if it's all linked?"

Hudson stood and turned to face me. "Explain."

"We know that whoever is fueling the blood magic spell is not opposed to killing children. Perhaps they are using the wildies somehow?"

Dave sighed and ran a hand down his face. He looked tired. "Let me get this straight. You are saying the wildies, the blood magic, the roses, and your aunt's kidnapping are all linked to you?"

"Yes."

"For what purpose?"

I bit my bottom lip, attempting to find an explanation that was the truth without exposing me. "I hold a specific power. A lock really." I looked at the cubs as everyone but them remained silent. "It would take a substantial amount of magic to overpower me and take it. It's linked to both me and this house."

Norbert broke the silence. "Is your power evil in nature?"

I shook my head. "No."

"Is it dangerous?" Dave asked.

"Only if it falls into the hands of those that wield it with malevolence."

"So we protect you and the house," Hudson growled.

"You make it sound so simple."

"It is."

"Would your protection involve wrapping me up in cotton wool and locking me inside this house?"

He shrugged. "Maybe."

"I can't live like that. It's my enemy, and a Roberts woman never runs from her enemy."

"You have a lot of enemies," Dave stated.

"It's not a bad thing, Dave. Having enemies means you've got standards, lines that can't be crossed. It means you have principles and values that are unmoved by evil, even if it's more powerful than you."

"And if that enemy destroys you?"

"Then I die knowing the color of my soul."

Chapter Sixteen

The top of the food chain.

"You said you didn't have a dungeon," Dave muttered behind me.

I rolled my eyes as I lifted back the heavy wooden doors. They flopped open, tearing some vines that covered them.

"Not a dungeon," I stated as I led the way down the creaky steps. I flicked on the light to show the brick archways. Seven in total, two of which were covered in bars as opposed to steel vaulted doors.

"Welcome to the Roberts personal vaults," I said with a wave of my hand. "We can hold Frank and Fred in one of those." I pointed at the barred arches.

"What's in there?" Dave said, swiping his hand close to the steel. He snapped it back as magic sizzled against his palm.

"I'm already trusting you with information about the location of these vaults. Don't push your luck."

"And we are grateful for that trust," Hudson said, eyeballing Dave with a *stand down* look.

Dave folded his arms and settled a firm frown on his face. Ugh, he wouldn't let this go.

"The cubs will need to be monitored," I said.

Norbert and Hudson dropped the cubs inside the room and slammed the gate closed. The little terrors ran to the bars and growled, saliva dripping from their mouths.

Norbert scanned the room, found a wooden stool, collected it and placed it down in front of the bars.

"I'll send someone down with food," I said. "And a more comfortable chair."

"I'd appreciate that," Norbert said, settling himself on the stool. "And a good book, if I'm not putting you out."

"Genre?" I asked as the rest of us started to exit.

"Oh, anything with a hero and a heroine. No sparkly vampires, but almost anything else."

"You like fairy tales?" I asked, pausing with my foot on the steps.

"Who doesn't? With mystery and a good old-fashioned love story, anything seems possible."

"That it does, doc, that it does."

Hudson and Dave finally left for their pack business. Sebastian was busy entertaining a princess. Rebecca kept watch over Aunt Liz, while Maggie kept the good doctor entertained with endless snacks and paperbacks.

That left me sitting on my sofa to ponder the shit storm in my room. The vines had grown thick; the sun was a mere blot of light through the windows. I contemplated cutting them down, but experience suggested they would grow back thicker and stronger. The magic fueling them possibly fed off the violence of their cut down. I needed to find their source, which meant finding the practitioner. I couldn't read the living, which meant I needed a body. That was dark, wishing for death so I could solve my problems. It was a slippery slope I didn't want to climb on. Which meant I needed help of the magical variety.

The orb of bright white light pulsed and expanded. I could no longer close the door and the walls had sustained cracks as they fought and lost the battle against the pressure. My options were limited; I could gather my aunts, fess up to my extracurricular activities and hope they didn't murder me for my trespasses against the natural order. Alternatively, I could tell Hudson—I was starting to believe he would accept my genetics and support me—but I didn't think there was anything he could do about the portal into heaven hanging out in my house. There was a third option—involve the head bitch. She had access to lore and researchers, which made my head spin. But the second she recognized me for what I was, I'd be dragged so deep into The Order's archives, I wouldn't see the sun again. I would be tested, experimented on, and ultimately killed.

My phone rang, disturbing the silence. I glanced at it. How the hell did she know? It was uncanny and a little creepy.

I hit the accept button with a sigh. "Grandmother," I greeted.

"Cora, how is the relationship with The Principal proceeding?" The Principal, not Hudson. My grandmother wanted to know if I'd successfully whored myself out to the head honcho.

"He still lives in the stables. He helped to rescue Dayna, and I believe he is invested in my welfare."

Silence stretched. I checked the phone to see if she was still on the line. Yup, still there.

"All of this," she said. "I already know. Tell me what I don't know."

Indecision burned within me. She was asking me to leak pack secrets, like the explosion of wildies. It was a betrayal I wasn't interested in committing. But I needed to give her something, something she would find out sooner or later, anyway.

"I slept with him," I blurted.

My grandmother sighed. "Cora, the game is only afoot if he hasn't already won the prize. I needed you to keep him interested."

I bristled. "He remains interested."

"Men like Hudson Abbott do not settle for a small town elemental. His mate will be a strong shifter, able to give him the offspring he sees in his future."

I blinked. Someone else voicing my fears was like gasoline to my burning doubts. She laughed. The sound was bitter. "Did you honestly think that would be you, Cora? Oh my, you have a lot to learn."

"Did you call for something, Grandmother?"

"We may as well strike while the iron is hot. There's a ball you need to attend."

I glanced at the wall as the fissure widened and tiny pieces of plaster dropped to the floor. "I'm kind of busy right now."

"Nonsense. Whatever ailments the shifters have, they can wait." I grimaced at her put down of my bread and butter earnings. "And Rebecca owes me for continuing to shield her - so she can run the guest house on your behalf for one evening."

"How did the negotiations go?" I asked. I needed to judge if I had to hide Rebecca somewhere else.

"What negotiations?"

"With Rebecca's parents."

"I haven't heard from them in some time. Is there something I need to know?"

I chewed the corner of my thumb. There were many things I'm sure she wished to know. But needed? No, absolutely not. And my confusion over where Aunt Liz had been and what she had been up to was one of those things. I wouldn't throw my aunt under the bus.

"Stop chewing your fingers," my grandmother snapped. I looked around the room. "I can hear it down the phone. Now tell me, what has you so worried?" Outstanding, Cora, now you really had to give her something.

"Someone is performing a blood magic ritual to gather power against the house."

"The house or you?" She was like a heat-seeking missile that never failed to land its punch.

"That's yet to be determined."

"Keep me posted. Now, back to the ball."

My head tipped back against the sofa. "Where, when, and with whom?"

"Sebastian's parents are hosting at their castle tomorrow night. Every powerful vampire, shifter, and elemental will be in attendance. Unfortunately, it clashes with a prior engagement for myself."

My hand tightened around the phone. The metal creaked under the pressure. I hated Sebastian's father, in particular. It should be no surprise he was in cahoots with my cold-hearted grandmother. "Why me?"

"I want you to make sure Hudson signs the treaty. He's a loose cannon, I already have the vampires backing. The shifters, however, are threatening to retreat into their refuges scattered in inhospitable environments. I need them here at the front line, not hiding with their tails between their legs."

Hudson was considering taking the packs into hiding? My heart panged with distress. When was he going to tell me? Was I a part of this plan? I better not be—I didn't run and hide no matter the foe.

"What treaty?" I asked.

"Between the three factions."

"We aren't at war," I pointed out.

"Not with each other, Cora. The world stands on a precipice. Supernaturals are on the verge of exposure to humanity. There will be riots, chaos, opposition. We must stand together if we are to come out where we were always meant to be."

"And where is that?"

"On top of the food chain, of course."

The phone clicked off. My hand slipped to the side. A treaty between the three factions to unite them against an attack from humans. The powerhouses in society were already aware of us, so why was she worried about a human—led revolt? What had changed? I glared at the white light, then at the vines outside my window. We'd suffered once. The witch trials were no joke. Many weaker elementals lost their lives at the hands of men that manufactured lies to keep women in line. Then the light dawned, brighter than the heavenly portal glaring at me. My grandmother had set her sights on being on top, not of the elementals or supernaturals. She wanted to be on top of everything and she was about to expose us to the world in order to reach her goal.

Chapter Seventeen

Sentiments and souls.

The morning bled into afternoon, and my butt made a permanent dent in the sofa as I contemplated all the ways I could prevent my grandmother from triggering a war. A world war. Because in today's age of social media, where everyone was a real time journalist, the explosion of misinformation would be felt for centuries to come. She was going to destroy any modicum of peace we had, with one big reveal. I wanted to slink into the shadows with the pack. Perhaps as Hudson's mate, I would be welcomed. Damn cat better make room for me. I shook my head. No, a Roberts woman didn't run and hide. She faced her problems, even if they were family.

Bella appeared through my open window, her pristine white fur marked with the blood of the roses. She eyeballed the portal, meowed her displeasure at the sight, then jumped up next to me on the sofa.

"You need a bath."

She hissed and backed up a step, tucking her ass into the corner of the sofa. "You'll get blood on the furniture."

She gave me a haughty look. I rolled my eyes and got to my feet. My legs were stiff as I made my way to the refrigerator. Cool air fanned my face as I perused the empty shelves.

Bella appeared and wound her way around my legs. "So, we are besties the second you think tuna might be involved?"

I slammed the door closed and stretched my arms. I wasn't solving anything sitting here and staring into heaven, not on an empty stomach. That was just stupid.

Me and the White Furry Menace made our way down the stairs, passing by a few new guests.

Maggie was checking in a couple I'd never met before. "Breakfast is served from seven to nine. But I can always grab you something if you guys aren't early risers. I make a mean omelet."

I grimaced. It was mean to make anybody eat it. They nodded and made positive noises as they took their key and darted up the stairs.

"We are full," Maggie declared.

My stomach rumbled in disapproval. I patted it in sympathy. "I'm not."

She frowned as she jotted something down in the guest book. She swiveled it to face me. I glanced down, my eyebrows hiking up. "Oh, I see. The house is full."

She nodded and turned the book toward her. "That's amazing, right?"

Amazing, but weird. We were never full. "Is there an event in town I'm unaware of?"

Maggie leaned forward and whispered. "Apparently there's a party at the vampire castle."

I swiped a hand down my face. "I know. But these aren't exactly the type to join a political soiree."

"No, don't be silly. They seem much too interesting for that. I have no idea why these guys are here."

God help me. Teenage shifters. "I'm going," I stated. She blinked. "To the boring political party."

She grinned. "Ooh, a chance to get dressed up. You'll love it."

She didn't see the irony or the jab at my apparent uninteresting life. If only that were true.

The front door burst open, and Dangerous Dave blew into the foyer with the force of a hurricane. In his arms lay an unconscious and bleeding wolf.

"I need you now," he growled as he ran down the stairs. His own wolf was close to the surface.

I darted after him and straight into my lab. He laid the wolf on my examination table. Vicious wounds sliced through her flanks and stomach. Her left eye was bloody and swollen shut, the same gouges across her face. I snapped gloves on and began inspecting her. She shuddered in pain. She should be healing, particularly in animal form—shifters carried a weighty magical source which was enhanced when in animal form. It heightened their senses, sped up their healing, and made them faster and stronger than their animal ancestors.

"What happened?" I asked, as I gently lifted her head and checked her skull. My fingers sunk too far. Dammit, her skull had been bashed.

Dave stood on the opposite side of the table, staring down at the wolf with a lost look.

"Dave," I snapped. "If I'm going to save her, I need to know what happened."

His eyes darted to mine, and he ran a hand through his hair. "Our holding cells have three, sometimes four, shifters in them. Two of them fought, Mary and Liam, and before we could separate them, he injured her." And they didn't have the doc because he was here cub sitting.

"Get the doc," I said as my feet squelched in the blood spilling onto the floor. "I need an expert in shifter trauma."

He ran out of the room, through my door, which led to the gardens. I tipped the wolf's head back, exposing her throat. A chunk of flesh was hanging off. I grabbed some swabs and padded the wound to staunch the bleeding before moving lower. My hands tangled in sausage-like appendages. Her intestines were exposed and spilling out of her abdomen. I worked quickly, grabbing a bag of fluid, hooking it on a stand, and inserting a line into her hind leg.

The door banged open, and Norbert narrowed his gaze on the wolf. He glanced at Dave with a grimace.

"Wait outside," Norbert ordered.

Dave shook his head. I gently pushed the intestines back into the wolf's stomach. She whined, low and pitiful. Dave took a step toward me, his features sharp with the promise of violence.

"You are stalling her treatment every second you stay in this room," Norbert stated.

Dave huffed and pointed at me. "This is your fault, save her or I will lay the blame at your feet. I will challenge you, Cora, shifter or no. You will answer for this crime."

"Then get out, and let us work," Norbert snapped.

He turned on his heel and strode out of the room. The door slammed closed behind him.

Norbert grabbed some gloves and stood opposite me. "What do we have?"

"Fractured skull, a nasty wound to her eye. She may have lost it. Multiple claw wounds on her flank, the major one has torn through her abdomen, exposing her intestines. She has a bite to her throat that is causing the majority of her blood loss, although it's not arterial, as she would already be dead."

He felt around her head. "Do you have an x-ray machine?"

I nodded. "Yes." I pointed to the portable machine in the corner. He rolled it over and positioned it above the wolf's head.

We exited into my office, closed the door, and I pressed the button to take the images. Hurrying back inside, we both grimaced at the results.

"This is going to be a close call," Norbert stated as he examined her abdomen injury. "There doesn't appear to be any organ damage. How good are you with a needle?"

"I'm not the prettiest, but I get the job done."

"Good enough."

We worked quickly, closing her wounds with stitches. My hands were steady and sure, but inside I was shaking like a leaf. We could sew her up, but that skull fracture wasn't something either of us were equipped to deal with.

I glanced at the clock. Twenty-one minutes, that's how long we'd taken to patch her up. I replaced the empty fluid bag. "Should I give her painkillers?"

Norbert shook his head. "It will make her healing sluggish."

I looked at the crimson puddle on the floor. "We need blood."

Norbert frowned and glanced at the door. "It would have to be a wolf. I'm not a wolf."

"Dave?"

Norbert snapped his gloves off with a sigh and deposited them in the yellow clinical waste bin. He washed his arms of the blood splatter in the metal sink, then opened the door. Dave had a hand on each side of the frame. His head was bowed and his back hunched.

"We need your blood," Nobert said as he put a hand on Dave's shoulder.

Dave sucked in a breath and lifted his head. I nearly stumbled in shock at his red-rimmed eyes and damp cheeks. Norbert ushered him to a stool I'd set up next to the wolf. I rolled up Dave's sleeve, inserted the needle, and taped it down. The blood flowed freely from his veins to hers. He clasped her paw, and his thumb stroked over the fur.

"Do you remember the time you got stuck up that oak tree when we were kids?" Dave whispered.

I blinked and shot a glance at Norbert. He shook his head, walked over to me and put a hand on my shoulder. "All we can do is wait now."

"You were jealous that Hudson could climb higher than you, and you wouldn't be told that wolves didn't climb. So up you went, higher and higher, following a cat. You were fearless and determined. Determined to show us nothing could stop you, determined to keep up with any species. I envied that determination. I still do. But what I need from you right now is to fight to stay alive. You have to live, Mary." He lifted his head and looked me dead in the eyes. "Because the world doesn't want to find out what I will do if you don't."

Whoever Mary was to Dave, she was precious and loved, which meant I was fucked if she died.

My butt was numb—again, this time matching the rest of me as I sat on the tiled floor across from Mary. Dave was in the exact same position opposite me. His blank stare scared me more than his anger. Norbert perched on the stool and kept watch over Mary, checking her vitals every few minutes. Hours stretched, and the sun gave way to the moon. That would help. While wolf shifters weren't ruled by the moon and her cycles, they drew power from it.

Mary convulsed, the tremors wracking her prone mangled body. I shot to my feet. Dave beat me to her side and blocked me. "Let her through," Norbert snapped. I pushed Dave, he slid to the side. His look of utter disbelief said I'd used far too much strength. I grabbed the prepared injection of anticonvulsants. Norbert held her leg, and I plunged it into her. We waited a beat to see if the medication would work. She settled for an entire minute. I let out the breath I'd been holding, and the universe spun and kicked me in the face as Mary fitted again.

I protected her head with my hands. Dave snarled expletives to the world, pain stamped all over his face. I'd not asked who she was to him, but it wasn't rocket science to know they were close.

"Do something," he growled, his fingers curling into claws.

"There's nothing more we can do," Norbert stated. "The head injury is something she will repair or it will overcome her."

Dave punched the wall, leaving a fist-sized hole in the plaster.

Mary jerked and then went still. Too still. I lifted my hands and backed away.

Dave spun on me. His teeth were extended—he was fighting his wolf for control. "Dave, calm down," Norbert instructed.

Dave prowled toward me. I edged around the table, trying to keep it between us. "Arm yourself," he barked. My spine rippled, and the sudden pain almost tore a scream from my throat. I inhaled and forced back my beast that was trying to break free and protect me. She yanked harder at the chains, several of them snapping, their links falling to the dark pit of my mind. Shit, shit, shit.

"That is the consort royal you are challenging," Norbert said, putting his arms up between us. I didn't want to hurt a man already in so much pain. But I would protect myself.

"Move, doc, as you pointed out, she is the consort royal, and therefore liable to the same laws and challenges as any other shifter."

"I am not the consort royal."

Three things happened at once, only one of which I predicted. Dave pushed the doc out of the way and flung himself at me. The door flew open and Hudson charged into the room with a roar of fury that shattered the peace and made prey scatter for miles away. He yanked me out of the path of Dave's claws. I stumbled, my hand reaching out on instinct to stop myself from face planting the floor and grabbed Mary's hind leg. The world fell away, and I entered a void of terror and evil that sucked my soul.

Chapter Eighteen

There's something in the water...

Sunshine streamed through the windows of the lodge as the boys ran around my feet, a wonderful combination of chaos and carefree. My mother floated toward me and handed me a bottle of apple juice. "Where's Dave?" I asked.

She waved a hand in the air. "Off saving the world with Hudson and his new mate."

I choked on my juice and wiped away the dribble with the back of my hand. "Mate?"

She smiled wistfully. "Yes, it seems the elemental our leader is smitten with has finally seen the light and decided to become his mate."

"Good luck to her. He may be pretty, but he's a lot to handle," I scoffed. "Is the pack aware?"

"No, I'm not entirely sure she knows. But she will. What about you? Anyone caught your eye?"

I ran my hand down my face, over the bumps and imperfections of my childhood with a sickening, heavy sensation in the pit of my stomach.

She sighed. "You're beautiful, Mary. Any man worth his salt will look past your scars."

"I don't want him to look past them, Mom. I want him to accept them."

Mom turned to me, tucked a strand of hair behind my ear, and smiled. "Wait for the right man. He will come along soon enough."

The cubs ran into my legs and knocked the juice out of my hands, then began slurping up the spilled liquid. I chuckled and gave Frank a scratch on his head. "I'll get a cloth."

I took four steps toward the kitchen before the pain hit and I crumpled to the floor. My head bounced with a sickening thud against the wood. Fred and Frank fell beside me. They writhed and growled. What the fuck was happening? Agony tore through my mind, something insidious squirmed its way into my soul. I fought, but it was insurmountable—the torment, the despair, the heartbreaking loneliness. It made me want to die.

I sank into the emptiness. My eyes were open but I was sightless. I could only feel. Whatever was here enjoyed that. It sucked at my energy, it devoured every emotion departing my mind until at last there was nothing left—only a shell ready to be filled. Except for love, I held onto the slither of light like it was my lifeline. If I let it go, the monster would consume me. I would be no more.

"Dave," I whispered. "Please, brother, hear my cries and save me."

Shadows moved in the depths, a shape formed as it came forward, its steps purposeful but unhurried. Its outline solidified and my brother emerged. His face contorted with disgust.

"Dave?" I rasped.

His eyes were glacial, crystallized orbs of hatred. "You are an abomination, Mary. You don't hold my blood. You are a pathetic little orphan that my parents took pity on."

I shook my head as tears fell in hot splashes of pain down my cheeks. "No, Dave, don't say these things. They are lies."

He knelt in front of me and tipped my chin up to face him. I'd never seen him so cold. "I never loved you. You're a broken, ugly bitch. That's why you remain unmated. Nobody desires to be in your company. We tolerated you because we felt sorry for you. That's all you will ever have, Mary."

The last shreds of my humanity slipped through my fingers, and the void welcomed me with open arms. I stared it in the face, obsidian eyes rimmed with a striking red, studied me. A smile stretched its mouth. "Now you belong to me."

Horrific scenes played in my mind, each more shocking than the last. The pack murdered, cubs and pups tortured, pack lands burned to ashes. It was apocalyptic and spoke of a dreadful future. All the predictions had a common factor. One person stood on the scorched earth covered in blood, with a malicious grin on their face. *Cora Roberts.*

The terrifying eyes rushed at me, going past Mary's mind and into my own. He did the impossible—breaching the barrier through the retro connection and finding me in the here and now.

"And now you know," he said, the words slithering like serpents in my soul. "And there's nothing you can do to stop it."

"No," I whispered. "It's not true."

"You don't believe what you see with your own eyes? Fine. Then see nothing at all."

Crimson dust puffed into my eyes, burning them as I tried to rub the substance out. I blinked. There were no shadows. No images. Nothing.

I gasped as air got stuck in my throat and fought a battle to enter my lungs.

"Breathe," a familiar deep masculine voice said. My hands flew out and grasped onto the only thing that was real, the only thing that was safe.

"Hudson," I cried out.

Warm arms enveloped me. "It's okay, Cora, I've got you." I shook with terror and twisted my head from side to side, trying to get a read on where I was.

"Move," Rebecca stated. "She needs sugar."

Hudson huffed and shifted me. His huge hot body was suddenly under mine. "Cora," Rebecca said. "Drink."

My hands moved and hit a cup. It clattered to the floor. "What's wrong with her?" Rebecca said.

"Cora, look at me," Norbert said. I twisted my head to where his voice came from. Something snapped to my left, and I jumped. A tiny switch clicked and air blew past my face. The good doctor was checking my eyes. "Are you blind?"

"Maybe," I whispered. Saying it out loud would make it real.

"Can you see?" Hudson growled.

"No."

"I'll fucking kill him," Hudson snarled.

I jerked in his arms. "The voodoo guy?"

"No, Dave. Who's the voodoo guy?"

A tremor went through me. Hudson gripped my hand and guided it until I touched a bottle. "Drink," he instructed. "Then tell us."

I guzzled the Gatorade, then wiped my lips on the back of my hand. Someone took the bottle away. "Thank you," I said.

"No problem," Rebecca replied. The plastic clunked against something wooden.

"Are we in my office?" I asked.

"Yes," Hudson answered. "Now start explaining, before I assume Dave caused your blindness and repay the favor in kind."

I grimaced and ran a hand through my hair. "Mary turned wildie the same time as the cubs."

"That's correct," Hudson confirmed.

"The guy that's doing it, saw me peeking in on the past. He didn't like it, so he performed some kind of voodoo and made me blind."

"Does he have a name?" Hudson asked.

"One would assume so, but I don't know it."

"Do you know where he is?"

"No."

"How about how we undo the spell?"

"No."

"What do you know?" Hudson snapped.

"I know how he's changing your pack into wildies."

"How?" Norbert asked.

"He's poisoning your drinks, maybe your food."

"Impossible," Hudson scoffed. "Our food and drinks are checked, and most of it comes from source."

I pressed my lips together. This was going to make me unpopular. "I can guarantee if I test your apple juice at the lodge from a few days ago, the one Mary spilled, and the boys lapped up, it would be spelled with some voodoo shit that allows the practitioner to enter their minds."

"Which means…" Hudson trailed off as he put it together. His arms tightened around me.

"It means what?" Rebecca asked.

"It means they have a traitor in the midst, a shifter whose loyalties no longer lie with Hudson or the pack."

"Well, shit," Rebecca concluded.

Cora Roberts—bearer of bad news, bad tidings, and bad juju.

Chapter Nineteen

There are worse things I could drink.

Everybody was staring at me. Even the dead. I could sense their damn pitying eyes burning a hole into my skull. "Will you all stop looking at me please?" I said through gritted teeth.

They had carried me to the parlor after I vetoed being taken to my rooms. I had to hide the ball of heavenly energy that was residing in my personal rooms at all costs.

"No one is looking at you," Hudson growled in my ear as his arm tightened around me. He'd stuck to me like glue. It was both endearing and enraging. I was conflicted.

"I'm looking at her," Sebastian stated as air breezed across my face.

I huffed. "Stop making rude gestures in front of me."

"I thought you were blind."

"I am, but that doesn't mean I'm stupid."

"Have some bread and honey," the doc said as a waft of delicious home-baked bread followed his steady, slow footsteps.

"I'm getting the bread and honey treatment? Am I dying?"

Norbert chuckled, the clean, sweet, warm yeasty aroma got stronger and made me drool slightly. It was like you were inhaling a blanket on a cold winter day. I didn't care. No one was going to pick on the blind chick for drooling. A warm plate landed on my lap. My hands found the bread, and I munched on it with relish.

"How long until Anita gets here?" Rebecca asked. "I don't like her vulnerable, particularly while the big bad is stalking her every move."

The house phone buzzed.

"An hour, maybe less," Hudson answered. "Nobody likes her vulnerable."

"I'm far from vulnerable," I muttered around bites of bread.

Maggie's sandals slapped on the floor toward us. "Um, Cora?"

I groaned. There's one person in the world who would make her hesitate after answering a call. I held my hand out, the cool phone slid into my palm.

"Grandmother, twice in one week. To what do I owe the pleasure? I'm currently entertaining the Principal, the Vampire Prince of North America, the Vampire Princess of the United Kingdom, Aunt Dayna, and the pack's chief medical officer."

"Quite the party you're having while you're blind."

Hudson stiffened next to me, because of course he could hear her. The bread and honey curdled in my stomach. How the hell had she found out? "I'm handling it."

"Clearly," she said as I pressed my lips together. "Your Aunt Anita is due to arrive with you shortly. I've sent my best medic with her. We need you fighting fit for the ball. Can't have my granddaughter attending blind and showing me up."

"Heaven forbid," I muttered as I pinched the bridge of my nose with my free hand.

"Explain to me how you became blind."

"I–" Had no answer that didn't involve wildies and throwing Hudson's secrets out in the air for my grandmother to make them into political capital. "It's complicated," I decided on. She'd hopefully read the undertone and mistake it for me being cagey in front of my current audience, not for me keeping secrets from her.

"I see," she said. "We can catch up once you are better. Where is your Aunt Liz?"

"I can't see her right now, so I don't know."

"Funny," my grandmother snapped. "When you locate my daughter, tell her to call me or I'll be paying a house visit."

The line clicked off. Great, more bonding time with granny.

Hudson shifted next to me. "Is your grandmother always so–"

I grimaced. "Caustic?"

Rebecca chuckled. "That's putting it lightly."

"Where is Aunt Liz?" I wondered.

"She's with Dave," Hudson answered.

"Oh." Dave wanted to murder me. I could smell it in the air, like a coiled heavy presence.

"He'll be okay. Give him time."

The wards clanged. Right on cue. "Here comes the cavalry," I breathed.

"Maggie?" an unfamiliar male voice shouted. I jumped.

"It's a guest," Rebecca said as Hudson massaged my shoulder.

"That's all well and good, but when you can't see a damn thing, intruders feel threatening."

"That's it," Hudson declared before lifting me into his arms. I gripped my plate of bread like it was giving me life.

"What are you doing?" I gritted out.

"Moving you somewhere more private."

"Not my rooms," I whispered.

He huffed as we moved. The front door creaked open, and we were out in the sunshine that warmed my flesh.

"No, not your rooms. The stables. But someday soon you're going to explain to me why you are dead set against anyone going in there."

When I've got rid of the damning portal, you can have all the access you want. I kept silent as we made our way across the lawn.

"Where are you taking her?" Aunt Anita called out from behind us.

"The guest house is full," Aunt Dayna explained. "So we are relocating to a less trafficked area."

"Who's the dork?" Rebecca asked.

Oh boy. "No," I told her.

"What?"

"No, you can't seduce him. He's here to help fix me, not scratch your ever present itch."

"Spoilsport," she muttered.

"You live in a building brimming with potential rendezvous. Go torment them."

"But I'm feeling like a nerd right now."

"I'm gay," an unfamiliar man with a high-pitched voice stated. "And not interested." Oh god, a challenge.

"Are you sure?" Rebecca asked. "I've been known to turn a man, and a woman, or two."

I groaned and buried my face in Hudson's chest. "Make it stop."

"Head in the game, or leave," Hudson growled.

The air grew silent as we stepped into the stables. I knew we were here because Hudson's woodsy scent got stronger. Plus, the sun had stopped coaxing freckles out onto my skin.

"I'm going to put you down on the sofa," he explained as he lowered me and left me on something soft.

"Right then," Aunt Anita said from in front of me. "Let's see what we have."

"This happened during a read?" the nerdy guy asked. It was no surprise that he knew about my gift, being sent by the head honcho herself, meant he was high up and likely privy to personal information. I had to tread carefully, as I'm sure he would feed every detail back to my grandmother.

"It did. I was treating a shifter who'd been involved in a fight. Her injuries proved fatal, and I accidentally touched her after her death."

"Was there anything unusual about the read?"

Silence stretched as I thought about how to navigate the truth.

"There's a voodoo priest screwing with my pack," Hudson growled. "He had something to do with it."

I pressed my lips together. Damn it, Hudson. If my grandmother sensed weakness, she'd exploit it for her own nefarious intentions. At least the devil was simplistic in his evil plans. He wasn't a wolf in sheep's clothing acting as the supernatural society savior.

"When she came around, she was blind," he finished. Someone gasped. My Aunt Anita, I think.

"Why are you shocked? It's not like it's a spoiler—we already know I end up blind."

"Did he do anything during the read?" nerd guy asked.

"He blew some dust in my eyes. Well, Mary's eyes."

"I see," the nerd guy said. Save me now. We have a comedian on our hands.

I rolled my eyes. Because being blind robbed you of sight, not my favorite expression.

"What do you need, Mike?" Aunt Anita asked. Ah, so he had a name.

"Arrowroot, mint leaves, Himalayan salt, the eyes of a mammal—preferably fresh—goat's milk, and a protection charm."

"It's a bit late for that," Hudson rumbled.

"It's for me," Mike clarified. "I'm about to go head to head with a powerful voodoo priest, unless I want to end up the same way as Miss Roberts, I need protection."

"Do we have those?" Aunt Anita asked.

"Apart from the fresh mammal eyes, yes. Anything you can't find in the kitchen is in the second cupboard on the west wall in my office."

"I'll be back," Aunt Anita declared.

"I'll sort out the fresh mammal eyes," Hudson offered.

I paused. "You have those lying around?"

He chuckled from next to me as his lips brushed my temple. "No, but I'm the best hunter."

Sebastian huffed. "Debatable."

"I'll be back soon," Hudson said, ignoring my best friend's bait. Good for him. "Try not to accidentally give her your blood while I'm out." Ugh, I take it back.

"Play nice," I grumbled.

Hudson's laugh could be heard as he exited the house, and the door slammed shut.

"Tea anyone?" Rebecca asked.

"Sweetened with honey for me," Norbert declared.

"Coffee, black if there is some," Mike said.

I shook my head. I was struggling with cool drinks and coordination; bringing boiling water into the mix seemed unwise for both my dignity and my flesh.

"What's your plan?" I asked Mike.

"I'm going to do an unveiling spell. Your sight hasn't gone, it's simply covered. Whoever this practitioner is, he wanted to scare you, but not permanently hurt you."

"You got all that from a few sentences?" Sebastian asked, his tone colored with disbelief.

"No, he got all that by reading me. He's a magical healer, more powerful than a doctor and able to unpick magical injuries, curses, and whatever other nasty is chucked someone's way."

The front door opened. Two sets of footsteps came charging down the hallway.

"A rabbit?" Sebastian questioned.

"It's a mammal. We can use the meat to make a stew," Hudson explained.

"Only a shifter would think of the culinary implications of a sacrifice," Sebastian muttered.

"It's the natural order, and food should never be wasted. It's attitudes like yours that are killing the planet."

My man was eco conscious. Color me proud.

"Stop arguing and get on with getting Cora's sight back," Rebecca commanded.

"Follow me to the kitchen?" Aunt Anita asked.

"Sure. Did you bring a blessed bowl?" Mike asked. "Oh, excellent, and what about a pan?"

My stomach flipped. "Am I going to have to drink this? With the rabbit's eyes?"

Someone squeezed my shoulder. "Best not to think about it," Aunt Anita advised.

"We can blend it," Mike suggested. My hand flew to my mouth as their footsteps disappeared into the kitchen.

I was about to drink blended rabbit eyeballs plus other shit that would no doubt enhance the taste. The sofa dipped next to me.

"I could ask them to add some flavoring?" Hudson offered.

"Stop trying to help," I gritted out as my stomach twisted and threatened to relieve me of my bread and honey. Damn it. What a waste. I should have saved the baked goods until after the bloody smoothie.

An electronic whirring drifted from the kitchen. I ground my teeth. In the words of teenagers everywhere: this was going to suck.

"Here we are," Aunt Anita sing songed.

I could down it in one go. Quick and easy. Right? *Cora Roberts—queen of optimism.*

"I'm going to start the spell," Mike explained. "Then you need to sip the mixture. The spell should take about four minutes. You need to make the drink last that long."

I grimaced as Hudson wrapped a hand around mine and opened it. A cool glass slid into my hand.

"It's cold."

"We could heat it?" Mike offered.

I shook my head. Hot or cold, this was going to be disgusting.

Mike began to say a spell in Latin. I brought the glass to my lips and took my first sip. I was wrong. It didn't suck. It freaking sucked hairy giant sweaty balls. I won the initial fight with my stomach and poured every ounce of concentration into sipping the gross globby mixture that slid down my throat worse than Maggie's mushroom lasagne. Oh, what I'd give to make that swap right now.

Four minutes had never seemed so long. "Last part," Aunt Anita declared. I tipped the glass back and swallowed everything that was left. Mike shouted one final word, and the world lit up like a firework on New Year's Eve. Power ripped through the room, knocking a colorful canvas of a cow off the wall with a clatter.

I blinked against the startling light. "Water, please," I begged as I looked around the room. Everybody was staring at me in expectation, including the Jimmy Neutron wannabe who was squatting in front of me. "I can see," I declared. "But I need something to wash this taste out of my mouth."

Hudson was sitting to my right. He pulled the empty glass out of my hand and replaced it with a new one. I tried not to dwell on the gray, green, and scarlet swirling mess that was stuck to the side of the glass.

I took a mouthful of the water, swirled it around my mouth and spat it into the glass with the remnants of the potion. "That's marginally better," I mumbled before I gulped the clean water down.

"How many fingers am I holding up?" Mike asked, waving his hand in front of me.

"Three."

Mike nodded and rose. "My work here is done," he declared.

I followed his retreating back. That was too easy. My stomach gurgled. Okay, not easy. But simple. And now the medic was slinking away.

"I have another appointment," he said to Aunt Anita. "Can you give me a lift to the airport?"

She studied me from head to toe. "You have your full sight back?"

I glanced around the room, glimpsing Harry hovering in the background with a worried scowl. He seemed more vivid. As if the veil between our worlds was thinner.

"Everything is good," I answered.

She nodded. "I'll be back in a couple of days, Cora. I have a few things I need to take care of. Stay out of voodoo priests' heads while I'm away, okay?"

I saluted her. "You got it."

Harry breathed out, his shoulders relaxing. He'd been worried that the only person who could see him had lost that ability. Aunt Anita walked with Mike out of the house.

Hudson smiled. "Thank god you got your sight back in time."

"For what?" I wondered.

"For the ball," he declared. "I need a date, and Dave makes for a grouchy companion."

I groaned and flopped my head back down on the sofa. Wonderful. I'd gained my sight and lost my night to formal dancing and weird canapés.

Chapter Twenty

Cursed legacies and secret plans.

"I can't choose," "I can't choose," I stated, waving a hand at the four beautiful dresses hanging on the curtain rail in Rebecca's room. I lounged on Rebecca's bed, having been waxed and preened to within an inch of my life.

Aunt Dayna fluttered a hand down the white gown. It was more bridal than ball. "Not this one," she muttered. "We can save white for your big day."

I rolled my eyes as Rebecca nodded in agreement. "The red is too bold. She's off the market now."

"Which leaves us with the green or the black," Maggie said with her hands on her hips.

"Green," I decided.

"You always do green," Maggie countered. The White Furry Menace meowed from her position on the end of the bed. She was doing an excellent impression of a loaf of bread.

"Fine, black."

"Excellent choice," Rebecca said, like I'd had a say in the matter. "It's sultry, sexy, and feminine."

I poured myself into the fitted black lace floor-length gown. Its modest neckline scooped over my shoulders and then left the length of my spine bare. I felt sexy, and a little buzz of excitement that I'd not known for a very long time buzzed beneath my skin. I wanted to knock Hudson's socks off.

"Hair up or down?" Aunt Dayna asked, picking up my copper waves and playing with them.

"How about down, but pinned to the side to show off her back?" Rebecca suggested. I stood like a mannequin and let them complete their finishing touches.

I glanced at the clock. He was late. Only by ten minutes—but my inside voice whispered it was because he'd lost interest. Damn my grandmother.

Harry burst through the wall and floated to a stop. "Bravo, Miss Roberts, he won't know what hit him."

My lips twitched as my confidence boosted. "Why are you smiling?" Maggie asked.

"I can't smile now?"

"You hate getting dressed up," Rebecca stated.

I smoothed my hands down my hips. "Not so much when I have someone waiting who will appreciate it."

"Speaking of waiting, Mr. Abbot has arrived," Harry declared.

A nervous butterfly took flight in my stomach. "He's here," I declared, as Rebecca slipped some earrings into my ears. She gripped my arms and spun me toward the mirror. I stepped closer.

"You've outdone yourselves, ladies. I feel beautiful."

"You're always beautiful," Aunt Dayna said with a smirk. "We just artfully arranged you to complement your natural beauty."

"Time to face the Principal," Rebecca said, taking my shoulders in her hands and guiding me out the door. My ridiculous heels clicked on the wood. I concentrated on staying upright until we got to the top of the stairs. A sharp intake of breath had my head snapping up. Hudson's golden brown eyes met mine. Damn, the man wore a tux like he was born into it. Each muscle rippled underneath, all that tailoring like it was begging for release. I licked my lips. His jaw had gone slack, and he was hovering with one foot on the stairs as he memorized every dip and curve of my body.

I found my confidence in his shock and glided down the staircase, pausing on the second to last step so we were eye to eye.

"You're late," I said.

"You're stunning," he replied. He wrapped one hand around my back and the other wound into my hair as he twisted, then dipped me low before stealing my breath with a dizzying kiss.

"Don't destroy my masterpiece," Rebecca muttered, hurrying down the stairs. "At least not until the end of the night."

Hudson pulled away with a grin, then set me upright. Rebecca looked me over and nodded. Apparently, I was still good enough to pass her high standards. I made it down the final two steps and out the door without incident. Hudson's hand skimmed the bare skin at the bottom of my back. The dress straddled the line between sultry and indecent.

"We will make this quick," Hudson said. "I have something to consider and possibly sign, then we can be back at the stables while the night is still young."

I grimaced as we made our way down the steps and toward the waiting Escalade. The treaty. He pulled the passenger door open for me and held my hand as I slid inside, gathering the train of my dress into the car before closing it. He shot around the front and jumped inside. Then we were off to the vampires' castle.

I bit my lip. I'd gone back and forth all day debating what to tell him. I couldn't enter a relationship with him and continue to shroud my identity; at least not my elemental heritage. My parentage was another story. But if he found out about my close relationship with The Order and it wasn't me who'd told him, he'd see it as a betrayal. Who could blame him?

"I need to tell you something," I stated.

He glanced at me, shrouded in the darkness, his eyes flicked to vertical slits before returning to human. "Okay."

I shuffled in my seat and scratched my nose. "I don't want you to freak out."

"Okay." He was eerily calm, and all the more terrifying for it.

"The Roberts bloodline. It has spanned centuries. Two hundred years ago, my great great great grandmother, Helen Roberts, got into a disagreement with a fire elemental. He'd deceived her into believing him available, and an affair ensued. She fell pregnant before she discovered he had, in fact, not one but two wives."

I pressed my lips together as Hudson suddenly pulled off the main road and took us down a dirt track. He pulled the car to a stop and cut the engine before swiveling to face me.

"What are you doing?" I asked.

"Giving you my full attention. This seems important to you, and I don't want to be driving while you share something like this."

He pulled one of my hands into his. His strength and warmth seeped into my flesh.

"Helen demanded that he leave his wives and be with her, as they had yet to conceive and having a child out of wedlock in those days was social suicide. She would be a pariah." He squeezed my hand, and I sucked in a breath. "Helen was powerful, more so than the other wives, and he feared her wrath. The other wives banded together as he prepared to leave them, and they cast a spell on her while she was pregnant. All Roberts women from that point forward, should they fall in love, would be at the whim of the male who they'd given their heart to. The man could, if he so wished, drain them dry of power."

He nodded. "While I wasn't aware of the origins, I knew the implications of your affections."

I smiled, but it didn't reach my eyes. "Throughout the years, many men have tried to win our love—we offer a wealth of power."

"I've already told you, I have no need of your power, and it would go against everything a mate stands for. I would never leave you powerless."

I let out a slow breath. "That's not the end of the story."

"Clearly, because Roberts women keep being born. And thank god, because here you are."

"Helen gave birth to Louise. She fell for a man called Eric. Eric wasn't a nice man. He had her pregnant and powerless within a month. Eunice was born magically impotent, because the curse had an extra spin—if the man took their power while pregnant, the baby lost theirs too."

"It's a curse that keeps on taking."

"Indeed. So Eunice, powerless as she was, became an expert spell caster. She tried for years in vain to reverse the curse. Eventually she settled on something which would alter the power structure." I swallowed. "Eunice found the most powerful elemental, a descendant of one of the original women who'd set the curse into motion. She became pregnant, and the altered spell drained him of all of his power and poured it into the baby—my grandmother. Upon her birth, he perished, as she had bled him of his life force."

Hudson inched back. "Why are you telling me this?"

"Because," I whispered into the dark. "That altered curse affects the firstborn of every generation of Roberts women. My grandmother made sure of it."

"Are you the firstborn?"

I nodded. "Yes. There's more."

"More?"

I glanced down at our entwined hands. This was it. He was going to leave me. "My grandmother, holding that power, climbed the hierarchy of elementals. Right to the top." I looked up, straight into his eyes. "My grandmother is Eloise Roberts, the president of The Order."

Hudson's lips twitched. I blinked and narrowed my gaze. He pressed his lips together, clearly trying to stop himself from laughing.

"What?" I snapped. "None of this is funny."

He roared with laughter. *Help, I broke the Principal. Dave would definitely have my head.*

"Did you think I didn't know?" he asked.

I tilted my head. "Clearly."

"The president waltzes into your home after you were attacked and has tea and cake, and you think I didn't put it together?"

My mouth fell open. "You said nothing."

"I was waiting for you to tell me."

"It was a test."

"No, it was me giving you the space to trust me."

"You're not mad?"

He shook his head and wrapped his free hand around the back of my head, drawing me closer. "I'm not mad. The altered curse puts a spin on things. But—"

He kissed my lips with a gentleness reserved for precious things. "But?" I breathed.

"Whatever is hiding inside of you? Whatever beastie you've got chained up tight? She would never hurt me. Would never leave me powerless, just as I would never do that to you as my mate. You would never do that to me."

"You are putting an awful lot of faith in a make believe monster."

His thumb slid over my pulse in my throat. "When you are ready, let her out. I promise to be gentle."

Said beastie raised her head and took him in. *Mine.* I sucked in a breath. She barely spoke, only acknowledging me when I was in danger. She didn't rankle at her chains.

Hudson's eyes flared with surprise. He'd heard her. Shit, shit, shit. How had he heard her?

"Stop panicking, Cora. When you are ready, I'll be here."

"There's one more thing."

He cocked an eyebrow. "What's that?"

"I'm meant to seduce you into signing a treaty with the other factions that I believe will pit you in an upcoming war against humans."

He barked a laugh as he turned the engine on and pulled away onto the main road. "Again, little witch, what makes you think I don't already know?"

Oh boy. My grandmother was screwed. She'd underestimated the Principal, and I had a feeling she was going to regret it.

Chapter Twenty One

I am exceptional, so screw you.

I'd give it to the vampires—they could throw a shindig which rivaled any celebrity. Lavish was putting it lightly. Everything from the thousands of candles lighting the way to the castle, to the hundreds of staff milling about offering champagne and canapés—it all screamed opulence without being gaudy. Crystals draped from the ceiling, creating a glittering ballroom under which the who's who of the supernatural elite gathered in a sea of silk, satin, and tuxedos. There was an even mix of the three factions in attendance, no doubt in the spirit of the treaty. History was about to be made, and it needed to be witnessed by those who could spread the word to the rest of the supernatural community.

I stopped a server as we entered the room and perused his tray. "Can I get a plate?"

He raised a brow and glanced between me and the hulking, scary man at my back. "Yes, Miss Roberts." He sank into the crowd in search of fine china.

"Hungry?" Hudson asked.

"Starving, and they expect you to take one of those measly little bites at a time. It's a travesty."

He snorted and put his warm hand on the bottom of my spine to guide me deeper into the fray. I nodded at a few familiar faces. My body grew tense as the sounds of Sebastian's parents holding court got closer. "Can we go in another direction?" I mumbled.

"Better to get it out of the way," Hudson advised as he propelled me toward them.

The crowd parted, and Leon's jaw ticked as he took me in.

Aira smiled at Hudson and stretched her hand out. He shook it. Royalty or not, shifters didn't kiss hands, unless they were mated, of course—then they kissed everywhere. "Good evening, Principal."

"Aira," Hudson greeted in return. She was a queen, but she wasn't *his* queen.

She turned to me with a wider grin. "Cora, I didn't realize you were coming."

I opened my mouth and was beaten by the Vampire King. "So you're together?" Leon said with a predatory grin. This was coming at some point. The day when he could force his son into the limelight, no longer protected by our fake relationship.

"We are," Hudson stated.

"Doesn't give you the right to meddle in your son's love life, though," I said.

Leon's grin widened, his slightly elongated canines on show. "It gives me every right. Do not lecture me on the ways of our people. You are nothing, Cora Roberts. A nobody with no power and even less influence. You were punching above your weight with my son, and now you think you hold the Principal's attention? He will only be interested in you until you open your legs."

Did he and my grandmother attend classes for this shit?

"Watch your mouth," Hudson snarled. "Cora is better than all of us. You will not disrespect my future mate."

Leon's eyes widened as he glanced between us. The silence stretched taut between the leaders, making the hairs on my arms prickle with power. "I see," Leon finally said. "My apologies."

"Let's do what we came here for," Hudson growled.

"The treaty cannot be signed in full this evening," Leon sneered. "The Order has sent no one from The President's bloodline to complete the process."

Hudson's thumb stroked down my spine in reassurance. I tilted my chin up and met Leon's stare head on. "Yes, she has."

Sebastian rolled into the group and took in the tense glares being thrown around. "Father, you promised to leave her alone."

Leon glanced at his son, then back at me. "Who are you?"

"Cora Roberts, granddaughter of Eloise Roberts, the President of The Order. I am here in her stead, to assess the treaty and sign on her behalf if I find the terms acceptable." Cat's out of the bag now. Everyone would know by sunup. Leon's mouth had fallen open, and he was struggling for words. He's known me for years and never figured out that I was part of the elemental powerhouse that governed my faction. This moment felt good. Aira blinked. She seemed less shocked, making me wonder if she knew.

Sebastian groaned and rubbed a hand down his face. He knew, he had for many years, but he'd kept my secret even from his asshole father.

"You knew?" Leon ground out. His jaw ticked as his gaze bored into his son's skull.

"Yes, father. And now so do you."

"So now we are all here, should we get this over with?" Hudson said. Clearly, his plan was still to deal with the treaty and have me in his bed before the party was over. I could get onboard with that. After a plate of canapés.

Leon shook his head and eyeballed me with newfound respect. "I have a few issues that need to be attended to before then. Enjoy the celebration. I'll call you once everything is ready." He spun and pulled Aira along. Hudson vibrated with violence next to me. Leon had given him his back. In shifter language he'd given him the middle finger and declared him a pussycat.

"Ignore him," I muttered as the waiter appeared with my plate and a blood-red linen napkin, because white would be too telling in a room full of carnivores. I took the plate with a nod of thanks. "He's trying to get a rise out of you. It's what he does best."

Hudson sighed and snatched the tray of snacks from a waiter. The waiter opened his mouth, then closed it, and made a hasty retreat.

"If I knew you were going to kidnap the food, I'd have forgone the plate."

"He's infuriating," Hudson muttered as he shoved something pink and slimy in his mouth. He grimaced. Note to self avoid the pink slimy thing. I helped myself to something that resembled steak. Licking my fingers of the sticky sauce with a hum of satisfaction, I readied myself for mingling with the bloodsuckers, elementals, and the shifters. We took in the attendees in companionable silence as we demolished the food. A studious waiter relieved us of our empty plates no sooner than I'd taken my last bite.

"Dance?" Hudson offered, holding his hand out to me.

I stared at it in horror. "What? No."

He grabbed my hand and tugged me onto the *deserted* dance floor. I fidgeted as he stopped dead center. His lips twitched as his eyes sparkled. "I don't dance," I muttered.

"Don't or won't?"

I cocked a brow and pressed my lips together as he wrapped his arms around me in a proper hold. "That's what I thought," he said as the music started up and he glided around the room like an expert. The band played a soft slow version of 'She Wolf' by David Guetta and Sia, which had me smirking. If only David and Sia knew. He pulled me closer than was strictly proper and spun me until I was laughing and the world fell away. He dipped me, landed an indecent kiss on my lips and then the room broke out in applause. Hudson Abbot had officially claimed me in front of society. *There's no going back now, Cora.*

Leaving the dancefloor, we made our way through the different groups. Hudson kept me happy with trays of canapés, while he spoke about political bullshit I wasn't interested in. The problem was they were so freaking tiny; I was still hungry.

"The cavalry has arrived," Hudson whispered in my ear. I spun as an army of people in black and white marched into the room carrying silver domed platters.

"Principal," a tall, lithe, middle-aged man shouted as he parted the crowd and slapped a hand on Hudson's shoulder. "I've been waiting to get you alone."

I eyeballed the trays, then glanced at Hudson. Ugh, now is not the time. Don't get between a woman and her food.

"Francis, one moment," Hudson said before leaning down to kiss my cheek. "Go fetch me some food, woman. I'll be right behind you, after listening to his complaints about territory."

"Fine, I'll go because I'm hungry, not because you told me."

Hudson's lips twitched as I left him and hot-footed it through the crowd, reaching the buffet table as the waiters revealed delicious food served in bigger than tiny bite size pieces. Excellent, I was here for the good stuff. There's nothing worse than arriving at the table late, only to discover all that's left is warm egg mayo sandwiches. I grabbed two plates and moved along the table while piling them high with goodies.

"He doesn't like tuna," a throaty feminine voice purred from next to me.

I glanced to my left with my hand hovering over the tuna and blinked. She was stunning in a navy satin gown. She was all long blonde honey hair, curves, ice-blue eyes and tall—she was so damn tall.

"Excuse me?"

She held out her hand. I shook it, because I'd been raised with southern manners. Inside, I wanted to drop the bitch to the floor for knowing something about Hudson I didn't, and because she had a long way to fall. It was bound to hurt.

"Cora Roberts," I said.

"Mercy Stephenson."

"Are you part of the pack?" I asked. She was a shifter. I'm not entirely sure what animal.

She nodded, and her lips pulled up in a smile, showcasing her perfect white teeth. "I've known Hudson for a long time. I'm the alpha of the leopard pack in Wisconsin." She wanted me to know she was mate material, a compatible species for Hudson. She was exactly who he should be mating.

They'll have pretty furry babies. It was an insidious thought that I fought a battle with, and I tried to keep it from appearing on my face. Jealousy wasn't an elegant look.

"I see," I said, grabbing the tuna cracker thing and putting it on my plate. He might not like tuna, but I did. "Are you enjoying your evening?"

"I am. I'm staying at the pack house while I'm here. Didn't Hudson tell you?"

No, he didn't tell me a blonde goddess was living in his home. But then again…

"He failed to mention you, probably hadn't noticed, given all the time he spends at *my* home."

She pressed her lips together. "He's a handful, right?"

Was she insinuating what I think she was? Or baiting me? "More than a handful," I winked.

She bristled and inched closer to me, so her arm brushed mine as she put three measly things on her plate. Never trust a person who doesn't eat, especially a shifter. "When he wakes up and realizes you're more trouble than you're worth, don't worry, I'll be right there to console him."

She spun on her heel and waltzed away into the crowd, leaving me staring at her back. Hudson was halfway across the floor, nodding at someone who was talking while waving their hands around. His eyes tightened as he glanced at Mercy, then back at me. Oh, he didn't like us speaking. I turned back to the food and continued down to the desserts. This called for sweet sugary goodness to wipe away the bitter taste of ex-lover.

"So, you're the one they are all talking about?" a gruff voice said next to me. What the hell now? Could a girl not stuff her face in peace?

"That's me," I said, side-eyeing him. Vampire. Stocky, with brown eyes and stubble. He wore a tux like it was a disease he wanted to shake off. So not one of the elite, but someone important enough to warrant an invitation to the treaty signing soiree.

"First the prince, now the Principal. What makes you so special, huh?"

His fingers trailed down my arm like oily tendrils of disgust. I shivered, which he misread as his fingers carried on and he grabbed my ass. Classy.

I grasped his hand, spun, and pushed him away from me. A wall of muscle wrapped in a black tux tackled him to the floor. Hudson's fist smashed into the vampire's nose. Blood went flying through the air, drawing the attention of every supernatural here. Hudson hit him again.

"Hudson, stop," I demanded. I reached for his arm, and his elbow caught my face. The force threw me backward, and I landed in a sprawling heap on the hard floor.

"Fuck," I muttered, pushing my hand against my jaw. I'd bruise but I'd be okay.

His head swiveled, and his wide eyes took me in. He abandoned the asshole vampire on the floor and hurried over to me.

"Are you hurt?" he asked.

I glanced around at our audience and dropped my hand from my aching jaw. Mercy wove between the enraptured guests, a pleased smile on her face. "No, I'm good."

His eyes tightened at my lie, and he held out his hand to pull me up. Leon and Aira pushed through the crowd and stopped in front of us.

"Show's over, folks," Sebastian said, emerging from the throng of people. "Go back to your champagne."

Soft murmurs carried around us as people milled around once more.

"Cora," Leon snapped. "Ever the center of attention."

I stood taller and tilted my chin. "It was your vampire touching me inappropriately that led to this."

Hudson was trembling at my side. He was seconds away from going fully furry. I touched his arm. "Let's get to the signing, then we can be done with the pretense."

"No," Leon growled before turning his darkening gaze on Hudson. "You have some decisions to make before my name goes anywhere near that contract."

Aira pulled on Leon's hand. "Darling, it's clear to me they are in love."

Leon's sneer twisted his face. "I won't be taken for a fool, and if you had a shred of common sense," he snarled at Hudson, "neither will you."

"Father," Sebastian snapped.

Hudson's jaw ticked as I wove my hand with his. "If we aren't signing the treaty, we should leave," I whispered.

Hudson's hand tightened in mine, and we began the trek out of the room. The sea of supernaturals parted for us, their accusatory eyes glaring at me like the whole incident was my fault.

We made it outside and into the waiting car before he leaned across the console and turned my face in his hands. I hissed at the pressure on my jaw. His eyes narrowed. "I'm so sorry, Cora."

"Why? You were defending my honor. It's the vampire that should be sorry."

He sighed and turned the engine on before peeling out of the driveway. Silence coated the air like an ominous, potent premonition. My stomach twisted with anxiety.

"It was nothing," I said to break the stony atmosphere. "And I will heal quickly."

"You're right, it was nothing. I should have predicted this."

That feeling intensified. "Predicted what?"

"I haven't fallen—truly fallen—for someone before you. Shifters are naturally jealous and fiercely protective of their mates." I stayed silent as he sighed. "There's never been a more politically volatile time for supernaturals. Your grandmother's meddling in our lives has backfired. Leon believes you are influencing me–"

"I would never," I whispered.

He glanced at me. "I know, not intentionally. But, it doesn't mean you aren't. I can't afford this complication right now, not when the shifters are depending on me to make the correct choices for them. Tonight was one vampire touching you. Tomorrow it could be another shifter who tries their luck. I would tear off their head and the pack would turn on us. I need to navigate these coming months with a clear mind."

I wasn't worth it. That's what he was saying. I wasn't worth the emotional baggage or the potential political carnage. "Don't do this," I whispered.

"It's not like I have a choice, Cora. Perhaps in a few months when the dust has settled from the treaty, when your grandmother has shown her true colors, and people see I'm not swayed by her beautiful granddaughter, that the decisions I make are for the good of the pack, not the combined interests of the elementals—"

"If you end this, there's no going back," I interrupted. "I won't sit around waiting for you to realize you made a mistake."

His hands tightened on the steering wheel. "That's a risk I'm willing to take."

I turned my stare to outside the window, watching the trees shrouded in darkness zip past as I hid the tear that slid down my cheek. He'd broken a little piece of my heart, a piece I would never get back. The car turned into my drive and the gravel crunched under the tires.

I grabbed the handle before he'd even stopped the car and threw open the door.

"Cora," he rasped.

I glanced back and leaned into the car. "For what it's worth, you are exceptional," I uttered. I sounded broken, but it couldn't be helped. "But you failed to realize that in return, so am I."

I slammed the car door and ran up the steps before darting into the house and dashing up the stairs to my room.

"Miss Roberts," Harry exclaimed as I fell onto the sofa. "What has happened?"

The flood gates opened, and I cried into the arms of a ghost, because the dead could hold my secrets, even the ones that shattered my heart.

Chapter Twenty Two

Is there anything a lemon cookie can't fix?

The sun rose with the never-ending optimism of *'tomorrow is another day'*. Except I didn't want optimism. I wanted thunder, doom, and misery. Maybe I should move somewhere miserable to match my mood. Regardless of the weather's mood or mine, I had work to do. There was the matter of the roses, fed from blood magic, clearly being channeled by the blinding voodoo priest. I had Lucifer on my tail … I cringed—not tail—no furries allowed. I had an aunt that disappeared on a mysterious mission that she lied about, as well as an encroaching grandmother who felt it was her duty to dictate my life. The wildies, while a pack problem, were linked to me in some manner. Then finally, the enormous issue that I faced alone, the glowing ball of energy that was consuming my personal space.

I threw back the covers and stretched my legs before swinging them onto the floor. That was a long list of problems, and none of them were being fixed while I laid in bed feeling sorry for myself. Teeth brushed, hair tied up, and fresh clothes, I felt like a new woman. *Bing bong.* An enthusiastic buzzer sounded in my head. Fine. I feel like a fucking mess, but fake it until you make it, right?

I swung open my bedroom door and frowned at the ball of sizzling white energy. "You will have to wait. I'm working my way up to multidimensional issues. First, I need to take out the trash."

As I made it to the floor below mine, Rebecca's door swung open. She eyeballed me with a frown and fell into step beside me.

"I thought I heard you up there," she said as we trotted down the steps. We were dressed like chalk and cheese. Me in jean shorts and a Guns n' Roses band tee, her in a sweeping summer floral gown that complimented her ethereal look.

"Yup, that was me," I stated, as we rounded the parlor and made our way to the kitchen.

"How did it go last night?" she asked.

I threw open the refrigerator door and grabbed some fruit and yogurt. Healthy body, healthy mind, and all that.

"Last night?"

"Yes, Cora, the ball. You and Hudson."

She folded her arms and gave me a 'spill the beans or be tortured' look.

I grabbed a knife and aggressively chopped the fruit, like it had played a part in my car crash of a love life. "Oh that. We talked, we danced, then he dumped me."

"Excuse me?"

"He dumped me. I'm single once more. But not available," I added to dispel any thoughts of her sorting me out with a rebound hook up.

"Oh, Cora." Her hands gripped my shoulders, and she spun me around to face her. "He's an ass. If he doesn't understand what he has right in front of him, then he's not worth your time."

I turned and finished making the two bowls of breakfast before handing one to Rebecca and sitting down opposite her at the dining table.

"Do you want to talk about it?" she asked.

I shook my head. "No, I have a long list of shit to do, and none of it involves talking about Hudson Abbot and his priorities."

"What's first?" Rebecca asked. I knew I liked her for a reason.

"Two things, but first, is anyone else awake in the house?"

She tilted her head. "The couple in the room opposite mine, but they are otherwise occupied."

"Excellent. For the first thing, you'll need to liaise with Sebastian."

"Okay, what for?"

I scooped up the last of my fruit. "Aunt Liz's impromptu mission to run interference between you and your parents at The Order? It didn't happen."

Her brows dipped. "They didn't come?"

I shook my head and collected our dishes before depositing them in the sink. "No, it didn't happen at all. There were no negotiations. I need you two to work together to figure out where my aunt went and what she did."

"Because she's acting weird," Rebecca concluded. "What if she's possessed?"

"Impossible. My wards wouldn't let her in."

Rebecca tilted her head. "What's the second thing?"

"For that, I need a copy of the tenant agreement for the stables."

She blinked. "You're booting his ass out?"

"Damn right. It's time to clean house."

Maggie found me in my office some hours later pouring over the tenancy agreement with a Google search open on how to evict tenants.

"What are you doing?" she asked.

"Figuring out if hundreds of shifters traipsing over my lawn counts as antisocial behavior," I muttered while skimming the passage in question. Failing that, I had to give a two-month eviction notice. Maybe I could take a sabbatical in the meantime? My aunts were scattered across the US—I could do a tour and return the day after he left. In the meantime, I had to hope the portal swallowed nothing.

"Fuck." I shoved back from the desk and ran a hand through my hair, tugging the end of my ponytail in frustration.

Maggie inched closer, clutching a glass of iced tea. "Did you take some to the doc?" I asked her.

She nodded. "Breakfast too. Would you like anything else? A cake? A cookie? I baked lemon, your favorite."

I eyeballed her. "You know."

She grimaced and shrugged her shoulders. "Rebecca mentioned it."

I tipped my head back and huffed. "Of course she did."

"She says she'll be down soon with an update on her task. The nature of which, she didn't tell me."

Trust Rebecca to spill the beans on my broken heart, but not my broken family. It wasn't like the whole of the party wouldn't have known something was up from the little fight fiasco.

"I'll take a cookie," I said. Because if that was a perk of getting your heart broken, then I was milking it for all it was worth.

Maggie beamed like the cursed sun shining down over the house and ran back upstairs. I perused another six websites, each confirming what I already knew. With a sigh, I downloaded the legal document I required and updated the date and address before printing it out.

"Did you find anything?" Rebecca asked as she floated down the stairs carrying a plate of cookies. Bella wound between her legs with a loud purr. I wasn't sharing my cookies with the cat.

"Two months," I stated, twisting the document so she could look at it. "I'm serving him with a formal eviction notice, but because I don't have any grounds to do so, I have to give him two months to find alternative accommodation."

She snorted as she placed the cookies down in front of me and sat in the visitor's chair as she read over the legal jargon.

"What about Aunt Liz?" I asked.

"It seems our devious aunty has been no further than The Big Easy."

I snagged a cookie and pushed away from my desk. "Why was she in New Orleans?"

Rebecca shook her head. "I have no idea. She drove down, checked in at a small local hotel. She ordered room service for all her meals apart from the night before she came back."

"What happened that night?"

"On that night, she dined at a Michelin-star restaurant. She met a man, mid-thirties, smartly dressed, and they enjoyed a three-course meal. Then she left. The morning after, she checked out and drove back here."

"No visits to weird voodoo priests?"

"Not unless that's who she had dinner with."

"Huh. Can we find out who the man was?"

"Sebastian is busy tracking down any footage he can find of him. As soon as he has it, he'll send it over."

Which meant I couldn't go any further with the Aunt Liz mystery at present. Which brought me back to my kitty problem.

Rebecca slid the eviction notice back to me. I signed it and folded it up before stuffing it inside an envelope.

"Perhaps he will leave sooner?" she said.

"Why? Because he's been so amenable thus far?"

She swiped a cookie from the plate and nibbled it. "Have you considered he's being a male?"

"Is that an excuse for stupidity?"

"No, it's an excuse for their knee-jerk reactions to situations they find hard to manage. Hudson is a control freak. He can neither control you nor the situation around you. So he did what he could to gain that control."

"Took me out of the equation?"

She waved her cookie at me. "Exactly."

"Your theory has some immense holes in it."

"Go on."

"First, he already knew who I was, and what my life looked like as he pursued me. It should have come as no surprise."

"I didn't say he was rational."

"And, he was fine until he realized two things: one, the power curse that plagues Roberts women is reversed for every first-born generation female."

"Shit."

I brandished my cookie and bit it in solidarity. "Second, he was fine with my crazy life while he didn't think it would encroach on his political sway. As of last night, Hudson Abbot realized the world would know I was Eloise Roberts' granddaughter, and they would think I had seduced him in order to bring the shifters over to the elementals side. The vampires wouldn't enjoy that."

"Wow, that's quite the revealing evening you had."

"Lastly, because of a handsy vampire, Hudson's beast lashed out and his jealous streak showed."

She tilted her head and pursed her lips. "What?" I asked.

"Shifters are possessive in nature. It's not unreasonable for them to react with violence to a threat to their mate. Hudson would know that, and so would the rest of the supernatural population. He wouldn't be judged for it. In fact, in shifter speak, it shows how damn serious he is about you."

I glanced at my desk full of papers which would extricate him from my life. "It would have never worked. It's better this way. Cut the cord."

Rebecca nodded. "Before someone gets hurt."

Too late…

Chapter Twenty Three

Get your towels in order.

"I can do it," Rebecca offered as I nibbled my thumb nail. She twitched the curtain in the front room to spy on the stables. "I'm not even sure he's home."

"He's home," I muttered with a sigh. "And no, I'm the homeowner. I need to do it. But thank you."

I grabbed the envelope and stalked out of the house. My sneakers crunched over the roses and thorns, their crimson sap seeping onto the rubber soles. I'd have to invest in some black ones. Black covered a multitude of sins.

Somehow I thought the walk would take longer, but what felt like a breath later, I stood on the doorstep knocking on the wood as I contemplated shoving the envelope through the letterbox.

A minute passed. Maybe he wasn't home? I took a step back. The door swung open and a raging fire spread through my veins.

Mercy arched a brow as she dried her hair with a huge towel. The other tiny towel was wrapped around her body, just about covering her ass. "Can I help you?" she asked. No, she needed help with which way you used the towels.

"I need to speak with Hudson," I stated. My voice came out monotone, surprising me. I'd expected to breathe fire like a dragon. The Principal was so tied up in knots about our relationship he'd sought solace in a pretty blonde. I don't know why I was so disappointed. I'd expected more from the man who ran when his political status was under threat. More fool me.

Mercy leaned against the door frame and smirked. My beast rose her head. *Kill her.* Always with the killing. Perhaps this time she had a point. "He's in the shower. Can I give him a message?"

Translation—we had hot sweaty shifter sex which he needs a long assed shower to recover from. I twisted the envelope in my hand. I didn't trust her, but I didn't want to see him.

"Mercy? Who is it?" Hudson shouted.

My heart pitter-pattered in my chest. I could shove the envelope at her and run? Right? That wasn't cowardly, it was self-preservation. Hudson rounded the corner clad in jeans, *only* jeans. His feet were bare, and so was his chest. His eyes widened at the sight of me.

"Cora, what's wrong?"

I slapped a fake grin on my face and offered my hand with the notice.

"Give us a moment," he stated to Mercy. His tone was warm as he spoke to her. She winked at me, then sauntered back inside the house. He plucked the envelope out of my hand and opened it.

"You're evicting me?"

"Yes, this is your official two month's notice."

He tore the letter in half. "What are you doing?" I spluttered as he continued to tear it up into tiny pieces which fluttered to the floor. Was it poetic, that's what he'd done with my heart? He stepped outside and closed the door behind him before maneuvering me so I backed up against the wall.

"No notice. No eviction," he said with a grin.

"You have no reason to stay."

"How about the threat to your life from whatever is fueling this blood magic? Or the king of hell that is hot on your trail?"

"Neither of those things are your concern."

"Just because I pressed pause on our relationship doesn't mean I don't care."

"There's no pause. I told you last night, you end it, then it's the end. You've already hurt me. Please don't continue to do so by being here."

He closed his eyes and a look of complete torment passed over his features before he leaned his arms on either side of my head and he touched his forehead against mine. My heart sped up, because while I was angry, I wasn't unaffected. I slammed my eyes shut, because I couldn't stand the look of longing on his face. "I'll leave once this threat is contained. Once I feel your life isn't hanging in the balance."

My life was always hanging in the balance. It was the nature of my beast. "Fine. We neutralize whatever the threat is, then you leave."

"Okay," he whispered.

He stayed against me for a few minutes. "Hudson," I muttered. He took a deep breath, then grazed his lips against my temple before pulling away. A ripple of pleasure ran down my spine.

He stepped back as Mercy opened the door and stuck her head out. At least she was dressed now, even if she looked like a catwalk model in high-waisted tight jeans, a floaty blouse, and heels. Like she needed the extra height.

"Cora," Dave shouted from the main house.

We spun to face him. His long stride ate up the distance, the roses splattered on his black pants.

He barely contained the look of disgust thrown in Mercy's direction. Huh, what had the leopard done to warrant the wrath of Dangerous Dave? Also, since when did I get the nice treatment? As far as I knew, he still wanted my head.

"This doesn't involve you," Dave snapped at Mercy. "Go back to the pack house."

Mercy huffed. "Hudson needs me."

Hudson eyeballed her. "No, Mercy, I don't."

Is it petty that I felt a warmth at his words? "But–"

Hudson put a hand on my back and walked with me and Dave toward the main house.

"That wasn't very nice to your new girlfriend," I muttered.

Hudson's head snapped to me, and his brows raised into his hairline. "Mercy is a friend, Cora. We ran together last night to blow off some steam. That's all."

"That's not all she thinks it is," Dave mumbled.

"What do you mean?" Hudson said.

Dave shrugged. "Mercy has had her eye on you for years. She upped the seduction once she saw you were serious about Cora."

"Well, he's free now," I offered. "And it turns out he wasn't all that serious."

Dave snorted and shook his head. "You're both clueless."

I reached out and touched Dave's arm. His gaze snapped to mine. "I'm so sorry about Mary."

He pressed his lips together and blinked twice. "It's not your fault. I overreacted to an impossible situation and lashed out, for that I am sorry."

Something that had been knotted inside me was released. "We will find the one responsible," I vowed.

Dave smiled. "No, we will murder the one responsible by pulling him apart limb from limb. I will remove his organs and keep him alive and awake to experience the utter terror and pain that he has inflicted on others."

And this is why he was called Dangerous Dave.

Hudson grabbed my arm and swung me around, halting the pair of us at the bottom of the porch steps.

"I'll wait inside," Dave said. "Don't be long. There's a crisis."

"There's always a crisis," I said with a sigh as the door banged closed.

"Do you not understand anything that I've said over the last few months?" Hudson snapped.

I tugged my wrist free and crossed my arms. "It all got wiped away the instant you tossed me aside."

He shook his head. "Give me six months. Let me get my house in order."

I narrowed my eyes. "You said the pack wouldn't be a problem."

"The pack alone won't be. It's my reactions, my jealous possessive reactions."

"Not uncommon for shifters, I'm told. The pack wouldn't think less of you."

"No, but others might."

I threw my hands in the air. I hated that he was getting me to defend my position as a worthy mate. "We are going around in circles. Mates are above everything, right?"

He nodded and narrowed his gaze. "Yes."

"Then if you considered me your mate, we wouldn't even be having this conversation because you would have put me above all else. The pack, the politics, the faction approval."

Rebecca threw open the door. "Figure your shit out quick. We need you in the basement."

I took two steps forward. "We aren't finished," Hudson stated.

I paused and looked over my shoulder. "Yes, *we* are, Principal."

He hissed at my use of his title. Professional boundaries needed to be restored—it would sting us both, but it was self-preservation. I entered the house and followed Rebecca down the stairs. I expected her to swing into my office, instead she headed to the makeshift training room. Dave stood outside the door with his arms crossed and his legs slightly apart.

"What's going on?" Hudson asked from behind me.

Dave's intense stare didn't leave mine. "Don't panic," he advised, as he reached the handle and swung the door open. My stomach flipped—shit was bad if Dangerous Dave was telling me not to panic.

I pushed past him and entered the room.

Aunt Liz snarled at me, her eyes flickering to obsidian as her neck twisted at an odd angle. She crawled along the floor and hit the edge of a hastily drawn protection circle. She flopped onto her back, then used her hands to imitate a human crab.

My hand slapped over my mouth as the foul stench of decaying meat slammed into me. "What the fuck?"

Chapter Twenty Four

Possession is nine-tenths of the law.

"Calm down," Hudson said as he leaned against my desk while I paced back and forth in front of him.

"Never tell a woman to calm down," I snapped as I rubbed my forehead. "My aunt is freaking possessed. If there was ever an occasion to freak out, now would be the time. This is serious, Hudson, her life is on the line."

"I don't understand how this could have even happened," Dave said from his position in one of my visitors' chairs. "She was fine when she left. What the hell transpired during those negotiations?"

I grimaced. Ugh, we hadn't told him yet. This would be fun. "There were no negotiations—she lied. She went to New Orleans."

His foot fell from his opposite knee onto the floor with a thump, and he leaned forward. Malice rolled off him like a tidal wave. "What did she do in New Orleans?"

"She met a man."

A low growl erupted from Dave, making the hairs on my arms stand up in warning. "Not like that," I said.

"What was it like?" he snarled.

"I don't know. Aunt Liz is a lot of things, but never a cheater."

"We are assuming this man is responsible for your aunt's possession?" Hudson asked.

"It will help once Sebastian acquires the footage of their meeting. Perhaps we will recognize him."

Dave nodded and studied the floor like it had all the answers. "There's one thing puzzling me."

"What's that?"

He glanced up and caught me in his gaze. I paused my pacing. "How the hell did she get past your wards? The boundary ones and the house. How did a demon waltz its way into Summer Grove House without you noticing?"

I blinked. Somewhere in the chaos, I hadn't even considered the implications of Aunt Liz being in my inner sanctum. The wards still worked—at least to warn me of visitors. Somehow she'd snuck through. Somehow *it* had snuck through.

"Didn't Dayna redo your wards?" Hudson asked.

"Yes. Shit," I said, running out of the office and down the hallway to the training room. We'd left Aunt Dayna and Rebecca demon sitting Aunt Liz.

Footsteps thudded behind me. I burst through the door, fully expecting a scene out of the exorcist with Aunt Dayna at the helm.

Aunt Dayna and Rebecca's eyes darted to me. "What's wrong?" Rebecca asked.

"Aunt Dayna, could I borrow you for a moment, please?" I asked.

She clambered to her feet and dusted off the knees of her bright pink dungarees. "Sure."

I darted a look at Rebecca. "What?" she mouthed behind Dayna's back.

Aunt Dayna passed me and the curious-looking shifters. "In my office," I instructed. I didn't want to give the game away in front of the demon. I had one shot at this.

I hurried after Dayna and the boys followed me. Dave closed the door and leaned against it. I strolled to my desk and rummaged around in the drawers, pretending to be searching for a pen. I glanced up as Dayna came closer, then grabbed the potion and threw it at her. It burst in a splat of bright purple across her chest. She looked down, then back at me with a raised brow.

"What the hell, Cora? These are my favorite pair."

"Not possessed then," I muttered.

"Of course I'm not possessed. What gave you that idea?"

"You redid the wards around the house. Someone let in the demon."

She frowned. "It wasn't me, and I did not redo your wards."

"You did. You offered, and I saw you."

"It's true," Hudson said.

I drummed my fingers on the table. "You couldn't have been possessed. You'd have never got in the house."

Dayna smeared the bright purple around in a pattern on her chest with her fingertips. "What are you doing?" Dave asked.

She smiled. "Damn potion will never come out, so I'm making sure it stains in a pretty pattern."

Definitely Aunt Dayna, no one was capable of imitating this craziness - it was Dayna's unique brand which we loved her for.

"You don't remember boosting the wards?" Dave asked again. "It was before we had the conversation about Aunt Liz on the back porch."

Dayna shook her head, then tilted it to one side. "Wait, I–" she frowned, then slapped a hand against her right temple with a yelp. "Damn that hurts." I took her arms and guided her to sit in the chair.

"Could she have been influenced without possession?" Hudson asked.

I pressed my lips together. "Possibly."

"How do we find out?" Dave asked.

"We need a psyche smasher," I muttered.

"That's an ominous name," Hudson stated. *You have no idea.*

Dayna's head shot up and her eyes went wide. She shook her head and grimaced at the pain. "No, Cora."

I squeezed my eyes closed and let out a sigh. "You might have more instructions buried in your subconscious. You spent hours with Lucifer before I arrived. Anything is possible."

"Do you know someone?" Dave asked.

Grimacing with resignation I said, "I do." I would never be forgiven if I hid any of this from her—after all, it was her daughters that were affected. "It's time to call in the big gun." I withdrew my cell from my pocket. Hudson and Dave looked on with interest.

The phone rang three times. My heart beat double time as the line connected. "Granddaughter, what mess have you fallen into now?"

It stung. Calling upon the woman who had been partially responsible for my relationship breakdown with Hudson. If I was a small town elemental with no familial ties to The Order, would his decision have been different? Maybe, but he'd always be affected by the possessiveness that plagued all shifters. He held himself to higher standards, which I understood—living under the rule of the queen of impossible expectations, I got it. Didn't mean I had to like it, and I still thought he was stupid to let it go, to let me go. But I wouldn't be chasing his tail ever. I'd been dumped, but I could carry myself with decorum and dignity. My grandmother wouldn't stand for anything less. As it was, she might flay him alive for daring to ditch me at all. Something I'd yet to inform her of. Oh boy, this was going to be fun.

We had congregated in the parlor, a gathering of supernaturals waiting for the doomsday woman of the hour to arrive. I fidgeted next to Sebastian, who'd been my second phone call. I needed the emotional support, and she was more likely to behave with a scattering of the supernatural elite surrounding me.

Dayna stared at the floor like she wished she could melt into a puddle and seep into the wood. Maggie kept up a steady stream of tea, coffee, and cookies. They didn't help, but I appreciated it.

The wards clanged in my head. They were up and fully working since I had revisited them. I did indeed find some gaps - loopholes really, not enough to allow anyone in. But a crack to let a specific demon slip through undetected. What I couldn't fathom was why. Assuming it was Lucifer behind the possession, what game was he playing sending my possessed aunt into my house? Was it the kudos of getting one by me? He had to know she would be discovered, and that the might of The Order would descend upon the house he was so intent on gaining access to. I tapped my fingers on my knee as Harry floated back and forth through the coffee table. The spirit version of pacing.

I stood and smoothed down my blouse and slacks. "She's here."

Rebecca and Sebastian flanked me as I went to the door. Hudson's jaw ticked as I passed him. Rebecca was my grandmother's favorite vampire, and Sebastian was the Crown

Prince of America. Hopefully, this would soften the inevitable blow.

I opened the front door and stood on the porch as the black Bentley pulled to a stop in front of the house.

"You've got this," Sebastian muttered under his breath.

The driver jumped out of the car and swung open the back door. Eloise Roberts emerged like a predatory wolf. She was immaculate, as always, in a sharp skirt suit that warned people of her serious intentions.

She glided up the steps and eyeballed my entourage. "Rebecca, Sebastian," she greeted with a small nod.

"President," Rebecca replied with her own nod. It was a calculated move. Factions didn't need to greet other factions with their official titles.

My grandmother smiled, and her eyes narrowed. "I see," she said. "Clearly, you have made quite the mess, Cora, if the vampires are deferring to me."

I fought to keep the frown off my face. That would piss her off more. "We need you," I stated, and stepped back to allow her into the house.

She eyeballed the people in the parlor, then turned to me with a raised eyebrow. "A mess indeed."

I closed the door and followed her as she stalked into the room and took her usual seat in the tallest armchair. "Principal," she said to Hudson.

He nodded. "Eloise."

I refrained from rolling my eyes. Stick with the plan, asshole.

My grandmother smiled. It was ten times warmer. "Good, someone who isn't trying to climb up my asshole. Tell me what's happened."

Huh, the Terror of Tennessee had won around my grandmother with one word. No one ever accused Eloise Roberts of being predictable.

Hudson tilted his head. "We rescued your daughter from the clutches of Lucifer and brought her back here."

My grandmother's eyes widened, and she shot a look in my direction as I sat down. Great, now she knew the devil was involved. *Nice going, keep digging my grave, Principal.* I had to steer her away from anything that would lead her to discovering my true heritage. My mother had done a fine job convincing the world my father was a lowlife scum that had slunk into the shadows and wasn't worthy of being named, and with my family being a gaggle of females, it was perfectly acceptable.

If I was an optimist, I'd say my grandmother would murder me quickly. However, I knew my grandmother, and I'd be stowed away in the deepest, darkest depths of The Order. They'd pick me apart until I was unrecognizable, then they'd piece me back together to do it all over again.

"Dayna reworked the wards, and left a way for a possessed person to enter," he continued. "Liz left under the pretense of dealing with Rebecca's parents when in fact, she went to New Orleans to meet with an unknown male. When she returned, she was different."

"Do you know who this male was?" my grandmother asked.

"Not yet," Sebastian answered. "We should have footage of their meeting within the hour."

She nodded. "Good, I will be present when you first view it." Not a request, a demand. "Where is my second born?"

"In the basement, inside a protection circle," I offered.

"Dayna," my grandmother snapped.

Dayna's spine straightened as she looked at her mother. "Yes?"

My grandmother sighed. "I need to see if you are still under the influence of the devil. If you are a ticking time bomb, we need to be prepared."

Dayna swallowed. "Yes, mother."

"What about Liz?" Dave asked, sitting forward with his elbows on his knees.

My grandmother arched a perfectly sculpted brow and eyeballed Dave. Her perceptive gaze took in his investment in Liz's welfare. She analyzed and concluded in a split second their involvement. Oh, Dave, you complete idiot.

"Liz is possessed," my grandmother said. "There are two ways of dealing with the issue."

Dave went stiff. He didn't enjoy the same analysis he gave everyone else. "Which are?"

"We perform an exorcism, banish the demon and regain Liz."

"Or?"

"*Or*, we kill it. Liz will die, but the world is a safer place."

Dave jumped up and snarled at my grandmother. She didn't bat an eyelid. It would take more than a growling grumpy wolf to shake the confidence of The Order's leader.

"Sit down, Dave. I have every intention of keeping my daughter alive. But we have to prepare for the possibility."

He sliced a hand through the air in front of her face. "It's not an option." Then he stalked out of the room, his footsteps banged on the way to the basement.

He had already lost a sister, he couldn't lose the woman he'd fallen for, and I couldn't lose an aunt.

My grandmother looked at the rest of us. "I need thirteen supernaturals for the exorcism. Gather your forces, we will conduct the exorcism at the peak of the moon. Anita is on her way back as we speak."

I looked around the room. With the doc and Maggie, we had eleven—two short.

"I'll sort it," Hudson said. I bet he would, but over my dead body would Mercy be involved in my personal business.

I frowned. "No, I'll call Rockhard and Lenson. They are discreet and capable." It would cost me, but it's not like we had powerful magical beings hanging around wanting to take part in an exorcism. They were dangerous, and anyone with half a brain would run as fast as possible in the opposite direction. I'd need something good to persuade the spell casters.

"What happens now?" he asked.

"Now," my grandmother stated, "I pick apart the psyche of my daughter and try not to fry her mind."

Chapter Twenty Five

My mind is a palace for you to smash.

There's something horrifying about prying apart someone's mind. It's a violation like no other, and it's the reason my grandmother holds her seat of leadership with an iron fist. No one would dare challenge *The Cracker*. Nobody was immune, not even me, and after observing a few sessions with her power in all its glory, I can safely say I never want to be on the wrong side of this woman I share genetics with.

"Is there a need for cuffs?" Hudson asked as Dayna laid down on my examination bed. Rebecca strapped the leather cuffs to her wrists while the other end was attached to the bars under the bed. Dayna stared at the ceiling, a slight tremble making her body vibrate.

I let out a long sigh. Hudson's shoulder brushed mine as he moved forward slightly, like he was ready to rescue Dayna.

"The process is painful, she will try to fight. No matter how willing she is, her instincts will kick in and she will defend herself," I muttered.

My grandmother produced a crystal from her bag, laid it on Dayna's chest and tied the cord around her neck.

"What's that?" Hudson asked. Curious cat.

"Bloodstone, used in reverse, it can suppress someone's power. We don't want Dayna burning down the house." I ghosted a hand over my chest where the same stone had once been placed against my flesh to keep my power contained.

"Her element is fire?"

I nodded and moved to the bottom of the bed. I tugged off her boots and dropped them to the floor. There was something I could do for her. It wouldn't be much. Dayna's eyes widened when she saw what I was doing.

"What are you doing?" Hudson asked, tracking my movements.

"Don't interfere," my grandmother snapped.

"I'll guard the door," Rebecca said, extricating herself from the situation. The door clicked closed behind her.

"Eloise, remember who you are speaking to. I am not one of your underlings who cower in your presence," Hudson growled.

Dayna's eyebrows hit her hairline. Nothing like a little supernatural political scuffle to take your mind off the encroaching pain. I cocked a brow and my lips twitched.

My grandmother sighed. "This is elemental business. I don't have to explain myself to you. But if you must know, Cora is going to share the pain to enable Dayna to cope with it better. Depending on how deep the suggestion goes will determine how hard I have to push. I suspect with Lucifer's involvement that this is going to be agonizing."

"Absolutely not, Cora, step away," he growled.

I tightened my grip on Dayna's ankles and swallowed. "You've lost the right to have any opinion on my decisions."

"Cora—"

I turned my head to stare at him, channeling the matriarch in the room. "Principal, if you are going to be a problem, then wait upstairs and let the women deal with this."

He shook his head, widened his stance and folded his arms.

My grandmother darted her gaze between the two of us. That's right, I lost him. I'm sure I'd hear all about how it was because I'd had sex with him too early. Apparently, I wasn't an elusive enough prostitute.

"Ground yourself in the present," my grandmother commanded as she stood by Dayna's head and placed her fingertips on her temples. I turned my attention to my aunt and met her eyes. "You are Dayna Ellen Roberts, daughter of Eloise Roberts," my grandmother continued. "You are in Summer Grove House, with your niece and your mother. Think back to being in your own house before Lucifer commandeered your home and demanded your niece."

Tendrils of my grandmother's power seeped into Dayna's mind. I winced. The mind was a clever thing. It knew how to protect itself and had many tricks to avoid facing unbearable pain. A psyche smasher relied on the mind resorting to these tricks, it dug under these layers to find the truth. A shudder ran down Dayna's body. I took the pain into myself and sucked in a breath.

"Good girl," my grandmother murmured as she slammed through a barrier, shredding it to pieces as she pushed further and deeper.

I gritted my teeth and tried to take the brunt of the pain so Dayna could hang on to the memory my grandmother was examining. My knees shook with the force of the power, but I stayed upright. I'd brought this on our family. The least I could do was take as much pain into myself as possible.

Dayna screamed, an earth-shattering, soul-clenching, torture-filled sound that drew tears to my eyes. I clung on tighter and yanked the residual pain from her body into mine. My mind urged me to let go, to avoid the agony. My fingers loosened as a sob broke free from my lips. Warmth engulfed my back and huge hands rested on my wrists. "You've got this," Hudson whispered in my ear. His woodsy scent enveloped me and gave me strength. I tightened my fingers with renewed determination.

"That's it," my grandmother said. "Show me what you are hiding." A wave of pain that brought bile up my throat rippled from Dayna to me. She was almost there, uncovering Dayna's deeply embedded unconscious suggestions that the devil himself had laid.

"There, you were told to let in a named demon, to crack open the wards that guard Cora and this house. Who have you let in?" my grandmother asked. This was important for the exorcism. Without a name we had about a twenty percent chance of getting rid of the demon and keeping Aunt Liz alive. With a name we could target the exorcism, and that probability rose to eighty percent.

Aunt Dayna thrashed as much as she was able to in her restraints, her mind resisting the intrusion. Blood seeped from her right nostril and down her cheek. "Grandmother," I warned. Eloise Roberts grimaced and pushed her power with a punch that gave the psyche smasher its true name. My knees buckled and Hudson's body pushed me against the bed, holding me up when I couldn't.

"She's been bound," my grandmother gritted out. "There will be a figurine close by. Most likely at a crossroads." She glanced at me as I searched my mind for likely places. There were several. My rooms, but I would have noticed a freaking voodoo doll making the magic wonky. There was under the house itself, in the vaults. They were literally built on such crossroads. But again, how the hell would Lucifer have gotten onto my grounds? My brain settled on something few people knew about Summer Grove House.

Aunt Dayna convulsed as my grandmother's magic wound tighter. "Any time now, Cora," my grandmother snapped.

"The stables," I said, shifting my gaze to Dave. "Probably near the back door. You are looking for a miniature lead coffin."

"What do I do with it?" Dave asked.

"Open it and unbind the hands and feet of the figurine," my grandmother said. "Under no circumstances break that figure."

"Why?"

"Don't ask," I muttered as I met my grandmother's eyes. Dave flew out of the room and I kept taking the pain from Dayna as best I could. The clock on the wall counted seconds, which seemed to be in slow motion.

Dayna suddenly relaxed on the table, and her mind became free of the entity which surrounded it. "Bune," Dayna rasped. "His name is Bune."

My grandmother's power slithered from Dayna's mind, retreating into its owner. Dayna sighed and passed out cold. I released her ankles and slumped back against Hudson.

"Is it over?" he asked as he scooped me up, bridal style.

"Put me down," I mumbled. Damn cat enjoyed carrying me around like a weakling. My limbs were like noodles and my struggles were akin to a newborn kitten clawing at a tiger.

"Hardly," my grandmother stated. "The good news is there are no further suggestions. The bad news is, Bune is no lower level lackey. He's a duke of hell, best known for moving the dead." She stepped away from the table and cocked her head at me. Her gaze narrowed. "Which begs the question, granddaughter, what the hell have you gotten yourself into?"

The office door burst open and in flooded vampire royalty. Sebastian's feet paused on the threshold. He waved a pen drive at me with a frown. "What the hell happened?" He eyeballed Dayna's unconscious form then swung his gaze back to me.

"Eloise Roberts happened," Hudson growled.

"My grandmother figured out who is possessing Aunt Liz and ascertained there are no more instructions lurking in Dayna's mind."

"That's good," Sebastian said. "I'm confused. Why is the cat carrying you?"

"Jealous?" Hudson said with a smirk.

I groaned. "Not now, please. We have enough going on without your alpha bullshit posturing."

"Is that the footage of my daughter's rendezvous?" my grandmother asked.

She snapped her fingers at Sebastian. He blinked and handed her the drive.

"Nearest computer?" she asked me.

I waved a hand at my desk. "Second drawer on the left."

She stalked to my desk and retrieved the laptop before placing it on the desk. I smacked Hudson's chest. "I'm fine, let me down."

His brow furrowed, then he gently set me on my feet. I wobbled a little before finding my footing and making my way to the laptop to help my grandmother. She folded herself into my chair like she belonged there. I refrained from rolling my eyes. It wasn't even posturing. She simply believed she had every right to be in the seat of power, no matter the room or audience. I spun the laptop toward me, turned it on and tapped in my passcode. My grandmother slid the drive into the side as I slumped in the visitor's chair. Hudson stood at my back, Rebecca joined us in the chair next to mine, and

Sebastian stood behind her. My grandmother's gaze roamed over us.

"What?" I asked.

"Manners," she scolded.

I sighed and sat up straight. Lord knows I didn't want my posture to be in question as well as my upbringing. "Apologies. I was wondering why you were looking at the four of us."

She grinned. "You make quite the powerhouse quad. At some point, Principal, you are going to have to explain to me why my granddaughter is not worth your time or effort. Was it just the chase you were interested in? I thought you wiser than a teenager."

That stung. For me and for him. She wasn't winning any grandparent of the year awards. She's certainly not the cookies and ice cream type of grandma everyone else seemed to get.

"That's between me and Cora," Hudson growled. I eyeballed the laptop. Come on, dude, work faster so we can get back to the supernatural drama and out of my love life.

"I see," my grandmother drawled. A little southern accent entered her tone, showing her true roots. My eyes snapped to hers. Oh boy, when the smooth southern belle came calling, you ran. Don't walk. Don't look back. Run, like your life depended on it.

"She's beautiful, intelligent, witty, she could bear your children, they might not be cats - but they would be powerful.

Hudson stiffened behind me. "Are you upset on your granddaughter's behalf, or because you lost your spy in my camp?"

"I was never a spy," I muttered.

"Because I came to live on your lands, giving you no excuse to go to mine."

My mouth fell open, and I twisted my head to look at him. And here was me thinking it was because he'd actually liked me. How utterly foolish I'd been. I'd fallen for his act, hook, line, and sinker.

"Don't pretend you weren't acting under the orders of your grandmother," he said, frowning down at me.

"My grandmother was asking me for information, but none of my actions when it came to you were under the guise of anything but following my heart."

His hand stroked my cheek. "Neither were mine. But your grandmother wants our union for different reasons, Cora. You know this."

"As touching as this is, it doesn't explain why you've jilted my granddaughter."

My head snapped back to her. "The outside world will see your manipulations for their true colors. People will believe a powerful elemental has influenced him and not take him seriously."

She arched her brow. "Is that so?"

I nodded and folded my arms. Just once, I wanted a non-complicated relationship with no strings, no influence, no games. I wanted normal. The white picket fence, a Labrador, and three kids normal.

"The reasons behind the pause in our relationship are many and private," Hudson ground out.

He kept saying pause, like he had the power to freaking press play whenever his highness decided. It didn't work like that. I guess he'd only learn I was serious when he tried pushing the button.

The laptop whirled to life, and the home screen appeared. Everyone stared.

"What is that?" Sebastian said with horror.

"Kittens," I said with my chin in the air. "Lots and lots of kittens."

"It's disgustingly cute," Rebecca stated.

"Childish," my grandmother intoned.

I huffed and clicked on the file browser before opening the video file. The clip played. My aunt was in a restaurant, alone. A minute passed before a waiter appeared, waving a man to the chair opposite her. He sat, and the waiter wrote several things on his pad before hurrying away.

"Is there sound?" my grandmother asked.

Sebastian shook his head. "No."

"Do you recognize him?" she asked, looking at each of us.

I leaned in closer. Come on, dude, look up. He tipped his head like he'd heard me and looked into the camera.

I gasped. "That's the voodoo priest who blinded me. That's him in the flesh."

My grandmother removed her spectacles from her bag and looked down her nose at the laptop. "Wrong," she sighed. "That's Stephen Proctor. Number one most wanted elemental in the world and a satanic priest. He's your worst nightmare."

Chapter Twenty Six

Nothing brings the family together like an exorcism.

Exorcisms predate the modern church by thousands of years. Some of the earliest recordings are from the people of Mesopotamia, which is now modern-day Iraq. They lived in a world of magical practices and believed in malignant supernatural entities which required protection and occasionally the exorcism of a demonic presence. Temple priests specializing in exorcism were called the *ashipu*. They developed a set of spells and incantations and recorded them on clay tablets. Today, ordained Catholic priests perform exorcisms which had to be ratified by the Vatican. There were fail-safes to ensure people needed a priest and not a psychiatrist. That said, if you had the right incantations and tools, it didn't prevent anyone else from doing one, and all major elemental power houses had at least one trained exorcist in their arsenal. Luckily for us, my grandmother was the best in America.

The door creaked open, and I looked over from the sofa where I was busy cleansing various crystals and blessing some water. I'd also retrieved the creepy mini lead coffin from Dave and purified the doll inside, so it no longer held any magical sway. Aunt Anita poked her head around the door before blowing out a breath and closing the door.

"Where is she?" she asked.

"Downstairs with Aunt Liz. She's making preparations."

Aunt Anita flopped into the chair opposite me, her body going limp as a noodle. I eyeballed her as she blew her hair out of her face. "You look like shit," I pointed out.

She arched her brow and smirked. "I feel like it. I'm trying to gather my wits."

I nodded. To deal with Eloise, one needed all their wits, plus any that were spare.

"Do we have thirteen?" she asked.

I nodded. I'd called in a favor, and like the good men they are, they came running—despite the danger. "Rockhard and Lenson will be here within the hour." I glanced at the clock on the mantle. "Actually, they should be here any minute. Time flies when you are preparing for an exorcism."

"It's definitely a fun family bonding activity," she agreed.

I snorted as the wards clanged again. My ward slithered against the newcomers, not recognizing them. The 'puff the magic dragon' car horn gave away their identities.

Aunt Anita snorted. "I have some final preparations to make," she said before swanning upstairs toward her bedroom. I flung open the door as Rockhard and Lenson hotfooted it up the steps. They were both eyeing my floral menace with curiosity.

"I take it you are aware of the blood magic saturating your house and grounds?" Lenson questioned.

I picked a low-hanging rose from around the door and squished the blood between my fingers. My inner monster perked up with interest. Down girl, no death was imminent. The roses had nothing to show me at the moment. It was like they had gone dormant and were waiting for a command. To do what, I wasn't sure. I wasn't sure of a lot of things, and that bothered me immensely. If I couldn't see the big bad, then I couldn't defend myself and those I loved.

"Fascinating," Rockhard mumbled. "I don't think I've ever seen blood magic this strong or covering this much ground before. Something powerful must be fueling it."

Yes, me and my stupid blood gave it a mega boost which hasn't helped matters. I let the petals fall to the floor. They might not be showing me visions of horror, but they were still icky. "They turned up a little over a week ago, first growing over a grave where the occupant had been put directly into the soil."

"That would give it a starting point," Lenson stated as he spun in a circle to take in the extent of the foliage. "But it doesn't explain how it's grown to such massive proportions. There's almost certainly been a ritual, a great sacrifice."

Rockhard frowned. He knew that wouldn't be enough, but he was too polite to push for my secrets. Time to get back to the business at hand. The murder-ridden roses were way down on my to do list.

"Thank you again for doing this," I said.

Lenson waved a hand at me. "Hmm, hmm, girl, we gotta talk about why your chakras are all outta alignment. Did that damn kitty get all up in your pussy and make a mess?"

Rockhard frowned at me as I grimaced. "Men are idiots, Cora, no matter the species. Eventually, he will understand the mistake he's made and seek to rectify it."

"I don't want him to rectify it," I mumbled as I stepped back and let them inside.

"Oh, sugar, you might not want him to, but it will feel damn good to watch him grovel," Lenson said as he looked around the house. "Have you heard of the revenge dress?"

Rebecca walked out of the kitchen and opened her arms to the pair of spell casters. "Boys, don't worry, I have the most spectacular revenge dress on order," she said in greeting.

"You do?" I wondered.

She winked over Lenson's shoulder and released the couple.

"What do you have for me?" Lenson asked.

I nodded. "Follow me." I took the stairs down to the basement and made a beeline for my office. Rebecca took the opposite direction into the training room, leaving me alone with the spell casters.

I pulled a key from the top drawer of my desk and continued through my office and examination room. Opening the outside door, I led them around the outside and then down into the vaults.

The doc looked up from his paperback and ran his gaze over the newcomers. "How are the boys?" I asked as I led the spell casters to an iron vault.

The doc glanced at the cubs who were currently curled up and sleeping in the far corner. "They've tired themselves out for now. It's a cycle, two to three hours of crazy snarling, followed by an hour of sleep. It's not healthy."

"We are tackling this one fire at a time," I said. A twinge of guilt pulled at my heart that I was putting my aunt ahead of the cubs and their trapped animal status. They'd live to see tomorrow. My aunt might not if we allowed the possession to continue. It was less one fire at a time, and more one huge inferno we were battling for control.

"I'm not even going to ask why you have two cubs imprisoned under your house and are entertaining the pack's chief medical officer," Rockhard mumbled.

"Good plan," I responded.

"An Austin fan," Lenson said, tilting his head to read the cover of the doc's book. "Are you a Mr. Darcy or Miss Bennet admirer?" Translation, which side do you bat for?

The doc arched a silver brow and glanced at me. "'There is a stubbornness about me that never can bear to be frightened at the will of others. My courage always rises at every attempt to intimidate me.'"

I folded my arms. So, news of mine and Hudson's demise had reached his ears and he was treating me to some advice via the infamous Elizabeth Bennet. Well, two could play that game. "'I am only resolved to act in that manner, which will, in my own opinion, constitute my happiness, without reference to you, or to any person so wholly unconnected with me.'"

The doc's lip twitched, and he tipped his head. "Touché. But for the record, I think you are matched in sheer stubbornness. One of you will need to concede."

"There's no battle here, doc. I will not fight for a man who puts political wrangling's above me. When I give my heart, I will pull out all the stops. I will come in like a hurricane and lay waste to anyone who threatens him, but I expect the same in return."

"That's fair."

"That's right, girl, you have your standards, ones the cat hasn't measured up to," Rockhard said with a snap of his fingers. I ignored the pang in my heart that said I wouldn't ever find anyone else like Hudson. It was a niggling doubt in my resolve that I quashed. I couldn't risk my heart to anyone who wouldn't give me theirs. Being with me meant holding many secrets. Secrets which could destroy me. No, it was better this way.

I unlocked the vault, it registered my unique magical signature and the bolts unclicked. I spun the dial in a specific direction, to an exact number of degrees. If I did this wrong, it would open but show a false, empty vault, a failsafe for if I was being forced to open it. The final lock clicked, and the door creaked open. Out of the corner of my eye I saw the doc lean back on his chair to look inside.

"Come look, doc, you've earned it," I said as I entered the room. Rockhard and Lenson hovered at my back as I entered.

"Don't touch anything," Rockhard advised the doc.

"Why?"

"There are things in here that would stop your heart," Lenson said.

"Make you blind," Rockhard continued.

"Summon your dead enemies," I said, pointing at a foot-high Greek vase. My gaze roamed over the many artifacts I'd collected over the years for times such as these. Elementals didn't deal in money. Our powers rarely left us short. The currency we traded was magical objects, and Lenson had a particular weakness for swords. The rarer the better.

I selected the long, thin metal case and carried it over to a table in the center of the vault. Lenson and Rockhard drifted closer with wide, curious eyes as I unclipped the case and pried it open. The purple velvet lining supported a long sword. "Fragarach," I declared. Lenson gasped. I smirked - gotya. "A sword forged by the gods, meant to be wielded with the stone of destiny." Which I also possessed, but I wasn't showing all my cards yet. "Also known as the—"

"Whisperer," Lenson breathed as he hovered a hand over the blade. It was a beauty, with an unusual bulb-style handle and Celtic symbols etched down the center of the blade.

"It also does this." I pressed my hand to the handle and the electric blue light ignited from the handle down the blade. The symbols glowed with power.

"Ooh," Rockhard said.

The doc tilted his head and pressed his lips together, clearly not impressed by a shiny sword.

Lenson swallowed and darted a look to Rockhard, who folded his arms and gave me a thousand-yard stare. Here it comes. "Where's the stone?" Rockhard asked.

I stood straight and rewarded him with the Roberts' hardass gaze. "This is enough for the exorcism."

Lenson swung his gaze between us and worried his lip.

"You have the stone?" Rockhard asked.

I inclined my head. "I do."

"How does one come across such rare, powerful, magical objects?" The doc asked.

My lips twitched. I played the part of sheltered little Cora Roberts well. The beast within me would terrify the strongest of men and the scariest of monsters. Being who I was meant I was trusted with items no one else on Earth was capable of protecting. "That is a story for another time."

I started to close the case. "If we don't have a deal."

Lenson reached out and stopped my hand as he cast a longing look at the sword. "We have a deal," he muttered.

Rockhard sighed. "I told you to let me do the negotiations."

"She's giving us The Whisperer. It's more than sufficient compensation for our help."

I pressed my lips together and fought a smile. "Fine," Rockhard said.

I let loose the grin. "Excellent."

The White Furry Menace shot into the vault carrying a small bird between her teeth. She eyeballed Lenson and Rockhard like she was trying to decide who was more worthy.

"I didn't know you owned a cat," Lenson said, kneeling down and offering his hand.

"I don't," I said, snapping the case closed. "She does as she pleases. I think she tolerates me because I feed her, but I'm not sure she's ever been owned."

"That is true of most headstrong females," Lenson said.

Bella eyeballed his hand like it was a rattlesnake, pranced over to Rockhard and dropped her offering on his boot.

"That's odd," Rockhard muttered.

"She is odd."

"She should bring you the gift of food," he said, tilting his head at Bella.

"She never brings them to me. She has an obsession with delivering these gifts to any males that come into the house. Hudson, Dave, Sebastian, and now you."

She nudged the dead bird with her paw, then began licking her fur.

"Huh, strange cat." *Isn't that the truth?*

I disappeared to the back of the vault, opened a cabinet and retrieved the original priceless ashipu clay tablets we needed for the exorcism. Nothing but the best for the Roberts family.

"Back to business," I stated as I made my way to the front of the vault. Lenson stroked the case. "It will be safe here," I assured him as I led the way out of my office vault. I reengaged the locks.

"It's time," I said to the doc.

The shifter and two spell casters followed me on my path to the basement. Maggie bounced down the stairs while brandishing a ladle in a big bowl and a squirty bottle.

"What are those for?" I wondered.

"The holy water, of course. The president wasn't clear on the delivery method, so I thought I'd give her options."

I opened my mouth, then snapped it closed.

Rockhard chuckled. "We brought protection charms for everyone," he said, pulling a bag of charms out of his pants pocket.

"Great, let's put them on before we start. Maximize the time they work for."

"Prepare yourselves," I muttered as I swung open the door and followed Maggie into the training room. "Shit's about to get real."

The smell flipped my stomach. It was so potent it settled on my tongue like fur on week-old rotten vegetables. "Jesus," Lenson said, holding his arm across his nose.

My grandmother spun from her position on the outside of the circle. She cocked a brow at us. "Good, you started with the praying. We are going to need it. This sucker Bune is buried deep inside my daughter."

"Phrasing," Rockhard muttered. The supernaturals collected a charm from him and then fanned around the edge of the circle, each taking a point at a lit candle. Four shifters, two vampires, and six elementals. With Aunt Liz in the center, we had our thirteen. She counted, she had to—because she had to fight. Aunt Liz's face had become gaunt, her bloodshot eyes bulging, and her cracked lips dribbling blood. The malevolence was eating her raw from the inside. Something niggled in the back of my mind. What was the point of all of this? I'd rechecked my wards, not even Lucifer could get through. So why send a demon in my aunt?

"Cardinal rules of an exorcism," my grandmother stated as she waved some burning sage in the air. "Cora."

I grimaced. Even now, she was testing me. "Once our hands are joined, don't break the circle."

"Good, continue."

"Don't address it directly. Avoid eye contact. Don't enter into conversion with it. It will try to goad you or bargain with you. Once you fall for it, it will know you and you will be vulnerable."

"And the golden rule?" she prompted.

"Don't step inside the circle."

"Why?" Dave snapped. He watched Liz with a deep frown. He already wanted to get in there and rescue her, and things were about to get much worse.

"We all hold power. We are about to use it to draw out the demon and banish him back to Hell. Collectively, we will channel this power into my grandmother who wields the spell to complete the exorcism."

"What's that got to do with stepping in the circle?" Hudson asked.

"The power loops through us and around the circle, effectively squeezing the demon from its host. If someone steps inside that circle, it causes a kink in the power line, the energy will back up at that point and the demon can feed on it and fortify its hold on Aunt Liz. With enough power, it could make it permanent, and damn her soul to Hell in its place."

"Don't step in the circle—got it," Maggie said, squaring her shoulders. I'd placed her between me and Rebecca. I was the most worried about our nervous little bobcat shifter and needed people who knew her to both support and keep control of her.

Harry shot through the wall. "Miss Roberts," he exclaimed. I closed my eyes. Not now, Harry, one supernatural crisis at a time please.

"Halfling, filthy, bloodsucker," Aunt Liz snarled. Her voice was inhuman and multilayered. The sound sent a shiver down my spine. Wait, who was she speaking to? My eyes sprung open to find her focus on Harry. "Heaven's reject, your soul is soaked in the stench of sin."

Harry gasped. "I'll have you know I was an ethical vampire that helped others to lead good lives."

Aunt Liz's head twisted. She put her hands down her blouse and tugged on the garment to expose her bra.

"Don't speak to it," I warned, both the living and the dead.

Dave snarled and shook his head. Aunt Liz freed one of her breasts to taunt the shifter. She turned to me once she'd failed to get a reaction from him. I stared it down. I wasn't under any threat of possession. I already housed a bigger and badder beast than the one staring at me. Bune hadn't just met his match in me. He'd punched way above his weight. The only thing stopping me from squashing him like a bug was my love for my aunt.

"You're all wearing your charms?" my grandmother checked.

A chorus of agreement echoed around the room. "I brought you a spray and a ladle for the holy water," Maggie said as she wrung her hands together and tried to look at anything but the mess of my aunt on the floor.

My grandmother blinked. Ha ha, finally taken aback by the little shifter. "The spray will suffice. Give it to Cora," she stated. Maggie grabbed the bottle and handed it to me. I filled it with the water I'd blessed and twisted the lid back on before handing it to my grandmother.

My grandmother nodded at me. "Ready?"

"Yes." I was her assistant.

She draped a purple scarf around her neck. Its Latin name is *stola*, essentially it was the symbol of eternal life through the divine. It helped to convey His power and enforce His will upon the demon before us.

"Join hands," she instructed. We formed a circle. I placed one hand in Maggie's and the other on my grandmother's shoulder. Aunt Dayna flanked her other side.

My grandmother chanted in Latin, some ancient words that called upon the higher power to imbue her with His grace. A rumble of energy echoed in the room. Aunt Liz paused her snarling and slurs and narrowed her gaze on my grandmother.

The candles flickered and my hair fluttered in the breeze as the spell gained traction and our combined magic channeled into my grandmother. She shuddered and gritted her teeth. She lifted the bottle and sprayed holy water over my aunt.

Aunt Liz flopped onto her back and arched her spine, her legs splayed obscenely wide as she gyrated and cackled. It was unfortunate she was wearing a skirt.

"Read with me now, Cora," my grandmother demanded.

I fell into sync with her as we recited the incantation which would send Bune back to Hell. Aunt Liz flipped onto her front and crawled to the edge of the circle in front of me. Her eyes were lit up with demonic energy, not red like the movies portrayed. This was like staring at black diamonds. The demon had altered her features, moving her bone structure to accommodate the insidious presence. It was bone chilling, even for me.

It smiled. "Daughter of death, do you enjoy playing with these lesser creatures, making them think they are your equal?" Ah, we were at the flattery stage. Except demons always missed the mark.

"Daughter of death?" Dave mumbled. Great, now the pack's chief of security was up in business again.

"Stay focused," Aunt Dayna snapped.

"Keep going and I'll tear and shred her from the inside out," Bune growled.

Dave's eyes shot from me to Aunt Liz. "It's lying," I told him. "Kill the host, and it loses its footing on earth."

"Doesn't mean I can't make it hurt," Bune snapped.

My grandmother's chanting reached a crescendo. This was it. "I command you, Bune, duke of Hell, in the name of our Lord, release this woman."

The demon's head snapped toward my grandmother, twisting slightly too much to be comfortable. "Pitiful witch, you can't banish me."

My grandmother yanked on the power from our circle. I sucked in a breath. "Bune, release Elizabeth Roberts, my firstborn. In the name of the Father, the Son—"

Bune cackled. "The Holy Spirit has long since abandoned you, Eloise. You made your bed when you did a deal with the devil. Did you think he wouldn't collect? Foolish woman."

My grandmother twisted the lid of the bottle and threw the contents at Bune. "Release her," she bellowed, shoving all her power at Bune. Bune flew back to the center of the circle, bits of the ceiling scattering onto the floor, and his roar rivaled Hudson's.

He threw a hand out and made a fist. My grandmother grasped her throat with her hands and coughed. Her shoulders lifted, forcing my hand to slip. "What's happening?" I ground out.

Bune smiled and pulled their hand up. My grandmother's feet left the ground as she gasped for breath. I grabbed her arm. "Let her go," I demanded.

"Your aunt or your grandmother, daughter of death, choose."

My heart pounded and sweat formed on my forehead. No, no, no. This wasn't happening. I wasn't losing anybody. I squeezed my eyes closed. Every second moved us a step closer to either of them dying.

I pressed my lips together and yanked on the power chain, pulling it from my grandmother into me. I needed to take control. My spine stiffened with the combined mass of magic.

"Release her," I boomed. Bune tightened his fist. My grandmother's feet kicked in protest next to me. When this was over, I would hunt Bune and eradicate him from any dimension.

"How's your faith?" Bune snarled. "Do you pray to Him?"

"This isn't working," Dave stated. I glared at him. He pressed his lips together. No, don't do it, Dave. He pulled the two hands he was holding closer together, so they were in front of his stomach, then pushed them together as he untangled his hands from Hudson and Rockhard.

"Dave, no."

He glanced at me, then dived into the circle. He tackled Bune flat to the floor and pinned his hands above his head. "Elizabeth Roberts," he snapped. "You are a powerful elemental who will not be taken down by a second-rate demon on a power trip."

Bune snapped his teeth at Dave's face. I glanced at my grandmother. She was levitating a foot off the ground, being strangled by an invisible force.

"Still not working," I muttered. Plus, he'd deteriorated the power source. I had zero chance of defeating Bune now. My inner beast stirred, reminding me I had a store of power which could turn Bune to dust.

"Do you remember our first date?" Dave whispered. "You wore a lemon dress, with your hair half up. I'd never seen such a vision of beauty and grace. You cooked your lamb shanks with rosemary and redcurrant sauce. It was hands down the best lamb I'd ever eaten."

Bune shuddered, and for a second I thought I saw a change in his face. "Keep going," I muttered.

"Later we took a walk by the river. Your hair shone in the moonlight as you recalled your dreams of being an ice skater. That was our next date. Turns out you're shit at ice skating, but we had fun falling. We are still having fun falling, Liz, so get back here and let me love you."

Bune bellowed a cry of anger as my aunt fought him. Dave leaned down and smacked his lips straight onto Bune's. Later I'd realize it was a very fairytale princess exorcism. My grandmother dropped to the floor with a clatter and sucked in a huge breath. I pulled on my power and pushed it onto Dave and Bune. "Release her, Bune," I screamed.

Bune roared. The walls shook, then a boom sounded in the room, like something had imploded. White rose petals floated from the ceiling. They rained down around us, outlining the circle where Dave was holding a limp Aunt Liz. The heavy floral scent chased away the rot and decay. I knelt down next to my grandmother and checked her pulse. She was okay. Next, I walked in the circle and checked on Aunt Liz. Her bone structure was restored, her eyes no longer bulged, and she was breathing. I closed my eyes and exhaled. Nobody died, that was a result.

"It's over?" Hudson asked.

I stood and spun to face him. "It's far from over, but we won this battle."

He frowned, and his gaze bored into my skull. My secrets were once again my own. Any barrier he'd managed to wear down, I'd re-erected with extra protection. Nothing was getting through this sucker. I wrapped my mind up in a super thick condom and I was on the pill. Okay, bad analogy, but you get my drift.

"I'll go fetch the broom," Maggie said, running from the basement.

"I didn't think we were getting a show and an exorcism," Lenson said, smirking at Dave.

I sucked in a breath. I was exhausted, but I needed to feel the sun on my face after facing that kind of evil.

"There's nothing more we can do today. I'll be upstairs," I said.

Hudson took a step toward me. "I'll come."

I put my hand out. "No, I need some space."

He huffed and ran a hand through his hair. He wanted to interrogate me about the things Bune had said. I wanted to pick apart some things myself, but with my grandmother.

I headed out the door, up the stairs, and through the house. I swung open the back door and sucked in a lungful of fresh Louisiana air as I stepped outside and closed my eyes, letting the sun warm my face.

"Cora Roberts in the flesh, color me honored, my dear. Now be an angel and take a seat. We have things to discuss."

My head snapped to the left and I found none other than the Satanic priest, Stephen Proctor, lounging in on my porch swing. Why me?

Chapter Twenty-Seven

There's a fox in my henhouse.

When dealing with satanic priests, one must proceed with caution—no sudden movements, no acting like prey—so a lot like handling Hudson. I'm doomed. However, he wasn't here to kill me. If Lucifer wanted me dead, I'd be dead. But the second I died, that portal would snap closed. I was safe, relatively speaking.

I folded myself into the seat next to Stephen. He was handsome, in an overly pretty kind of way. Dark hair, dark eyes, olive skin, long limbs tucked into a sharp suit. Too clean, too groomed—like a Calvin Klein ad campaign.

"Your roses are making a mess of my house, Stephen," I stated as a fat droplet of blood clung to the bloom hanging from the porch.

The petal shuddered in the breeze and released its crimson fruit onto the floor. Another rose instantly sprouted from the blood.

Stephen smiled. "Ah, I see your grandmother has made the link. No matter. I'm no demon, Cora, you can't banish me from this plane. It's my own, after all."

"For now."

He sighed. "Don't bore me with tales of religion. We both know there's a Heaven and a Hell. I don't need to hear the Ten Commandments to know which realm I am destined for. While the destinations and characters are real, religion is a man-made mass illusion, fed by the fear that every act will be judged and weighed."

I turned to face him. "Won't it?"

"You know better."

"Religion at its core is about living a good life, being compassionate, kind, generous. It considers human vices and makes room for them. The part you speak of was written by men to keep women in line and rule over leaders of nations. We've come a long way since then."

"Yet as your race stands on the precipice of war, you worry they will cast you out of this fabricated religion."

I inclined my head. "No, I worry that humankind will think religion is specifically for them, and them alone. It will give the haters fuel, that we are abominations that need to be eradicated. History has proven the few influence the masses."

He stretched his arms out, like he was welcoming my conclusion. "And so we have a quandary. Your grandmother needs to be stopped."

Huh, this was an angle I hadn't expected. Stephen Proctor was here because of the blood magic and the Lucifer mess he was entangled with, not because of the political wrangling of the supernaturals. What was I missing? Was this linked to the deal Bune spoke of with my grandmother? Ugh, so many unanswered questions.

"My grandmother has legions of elementals and is poised to have a landmark treaty signed between the three factions. If that happens, it will take an act of god to stop her."

"What are you going to do about it?"

This was surreal, chatting with the menace that was wreaking havoc in my life about my family issues. I sighed. Sadly, it wasn't the weirdest moment I'd ever experienced.

"Let's focus on more pressing matters, Mr. Proctor."

"Like?"

"The blood magic you have cast over my property. What is its purpose? If you think I'm scared by a little murder and gore, we clearly haven't met."

He chuckled. It was a warm dark sound that caused goosebumps to erupt down my arms. "Perhaps I underestimated you. But if I wanted you frightened, I could have done this."

He snapped his fingers, and the world fell away. I gripped the seat, lifted my feet and gasped as the floor disappeared and in its place was a vast labyrinth of fire, destruction, and suffering. The sulfur burned my nose. He was showing me Hell. My spine itched as my monster fought me for control. She wanted to obliterate the threat and save me. I closed my eyes and forced my heart to slow. I was safe. Visiting Hell wasn't as simple as snapping one's fingers, no matter what company you kept. My eyes sprang open. No Satanist was going to have me running scared. That path led to my enslavement by Lucifer. I'd be damned if I let that happen. I ignored the lurch in my stomach and put my feet back down, then stood, seemingly in midair, hanging above the web of agonizing pain. The thing was, I'd experienced pain that broke the mind and terrorized the soul, and I'd survived it.

I twisted to face him and folded my arms. "You are going to have to do better than that."

He tilted his head and studied me. The illusion fell away to my back porch. "Yes, I have underestimated you. Only a scarred and dangerous psyche could withstand my power."

Perilous ground, steer him away, Cora. "What did you do to that boy?"

He leaned back in the swing and smirked. "His sacrifice was necessary."

"The words of a true sociopath," I mumbled as I leaned against the railing.

"In some cultures, it is believed we are born with a finite amount of luck and power. As we progress through life, we deplete that source until finally we die."

"You sacrificed a child because his luck bucket was full?"

"Each religion and belief system has its own rules and rituals. If you perform them correctly, that belief system translates into power."

"Giving you the opening to bastardize any culture to meet your demands."

He inclined his head. "No matter the underlying heritage, blood magic will always hold power."

"All so you could grow a pretty display?"

"No, I have no interest in the aesthetics of your home. Although I like the symbolism." This wasn't getting me anywhere. I needed to goad him into parting with information.

"White roses and blood, the ultimate symbol of death for The Undertaker. Well, aren't you a clever little puppet Satanist?"

His stare turned flinty. One thing you could count on for all these power-tripping idiots, they hated people pointing out that there was someone pulling their strings. "It's an honor to serve him."

"Sure, and when he gets what he wants, he's going to give you a place ruling at his side and shower you with riches and gold? Perhaps a few virgins to sweeten the deal?"

He pressed his lips together and leaned forward. "You know nothing, Cora Roberts."

I laughed. "I know more than you think. Do you realize who I truly am?"

He blinked. Ah, clearly not. Another thing sociopaths hate—not knowing all the facts. "Ask yourself why the King of Hell is interested in a southern girl with a retro gift?"

"You are holding open a portal to the promised land."

Okay, so he knew a little. "A bit much for an elemental to manage, don't you think?"

He frowned and stood. "What are you?"

I smirked. "That would be telling. Now you find yourself in a situation with an unknown foe. Remove your magic from my grounds and I won't retaliate."

He quirked a brow. "It doesn't matter what you are, no being on Earth could stop what is coming."

"I could easily stop anything from reaching my house. You aren't even here." I reached out a hand and swiped it through his body. "Your magic can seep into the dirt I stand on, but you can't reach me. No matter how many sacrifices or rituals you perform, I will always be stronger."

He grinned. "Except the danger isn't outside your house, Cora." He disappeared.

Oh fuck. What the hell was in my house?

Lenson and Rockhard had left with their new sword. My grandmother was recovering in her room, being attended to by Aunt Dayna and Aunt Anita. Dave had strode into Aunt Liz's room with her draped in his arms and slammed the door closed behind him. They had people, people who loved and cared for them. I was glad, but also a little jealous. It was an ugly emotion, but as Hudson retreated to the stables, my heart sank. I'd survived without him before. I would go on again. It wasn't like I was alone. I had my vampire entourage and spiritual guide, who was currently floating around the sink and staring out across the garden. He was pivotal in the next step of my plan and I'd had enough of being on the back foot with Stephen Proctor. Starting with getting rid of the blood magic infiltrating my grounds, I was going to do everything I could to negate the threat he posed. I think it had already served its purpose by letting in a demon. I wasn't sure of the point of that possession. Perhaps we had banished Bune before he enacted whatever evil plan he had stored up his sleeve? I wasn't that lucky, but I was that hopeful.

"Why are you wearing those?" Sebastian asked as he came striding into my kitchen.

I tugged on my other pink spotted rain boot. "Thick soles, and protection for my legs," I explained.

"Are you doing something which requires protection?" he asked, leaning against the door frame.

"I had a visit," I started.

Rebecca breezed into the kitchen and eyeballed my quirky rain boots. "From who?" she asked.

"Stephen Proctor, the Satanic priest responsible for Aunt Liz's possession."

They both froze. "When?" Sebastian snapped.

I sighed. "Don't get your panties in a twist. It was after the exorcism. But he wasn't actually here. It was a projection."

"What did he want?" Rebecca asked as she filled the kettle and popped it on the stove.

"What all evil nemeses want, to gloat."

"But we beat him, Bune is banished, and we saved Aunt Liz," Sebastian stated as he came to sit next to me at the kitchen table.

"Excuse me, Miss Roberts, I believe I have sighted our target. I shall return soon," Harry said as he flew straight through the wall and out into the garden. Excellent, and just in time. First, I needed to fuel up, because this next part was likely to suck big hairy balls.

"It's not that easy," I explained. "I'm not clear of the purpose and therefore we can't be sure if he was successful. He hinted that the threat exists within my house, so with that in mind I'm cleaning house."

"You're going to unpick the blood magic?" Sebastian guessed.

I nodded. "That's a good place to start."

"You'll need to eat," Rebecca stated, opening the fridge. She compiled a plate of sugary goodness together in two minutes. My stomach rumbled in anticipation as I picked up a slice of lemon cake.

Rebecca rolled her eyes. "Always going for cake first."

"Or cookies," Sebastian said, swiping an oatmeal cookie from my plate. Rebecca smacked his hand, but he ate it anyway.

"Hey," I complained. "Only the crazy elemental about to unpick a blood spell gets cookies."

He chuckled as he stuffed it into his mouth. I made quick work of the rest of the meal, dosing myself up nicely to negate the inevitable downer.

Harry reappeared with wide eyes. "I believe I have found our foe, Miss Roberts, if you would follow me." He floated straight through the wall. Then shoved his head back into the kitchen. "Not exactly follow me, but I will meet you outside."

He was taking death in his stride, and had seemed to find a purpose in his afterlife that he didn't have in life. He might even be happy.

"When are you doing it?" Sebastian asked.

I stood, took my plate to the sink and washed it. "No time like the present." Rebecca and Sebastian looked at me expectantly. I shook my head. "No, you aren't coming."

"Why not?" Sebastian snapped.

"I'm going to be exhausted and strung out after this. I don't need you overreacting and trying to heal me," I told him before turning my gaze to Rebecca. "Blood freaks you out."

"When it's coming from a carcass. The roses are macabrely beautiful."

I eyeballed her silver strappy sandals. "You'll need better footwear."

She snapped her fingers. "We are the same size. I'll borrow your other pair." She darted out of the room and returned thirty seconds later carrying my bee print rain boots. She toed off her sandals and slipped them on. Only Rebecca could look elegant in a sundress and rain boots.

I groaned and tipped my head back. "Fine. Neither of you freaks out or intervenes. This won't be a straightforward task."

They nodded and followed me out of the kitchen, down the hall, and past the living room full of supernaturals. I grabbed a shovel leaning next to the back door before exiting into the garden. A few clouds dotted the sky as the late afternoon sun bid farewell to the day in streaks of pastel pink and orange. I shivered, still only in my jean shorts and band tee. It's not like the cleansing of blood magic requires formal wear. Something warm settled on my shoulders. I glanced to my right, finding Rebecca smiling, and she encouraged me to shrug on a pale pink hand knitted cardigan courtesy of Maggie's latest hobby. It was warm and soft, but a little misshapen and holey.

Harry darted around the corner and waved at me. I'd given him one task. Find me the boy's bones. I knew without a doubt that they were buried on my ground somewhere. If I removed the catalyst, the magic would unravel. Something this complex and vast would take time, but I had to pull on the string that was holding everything together. The rest would follow.

I stalked after Harry across the thorny rose-filled lawn. We passed the unmarked graves, rounded the largest magnolia tree, and halted near the border of my property. Harry pointed under a bush. The air smelled damp, like decaying compost.

I slammed the shovel in the ground and began digging. Sebastian elbowed me out of the way and took up the task.

"How do you know where to dig?" he asked as the pile of dirt increased next to him.

"Lucky guess," I mumbled. Rebecca took a step back and Sebastian paled. Oh boy. Ten seconds later, the cloying stench of disease and decay hit me. It brought tears to my eyes and made my nostrils sting.

"There they are," Sebastian said as he stepped away from the hole he'd created.

I came to the edge and peered down at the hessian drawstring bag covered in dirt. Look at that, they bagged them up for me. Satanists in the south were clearly considerate. Lucky me.

I plucked the bag out of the hole, being careful not to touch its contents.

"Now what?" Sebastian asked.

I frowned. There were several ways to destroy the blood magic, the most effective being to burn the bones and scatter the ashes in a body of water. But that wouldn't give his soul any peace. In fact, he'd likely be in permanent torment, and that wasn't acceptable. Not to me. They imbued the bones with the horrific ritual. The power was in the terror from the act. If I relived that act with the spirit, I might be able to take that pain and help him to not be in a permanent state of terror, which was fueling the spell. Of course, with Stephen Proctor in charge, it wouldn't be that easy. The guy was a master of mental booby-traps.

I undid the string and prepared myself. "What are you doing?" Sebastian asked.

"I need to relive the death, like a retro read, and try to detach the spirit from the blood magic. If I can help find him peace, it will stop fueling the spell."

His hand shot out and grasped my wrist. "Wait, you want to go head to head in mental warfare with the Satanic priest that blinded you last time?"

"It was a solid plan until you said it out loud," I replied.

"There's got to be another way," Sebastian said.

The boy appeared a few feet in front of me, his mouth open in a silent scream as blood covered his face. "Oh my," Harry said, hovering a little further away from the tormented spirit. "We must help him."

I knew I liked Harry for a reason. We were both set on saving the world, one soul at a time. I shook my head at Sebastian. "I can do this. It's another death memory. I've lived through hundreds. Now I know Stephen is lurking around, I'll be careful."

I tugged my wrist free of his grip and tipped the bones into my palm. I was dropped into a dark room, my body trembling on the damp, cold stone floor. The porridge in the metal bowl had gone hard and stale. I couldn't eat, not when I didn't know what horror awaited me at the end of this. Mother had said I was going on a trip with my uncle to America. The trip had been long. Then my uncle had met with a man in a suit. After some talking in a language I didn't understand, the man in the suit grabbed my arm and threw me into the trunk of his car. I'd stayed quiet. My uncle would beat me if I created a fuss. I'd struggled to hold my bladder and had paid the price once the man discovered the mess. Now I was waiting, all day, all night, every day waiting in a room with no windows, being kept by a man who had evil lurking in his eyes.

The metal lock on the outside of the door clanged, then it swung open with a deafening screech. I peered at the evil man from underneath my eyelashes. He walked into the room and bent down next to me.

"It's time for you to prove your worth," he said in my language.

I shuddered and curled in on myself. Two more men filled the chamber. One grabbed my ankles while the other hooked his hands under my arms. They carted me out of the area, down a dingy hallway, and into another room with the same car I'd come here in. They dropped me in the trunk, then bound my wrists together with a tight rope that burned my flesh. Next they bound my feet. I let out a yelp of terror. I couldn't help it. The evil man appeared above me and tilted his head. "All these weeks, and now you decide to start whining?" He sighed and whispered some words above me. My throat tightened. I gasped and sought to scream, nothing came out. It was too late. Deep down, I knew that before this day was through, I would no longer be alive.

The evil guy's gaze roamed over my face, a slow grin tilting his lips. "Cora Roberts, sticking your nose in my business again? You want to know what happened to the boy?"

I tried to scramble out of the memory before he unpicked my mind and got inside. He tutted. "Silly girl, I'm not going to hurt you. But I am going to make you feel every inch of this boy's pain. After all, you are responsible."

Time jumped, and I became disoriented as two immense men dragged me into the middle of a stone circle. I struggled, but with bound hands and feet, it was useless. Stephen grinned as he welcomed me into the center of the circle. Gigantic trees surrounded us. Familiar trees. We were on the edge of my property, on the border of my wards. I looked up.

The moon was enormous, like I could pluck it from the sky. A super moon.

The men dropped me to my knees, and one of them pried open my mouth while the other grabbed a rope hanging from a sturdy tree branch and fashioned a noose. Stephen approached me and chanted some strange words over a bowl before he scooped out a claylike substance, stuffed it into my mouth, and forced it down my throat.

"Swallow," he demanded. I gulped down the burning goo and was almost sick. Stephen watched me, then nodded at the man holding my jaw. He released me. The other man grabbed the noose hanging from the tree and brought it toward me. Terror suffused my veins, making my body shake and teeth chatter. I wanted out of this memory so badly, but I clung on because it was the least he deserved—to be seen, for someone to know his story.

He grabbed my bound ankles and looped the noose around them. He signaled to another man with a thumbs up, and my stomach lurched as I was dragged along the floor, then the world tilted, and I was dangling upside down.

Stephen approached me. Moonlight glinted off the machete held in his right hand as he twisted it. A jumble of words spewed from his mouth. Power pressed in on me, squeezing my already frantic lungs.

Stephen smirked. "Feel his pain, Cora." Then he sliced through the air and my throat stung before blood gurgled and spilled, covering my face before seeping into the ground below. It sought the roots which straddled my property and encroached on my land. My struggles lessened, then stopped. Death had come, but hadn't released me. It held me in the grip of terror with no end in sight.

I hurtled out of the death memory and was spat out back into my garden. Sebastian caught me as my knees gave out.

Harry hovered over me. "Miss Roberts, I was incorrect—the child's bones aren't only located here. I've found another three sites."

My head tipped back, and I groaned. A terrible roar split the air. Oh good, the Terror of Tennessee is here. We were all saved. Then I promptly passed out.

Chapter Twenty Eight

Game on.

Magic has been around since the dawn of time. Early religion taught us to fear it. However, as we long to have faith in miracles, we also want to believe we have power over that which we can't control. Time, the future, death, love - people have sought practitioners of magic to bend the natural order to their liking. No one has control over these things, and those who claim otherwise are taking advantage of the desperate and giving the rest of us with power a bad name.

This need for control was how we'd arrived at our current standoff. Me seated on one side of my desk, Hudson, Dave, and Sebastian on the other. Everyone else was busy dealing with my booming guest house.

"There's got to be another way," Hudson growled with a frown.

"There's not," I answered. We'd been going around in circles for about forty minutes. Having decided my property was overrun with blood magic, and that it was too strong to destroy by simply removing the boy's bones, I'd concluded that the property needed to be blessed. Stephen Proctor was a nasty piece of work. I wouldn't be surprised if multiple spells were in play. A blessing would out any and all nefarious magic.

"Can someone else do it?" Hudson asked.

"The property is in my name. It will have the most impact coming from me."

"So, someone else could do it?" Dave said.

"Technically, yes. Realistically, no."

There was also the other minor problem, the one where the boy's bones had been scattered around my property. Harry hovered in the back and wrung his hands together with a frown marring his face. If he was alive, I'd warn him he'd be at risk of wrinkles. I didn't think it was a concern for the dead.

"What are the risks?" Hudson asked.

I studied him. Tightly coiled muscles, narrowed eyes, ticking jaw—Hudson Abbot was a hairbreadth away from going furry. "The risks are my own. I don't owe you any explanation. You aren't here to weigh in on my choices. In fact, I don't know why you are here at all."

He opened his mouth to argue. I stood and sliced my hand through the air. "No, you gave up the right to have a say in my decisions and in my life when you chose the pack over me. Save your concern for someone you deem worthy."

Sebastian shoved his hands in his pockets. "What about your best friend?" he asked. "Do I get a say? Or is it Cora's way or the highway?"

"This isn't a democracy. My home needs protecting; it's also my livelihood."

Sebastian sighed as he nodded. "So tell us what we can do to help, and how we can minimize the risks."

I pressed my lips together and gave the trio a hard stare. "We have four people. We can do it via the elements if each of you represents them."

"We aren't elementals," Dave pointed out.

"It doesn't matter, you still hold a source of magic. I can tap into the power for the blessing. You act as a conduit."

"Fine," Hudson muttered.

"I've literally gone my whole life without being drawn into one magical spell," Dave said as he looked at the floor. "Then I become entangled with the Roberts' women and I'm involved in exorcisms and blessings. I lost someone I love." Thick silence coated the room before he snapped his head up and pinned me with his gaze. "I'm so angry at you."

I swallowed and Hudson tensed. "I know." Saying sorry wouldn't take away his pain, and it was too little of a sentiment for his loss.

"Promise me we will kill the bastard and make it hurt."

I moved toward Dave and wrapped my hands around his tight fists. "He will die screaming. I will make sure of it."

He stared at my face and saw my resolve. He nodded and rose to his feet. The door burst open and Aunt Dayna came bounding through. "It's back," she declared.

"The demon?" Hudson asked as he jumped to his feet. Now everyone was ready for battle.

Aunt Dayna spun in a circle, her fluffy skirts floating around her, and giggled. "My house, silly man."

The boys blinked. "The house that got sucked through a portal to Hell?" Dave checked.

She parked her hands on her hips. "What other house would I be referring to?"

Dave ran a hand through his hair. "I'm too old for this shit."

"We need to reset the wards," Dayna chatted on. "Should only take a day or two."

"You're leaving?" I checked.

She nodded. "Yes, and my sisters. Plus my mother," she muttered with a dark look.

"Excuse me," Dave snapped as he rushed out of the room. I didn't envy my Aunt Liz. He looked like a man on a mission.

My heart sank, and I squeezed my hands into fists. Without my aunts and grandmother, I'd be vulnerable to the encroaching evil. But my family didn't know the stakes. "We've banished the demon. You are about to bless the house—that should sort out the blood magic. Surely you can hold the fort for forty-eight hours? There's a waiting list for our rooms, so you'll be able to make some extra cash."

I forced myself to smile. "Sure."

Hudson was studying my face like it was a map to my inner thoughts. He was too perceptive and could see through to the bubbling anxiety sitting beneath my flesh.

Aunt Dayna headed up the stairs after Dave. I tilted my head toward the examination room and broke the awkward silence settling between my best friend and ex-boyfriend. Although we hardly got off the ground, so I guess he doesn't warrant an ex status. "I need to gather a few items and prepare. I'll meet you in the garden in half an hour."

They'd left. Including Dave, which meant I'd had to rope Rebecca into the fray. We stood in a circle around the grave where Tom's bones had been laid, the place where the roses had first grown. Each of us held a white pillar candle and as I began the blessing, they lit them one at a time on my signal. The elements answered my call, and power flooded the circle. It was a good thing my family had left. By all rights I should be tapped out of magic, with an exorcism and a retro read in twenty-four hours. The truth was, I got tired, but my well of power never ran dry, it rarely ran low. My family would expect me to pull on the magic of those in the circle to supplement my own and conduct a successful blessing. I didn't need their power. The portal upstairs was a testament to that.

I finished the blessing with an extra burst of power that seeped into the ground and raced along the network of roses. My magic twisted with the blood spell and tugged. It latched onto the satanic priest's signature and the boy's genetic code and disentangled it from my own more primordial lineage. A rumble shook the earth, causing the four of us to look around. Was it natural or unnatural? Benevolent or malevolent? The vines snapped around us and out of the earth rose hundreds of bones. They shook themselves free of the dirt and continued rising to waist height. They covered my grounds in every direction. Some were those I'd laid to rest, many weren't.

Hudson eyeballed the bones like they were branding irons. "Where the hell did they all come from?" He sniffed the air. "Some of these are fresh, Cora."

A deep scowl settled on my face. "Our resident Satanic priest has been a busy man. No wonder the blood magic was so strong. He's been feeding it daily."

Rebecca swallowed. "Now what?"

I placed my candle on the floor. This was going to be horrible, but there was only one way to fix this. I reached out and grabbed the first bone. Instead of falling into a retro read, I slammed my walls down and forced my power through the connection. Stephen felt me, and I braced myself for the impact of his rebuttal. It never came. The bones shivered in the air as a burst of cleansing energy flowed from me. Flames ignited every single bone, creating an impromptu firework display. "What on earth?" I said.

The flames shot high, then the bones turned to ash and scattered over my grounds before sinking into the dirt. The bloodied roses shed their crimson, and the blooms turned obsidian.

"Oh shit," I muttered, spinning in a circle. A whip of soul-sucking magic stole my breath, leaving me feeling both weaker and stronger. My fingers twitched as I attempted to call upon my element. The water in the Mississippi no longer listened. Stephen Proctor had stripped my elemental power and left me feeling bereft of my matriarchal lineage. This was Lucifer's doing. Now I was my father's daughter, and shit was about to go down.

"They're not bleeding anymore, that's a good thing, right?" Sebastian asked.

"Bleeding, they were still alive. Now they are death."

"You mean dead."

"No, I mean they are *death*."

Game on Lucifer. You want Cora Roberts, Daughter of Death? Then you will damn well have her.

Chapter Twenty Nine

My heart is a sucker.

A storm was coming. My wards were down and, as far as anyone knew, I was powerless. We were sitting ducks, waiting for Lucifer to arrive with an army.

We were back in the parlor with Hudson seated next to me.

Sebastian looked at a message on his phone and sighed. "I've got to go," he said. "My father is losing his shit. He wants the treaty, but doesn't want to be at the beck and call of your grandmother. I need to talk him down from whatever he's planning."

My eyes closed, and I fought the rising panic. Everyone was leaving. "Of course. Don't let him sign it, Sebastian," I said, opening my eyes. "My grandmother doesn't mean well with that treaty."

His eyes tightened. "What are you talking about?"

Hudson took a sip of the lemonade Maggie had brought him, then leaned forward and leveled Sebastian with his Principal stare. "Eloise wants us united in a war she's about to incite between humans and supernaturals."

"To what end?" Sebastian asked. You can take the prince out of the politics, but not the politics out of the prince.

Hudson glanced at me. I gave him a nod. We might not be together, but I still cared and wanted to avoid the bloodshed my grandmother planned. "Eloise wants to be at the top of the food chain. The other factions are cannon fodder for her war."

Sebastian went so still you'd think he was part of a Madame Tussaud's display. "I was going to tell you," I whispered.

A frown appeared on his forehead, and he avoided my gaze. "I need to go." The door swung open, and he was gone.

It was a good thing, the fewer people around to witness Lucifer's attack, the better. Less people to keep breathing. It was safer this way. Now to get rid of the Principal.

"I have research to do," I stated. "So you can go back to the stables, or the pack." *Or Mercy.* He didn't move. I turned my head and glanced at him. He leaned in, causing my breath to hitch. *Don't kiss me. I don't have the willpower to say no, even when I know you are bad for me.* "There's nothing happening here, anyway. The blood magic has lost its traction." *Lies. Huge stinking lies.* He tilted his head and ran his nose behind my ear, causing shivers to dance down my spine.

"You smell different," he growled.

I laughed. It was a nervous sound that struggled to cover my panic. "Your nose is off. I suggest you stick it close to someone who wants you in their personal space."

He inhaled, then leaned back. His pupils had turned vertical as his prehistoric cat sought to decipher my scent. "What's changed, Cora? What did that cleansing do to you?"

I swallowed, sucked in a deep breath, and fought with my beast. She was clawing at my insides, trying to get out and protect me from harm, any harm. His eyes narrowed and a green sheen ran over them. My beast paused in her struggles and examined his lurking monster with interest. Fuck. Houston, we have a problem.

I trembled with the harassed power I was restraining. His eyes tightened, and he leaned his forehead against mine. "Whatever it is, you can tell me."

Wrong. How can anyone say that when they don't know what it is? It's an empty promise that would turn to ashes the second he learned the truth. If he wasn't with me, he wasn't invested in my life, in my care. He didn't love me like I could have loved him. *Because you are unworthy.*

"I need," I breathed.

"Yes?"

"For you to leave."

His head shot back, and darkness clouded his gaze. He stood and stalked toward the still open door. That was easier than I thought. Like he could hear my thoughts, he paused, spun on his heel and prowled back toward me. I jumped up and took one step back before he caught me around my waist and slammed his lips against mine. It was ferocious, fevered; it promised violence and peace, love and sorrow. It stripped me bare and forced me to witness his vow, that he was in love with me, that he wanted me, that he would kill for me.

I ripped my mouth from his and panted. "No," I shook my head. "I won't be some dirty little secret you come calling on in the midnight hour while you weave your power over the pack. It's all or nothing."

He sucked in a breath. I'd said I wouldn't take him back, and now I'd given him an in. I was weak. But we all made mistakes. He squeezed his eyes closed, and I knew his answer. I pushed on his chest. He let me go with a pained look. "Leave," I stated.

He ran a hand through his hair, and his gaze blazed with longing. "I need some time."

I shook my head and wrapped one hand around my waist while I pointed at the door with the other.

"Stubborn female," he muttered. "Would it kill you to see it from my perspective?"

"I already do, which is why I am asking you to leave. Not the house, but my stables."

"No."

I groaned and glared at him. "You have the emotional intelligence of a toad. I am not joking. You said you'd leave once Aunt Liz wasn't possessed—well, she's not possessed."

He folded his arms. "I said I would leave once you weren't in danger. Death has come stalking you, Cora. That is the nature of danger."

"Death isn't dangerous, evil is."

"This isn't over," he growled before turning on his heel and striding out of the door. Perhaps when this was over, I could get myself a nice little house somewhere remote. Everywhere needed guest houses, right? The door banged closed. He wouldn't follow me, not with the pack demanding his attention. I would be blissfully alone, like now. Time to do some research. Lucifer fucking Morningstar had met his match. He thought me to be vulnerable and weak, he should know better. A Roberts woman was never vulnerable or weak. Even laying bloody and broken in the dirt, we would always be stronger than evil.

Chapter Thirty

Pineapples and primordials.

I shoved another book away from me with a huff. There was nothing in the lore about bloody roses that turned black. I'd been at this for hours and had devoured too much useless knowledge and far too many cookies. But other than restocking my plate, nobody had disturbed me in my office.

Maggie barreled through the door brandishing a tea towel like it was the Olympic torch. I spoke too soon.

"What's wrong?" I asked.

She darted a look around the room. "We got ourselves an Elvis."

I frowned. "A what?"

"An Elvis," she repeated with a huff.

I glanced around the room currently devoid of spirits—because while I can see dead people, no one famous had turned up yet. "Where?"

She jerked her head at me. "Come, I'll show you."

She hustled down the hallway, past the kitchen and sitting room. I waved to the Sampleton's, a pair of vampires who visited three times a year and never failed to tune in for the reruns of Cheers. The sofas around them were packed full of supernaturals, all chuckling at the classic show. Most probably remembered it the first time around.

Maggie turned right. Where the hell was she going? The only thing down there was…

She threw open the toilet door, and suddenly everything made sense.

"He's dead," she told me. Thank you, Captain Obvious, thank you very much.

"That's Colin, the mailman," I hissed, moving closer and grabbing Maggie's arm to draw her into the cramped bathroom before closing the door. "Why is Colin the mailman dead with his pants down around his ankles while he pops a squat on my toilet?"

Maggie squinted at me and wrinkled her nose. "Don't you take your pants down when you go to the toilet?"

I pinched the bridge of my nose. Why me? "Why is he here at all?"

She blinked and looked back at Colin. "He said he felt unwell. I asked if he'd like some homemade lemonade. He came in, drank the lemonade, went to the loo and didn't come out. I gave him fifteen minutes and four knocks before I forced the door. Then I found him like this and came to get you."

"Your lemonade?" I wondered. Had she finally killed someone with her cooking?

She shook her head. "No, one of the aunts made it."

I dug into my pocket and pulled my cell out. "What are you doing?" Maggie asked.

"Calling the sheriff."

"Why?"

It's a testament to how severely messed up my life is that people would find it odd for me to call the police when someone dies.

"Because," I explained as I brought Robert's number up, "human death means human law enforcement."

"What's wrong?" he asked on the second ring.

"Colin's dead."

"The mailman?"

"The one and only."

"Your place?"

"Yes, come through the front."

He sighed. "Give me ten minutes."

The line cut out. "Stay here," I said to Maggie as I pushed open the door. "Guard the body."

She cast an anxious glare at Colin. "Why? What's he going to do?"

"Nothing. I don't want our guests to find him."

"Ah, good thinking."

I clicked the door closed, then thought better of it and reopened it. "Why don't you wait out here?"

Maggie rushed out and shut the door behind her. "Good idea."

Seven minutes. That's how long it took until the sheriff's car was rolling up my drive. Of course, my life wasn't complete without the Terror of Tennessee exiting his house and casting a dark look at the sheriff as he got out of his car and popped his hat on, keeping the worst of the sun's glare off his shaved head. Nothing to see here, Principal. Move it along and go flex your muscles at some poor unsuspecting little shifter woman. Leave the death and destruction to me… because that's all you've left behind. Asshole. Yikes, I didn't realize I was this bitter.

Robert jogged up the steps and swept his gaze around the house. "Do I want to know about the black roses?"

"No."

"I didn't think so. Where's the body?"

I swung the door open as Hudson jumped the porch railing and landed next to us. I rolled my eyes. "What do you want?"

"There's a body?"

"Human," I snapped low. Not wanting to air my dirty laundry to the entire house. "And therefore, not your concern."

Hudson's eyes tightened. *Your fault douchebag, if you wanted to be part of my life, you actually have to be part of my life.* Of course, he ignored me. He waltzed in like he owned the place. Whatever, I'm over his bullshit already. Probably. Maybe. Well, no, but I will be soon. There are things women do when they've been rejected, right? Girls' night? Rebound guy? I sighed and closed the door before leading the way to the bathroom. Maggie's eyes widened at my entourage.

I waved at the door. She opened it and tried to blend into the wall as poor Colin was revealed.

"Damn, you got an Elvis," Hudson muttered.

I swung my glare to him. "Is this a weird ass shifter thing? Wait, was Elvis a shifter?"

Hudson's eyes sparkled with amusement, and his lips twitched.

"Natural causes?" Robert asked me as he stepped into the bathroom.

I shrugged. "How would I know?"

Robert knelt in front of Colin before quirking a brow at me. "There's a lot of weird shit that happens around you."

I folded my arms and leveled him with the Roberts stare. "So I've been told."

"What happened?"

"Colin felt unwell when he came to drop off the mail. He asked to use the toilet and then didn't return. Maggie discovered his body."

"Just like that?" Robert asked.

I narrowed my eyes. "Yes. Just like that."

"Fine, I'll call the coroner."

I huffed. The coroner was a cantankerous bastard with a chip on his shoulder the size of the Empire State Building.

"You don't like the coroner?" Hudson asked.

"I like him fine. Ray just doesn't like me."

"You showed him up in front of the entire department," Robert pointed out.

I shrugged. "I don't joke about death. If I say someone didn't die of natural causes, then I expect to be listened to. The lazy old git wanted to get home to his wife and the roast lamb she had ready and waiting. My thoroughness put a dampener on his plans. So now he hates me."

"You got between a man and his meat," Hudson stated with a nod. I pinched the bridge of my nose. Save me now.

"How long?" I asked Robert.

Robert leveled me with his own stare as he straightened. "You got somewhere to be?"

"No, I have a full guest house of vampires and shifters that will smell the decay soon."

"Too late," Hudson muttered. "They are being polite about it."

"Don't try to help me," I growled.

His hands rose in the air. "I'm not."

Robert's eyes darted between me and Hudson. "What did I miss? I thought you two were–"

"We were. Now we're not.," I stated. Hudson's smirk dropped along with his hands. "Mr. Abbot was leaving."

"The stables or the house?" Robert checked. The sheriff was an information gatherer, after all, and it was widely known that knowledge was power. What many failed to realize was that knowledge without wisdom was dangerous.

"Both," I stated.

Hudson's gaze bored into mine. "The house."

I suppressed a growl and lifted my head. "I'll be in my office. Let me know when the coroner gets here."

I stomped away from the bathroom and practically jogged downstairs. The cat didn't make a damn sound behind me, but I knew he was stalking my every move.

I threw open the door to my office and spun to face him. He clicked the door closed behind us.

"Really?" I started as I clenched my fists at my sides and paced in front of him. "You want to do this here? Why stay? Are you trying to torture me?"

His eyes softened, and he reached for me. I took a step out of his reach. I would forever be out of his reach. "I don't want to hurt you."

"Too late."

He ran a hand through his hair. "It's not easy having all this responsibility and juggling all the different political wildfires."

"Let me make this easy for you. Leave. Don't call, don't look me up, don't even say hi to me on the street. If I pass you by, look the other damn way."

"Impossible," he stated. "That's like asking me not to look at the sun."

"Then I suggest you take up night strolling."

"Or the moon."

I threw my hands in the air and stepped in front of him. "Move to freaking Alaska."

"I can't leave you alone."

"You made your choice. I warned you."

"And the reasons still exist."

"You think I don't understand the restraints and pressures of the factions, that I hadn't thought through the ramifications of us being mated?"

"Clearly you don't and you haven't."

"I have. It's the reason I stayed away from you for months. The difference is—I stopped caring what effect it had on other people. I put you first, whereas you put yourself and your pack before me. In fact, everyone is before me."

"That's not true."

Ugh, I was so mad I could bring my house down with the force of my emotions. "Prove it," I roared.

"It's not that easy, and it doesn't mean I'm not struggling with it."

"Try harder, because I can't tolerate you looking at me this way."

"What way?"

"With regret. With indecision. With passion."

"I can't help the way I feel."

I'd had enough. He'd made his bed, and now he had to lie in it—without me. I couldn't stand this longing, this need—it would destroy me on a level no other had before. "Forgive me for not having any sympathy," I snapped.

"You're young."

I rolled my eyes. "Ironic that you are blaming your lack of adulting on my youth."

"No, I'm blaming your youth for your narrow-minded view on the weight of responsibility."

I snorted and stepped toward him. "That's rich. You have zero idea of the responsibility on my shoulders."

"Yes. The poor little lamb, sent to slaughter for the advancement of her powerful grandmother." Ouch, that stung.

Primordial power nipped at my fingers begging for release, wanting to show this man how powerful I was, and exactly what he'd let go. The beast inside me lifted her head to peer at Hudson and fought me for control. My voice came out multilayered. "That's a drop in the ocean compared to the overwhelming power we wield. You have thousands that depend on you to make the right decisions, Principal. We have billions. Not one soul would be untouched if we made the wrong fucking choice." I slapped a hand over my mouth as his eyes widened. Shit, shit, shit. I yanked on the chains, but the bitch had said her piece. She was content with making it known what he'd passed up. Thick silence coated the room as I waited for the judgment, the rejection, the loneliness that was ever present.

"What choices are those?" he whispered, stepping closer and tucking a stray strand of hair behind my ear. He'd seen, he'd heard, and he still wanted to be closer? Did this man have a death wish?

"The type of choices," I breathed, letting my hand fall from my mouth and onto his chest, "that I would have trusted my mate with before he ditched me for political gain." I pushed away from him and rounded my desk, needing the furniture between us.

"Except you didn't trust me."

"Not yet, but I could have. Now we will never know." I knew deep down it was true. I would have given him everything in time, trusted this man with my deepest, darkest secrets.

"Cora," he said, rounding the desk and entering my space again.

I tipped my head back but didn't move. I was done running from him. "Pack and leave the stables. Don't torture us both with your proximity."

Harry flew through the closed door into the room. "Pineapples," he shouted. "Miss Roberts, we have pineapples."

It took a second for my mind to catch up as I frowned.

"Pineapples?" I directed at Harry.

Hudson spun around in Harry's general direction. "Your resident ghost?" he enquired. Why was he still here? Hudson, not Harry.

Harry nodded. "The guests." God help me, if this was something about a fruit salad, I couldn't be held responsible for my actions.

"What's wrong with the guests?"

A howl ripped through the air, and furniture smashed above us. I darted a look at Hudson. "What the hell?" We tore up the stairs, following Harry's rapidly moving form.

Destruction and chaos reigned supreme in my home. Rebecca slammed a fist into the head of a large fox. "What is happening?" I asked.

"They're wildies," Rebecca stated as she downed a wolf with a strategic flick of her wrist. He crumpled to the floor and was out cold in three seconds flat.

My eyes widened as I took in the tens of shifters fighting each other in their animal form. Somehow Stephen Proctor had gotten to them all. A bobcat rounded the kitchen doorway and prowled toward us. Her tail twitched in the air as her eyes narrowed.

"Maggie?" I whispered. No, no, no. He couldn't have my girl. I wouldn't allow it. She snarled as Rebecca jumped in front of me and pushed me against the wall. Maggie prowled closer, her head low, and a look of malice was settled onto her features. This was bad, so, so bad. Two bear cubs came barreling through the crowd, snarling and baring their teeth at us.

"Don't kill Maggie," I said.

"Of course not. But if you have any ideas, they would be gratefully received," Rebecca said. "I knock them out and they keep getting back up."

She moved like a ninja as she batted Maggie off, her dress tore, and claw marks slashed across her forearm.

"I'm thinking," I muttered. A low animalistic rumble that made my teeth hurt and my bones ache echoed in the house. Harry froze and paled—impressive for a dead vampire.

"Pineapples," Harry whispered.

I swallowed the lump of fear stuck in my throat. "Hudson?" I whipped my head around and found golden eyes staring at me from a prehistoric beast.

"Where is he?" Rebecca asked, her attention absorbed by the constant flow of challenging shifters coming down the hallway.

"We have a problem," I stated.

"Understatement of the year."

"A bigger problem."

Rebecca punched a white wolf on the nose with a sickening crunch. Shifters were tough, but not made of steel, like vampires. It fell to the floor and pawed at its bloody snout. She swung her head back and caught sight of the terrible sabretooth tiger eyeballing us. He wasn't fighting like the rest. He was watching me, waiting for the moment I became vulnerable. I glanced at the front door, which was wide open.

An army of shifters turned wildies covered my lawn. So this was Lucifer's plan? He didn't want the hassle of raising a demon army, so he created his own using the hundreds of shifters that lived in the area. Worse, he'd sent in shifters to my guest house like a Trojan army and I'd failed to connect the dots and see it coming. Well, if we couldn't get out, we'd have to go up.

I put a hand on Rebecca's shoulder and began edging us toward the empty stairs that led up. "My rooms," I said. The wards there didn't rely on my absent elemental magic, they were set with something more powerful and primordial. It was the safest place right now, but it also meant showcasing my secrets to Rebecca. It was a risk I was willing to take.

We backed up the stairs. The snarling shifters followed, led by Hudson. "What's the plan?" Rebecca asked as we hit the first floor hallway. Hudson's eyes didn't move from me. Every step I made, he made. I was being stalked.

"Do you have a plan?" Rebecca gritted out as she herded me backward and kept herself between me and the gang of crazy shifters.

We started backing up the final steps. "My rooms are warded. Anyone who wants to hurt me can't get through."

"I thought the wards were down."

Now is not the time to be a perfect perceptive vampire princess. "These ones work differently."

"Huh." I wasn't getting away with that explanation. If I lived through this, I had some explaining to do. I reckoned it was a fifty-fifty chance.

Hudson's eyes narrowed like he'd figured out my plan to barricade myself in my rooms. "Rebecca," I mumbled.

"I know," she whispered.

A white ball of fur shot from behind me. It exploded into a terrifying menace the size of a fully grown lion with snarling teeth, silver eyes and curved ears that were flicked down in warning. Its tail twitched. "Bella?" I knew there was something off about that cat.

Hudson pounced, Bella inserted herself between him and Rebecca. He knocked them into the wall and they went down like a sack of bricks. Rebecca's head lolled to the side, and the overgrown White Furry Menace was sprawled in a heap of unconscious fur over her. I take it back. Most shifters weren't a match for vampire steel, except those that predated modern history. My heart twisted. I couldn't let Rebecca die, not on my watch. Power ripped from me and I cast a net of protection over Rebecca and my cat, saving them from the encroaching shifters that were trying to tear them to shreds. My other power, the one that both ignited my soul and terrified my heart, was easier to reach for without my elemental shroud of magic. Stephen Proctor made a huge mistake when he unwrapped this little gift. I tripped backward and my ass bounced off the edge of the wooden steps. Pain reverberated up my spine and down my legs, making me hiss. A second later, hot breath blew over my face and I was staring into the face of prehistoric nightmares.

"Hey there, your furry majesty," I whispered.

A snarl worked up his throat, and his fangs elongated. What in the ever loving fu-

"*Cora?*" Hudson's voice echoed in my mind, like he was shouting at me from miles away down a long tunnel. My hands skimmed up the giant paws and legs of the beast lurking over me before I buried my hands in the fur on his neck and gazed into his eyes. He was trying to reach me. I stretched out my mind and fought to get past the beast to the man. Maybe, because he wasn't like a normal shifter, I could reach him.

"*Come back to me, I need you,*" I aimed at him. It wasn't a lie. I was alone and terrified. My world was collapsing and everyone that could help me was gone or incapacitated. I *needed* him.

He snapped his teeth at me and growled. I clung tighter to his fur, not willing to believe that anything, including a Satanic priest, could come between us when it mattered the most. It was like staring into the face of death, and I should know, I'd done it enough.

"*I'm trying to–*" Hudson's voice cut out, and the beast shook his head. His fur rippled. I released him and shuffled back. A lion tried to muscle past Hudson. He turned and bared his teeth, making the horde of shifters shrink back. They recognized when they were outmatched and out-muscled. I glanced at Rebecca, still out cold under a glowing net of protection. Still safe. I closed my eyes and sent a wave of power out that made the shifters behind Hudson whine. The floor under me creaked. The more power I used, the bigger the target I put on my head. I was like a beacon for the creatures that hunted me.

Someone swept their arms underneath me and lifted. My eyes flew open in time to see the shifters pawing at their heads from the unearthly force I was flooding them with. The door slammed closed and Hudson's arms tightened around me.

"Can they get in?" he checked.

I shook my head and detached myself from him—a very naked Hudson stood before me. *Don't look, don't look—too late.* He froze, every single muscle stood rigid against his flesh. Oh good, he'd seen the light. Literally.

"What is that?" he asked in wonder. He took a step closer. Who wouldn't? Heaven was hard to resist. The promise of peace and serenity was a seductive lure that would lead even the strongest into its arms.

"If you plan on living, don't touch it," I said, pushing his arm away from the portal.

"That's not what I asked. Wait, is this what was hiding behind the door, the one you wear the key to around your neck?"

I glanced down, tore the chain off, and dropped it on the kitchen counter. "It's redundant now."

A howl of agony ripped through the air. I rushed over to my balcony, threw the doors open, and leaned outside. Hudson was at my back as we surveyed the gardens.

Stephen Proctor stood amongst the black roses, concentric rings of shifters kneeling before him like he was their master. Hudson let loose a growl, drawing Stephen's gaze to me. He smirked, raised his hand, and snapped his fingers. The shifters closest to him lifted their heads, then exploded. Their blood decorated the air before sinking into the ground. The next ring of shifters tilted their heads in the same manner. Oh shit.

Hudson trembled. I put my hand on his arm as I searched the rows of animals for anyone familiar, for the bobcat that I'd taken under my wing.

"If you go down there, you will be killed," I warned him.

"He's murdering my people," he snapped. I drew in a breath and gazed at the horrific scene below. Why was he killing the shifters he'd fought so hard to control? The ground beneath him rumbled at the same time as the portal behind us stretched. He was fueling the blood magic, squeezing open my portal and preparing for battle. Something big was coming. An echo of chanting sounded from Heaven that made the hairs on my arms stand to attention. They'd felt my power and were coming to obliterate my unnatural presence from the universe. Shifter after shifter fed the ground their blood, and the earth peeled away from Stephen, leaving him standing before a cavernous crater that disappeared into the unknown.

"Maggie," I whispered as a bobcat came staggering out of the house, down the steps and onto the grounds. Not that her life was worth more than the other shifters. It was that I couldn't conceive of a world without the little shy girl I'd watched grow into a confident woman. I glanced behind me as the portal breached the roof. Plaster toppled onto the wooden floors. It was too late now. They were coming come hell or high water. The least I could do was save those I love. I loosened the chains, my beast stirred and looked at the scene with interest. She narrowed her gaze on Maggie. She cared about what I cared about.

"Ours," she confirmed. I redirected our gaze to Stephen Proctor. "Kill." I gripped the railing and threw myself down to the ground, clearing three stories with ease.

"Fucking hell," Hudson muttered as he landed beside me. I turned my gaze to him, knowing I was displaying the ethereal eyes of my ancestors. He swallowed but didn't move back.

"Get the shifters off my property. While they are here, they are vulnerable," I commanded.

"What are you going to do?"

I grinned and my voice echoed with my beast's. "I'm going to tear the priest to shreds so he can meet his Lord in Hell."

I ran toward where Stephen waited. He eyeballed me with a smirk stuck on his stupid face. He thought himself safe on his self-made island. *Wrong Stephen, you might have been safe from an elemental, but not from me.*

I barreled through the remaining shifters and spied Hudson with his beast at his side, pushing those they could reach toward the gates. I pumped my legs faster. Stephen's gaze narrowed as he saw I wasn't slowing down. A foot from the edge of the cavern, I bent and leapt into the air. My beast helped to propel me toward our target. He whipped out a hand as I cleared half the space. I prepared to land and tackle him to the ground. I'd make this quick and brutal. I had no time for pompous posturing. Heaven's army was on its way, and I needed to be ready.

Heat scalded my leg, and my flight was interrupted as someone yanked me down. The world disappeared, and the breath left my body as I descended. I glanced down and found a monstrous three-headed black scaly beast with its claws wrapped around my calf and its jaws hanging wide open to display row upon row of sharp needle-like yellowed teeth. Dear god, he'd opened the pits of Hell and unleashed a legion of creatures which would lay waste to this world.

Jagged rocks caught my arm as I tumbled down the black rabbit hole. I looked up. The sky was a rapidly shrinking bolthole, and I knew in my heart once it winked out, I would never see it again. My spine ached with the force of my beast. She wanted to be free, to save us. If I unleashed her now, I might never be able to return to the self-imposed restraints. I could take my chances in Hell. It would be safer than what was coming. But Maggie needed me, my family needed me. The three-headed monster's claws dug deeper. I screamed in frustration and pain before unleashing a wave of power. The monster's six eyes widened before he released me. His scales rippled with fire as my power buried deep. Then he was incinerated, his ash floating above me as I spun past.

I closed my eyes and readied myself for the inevitable landing. Hell was buried in the crust of the Earth. It was a different dimension that required a journey, sometimes a fall, sometimes a tunnel—occasionally I'd heard of people actually going up to Hell.

"Cora!"

My eyes flew open. No, he didn't, oh you stupid, stupid fool. Hudson grinned at me as his body hurtled toward mine.

"What the hell are you doing?" I shouted as the wind whipped my face.

He cocked a brow. "Falling with you. Where you go, I go. I got the surviving shifters off your property lines, including Maggie and the cubs. Didn't think you could run off on fresh adventures without me, did you? We're a team."

I smacked a hand over my forehead as my hair whipped around. "You're insane."

"Where my mate goes, I go."

Ugh, he wanted to do a U-turn on our relationship while falling down a hole to Hell. Talk about under duress. *He jumped for us,* my heart argued. Yes, yes, we can discuss the finer details if we live to see the next sunrise.

Hudson twisted his body and dived toward me. His hand snapped out, and he grabbed my arm.

"Good going, hero. Now we are falling together."

"Who said you weren't a romantic?"

"Ha ha."

"What's the plan?"

"Plan? I don't have one."

"Right. Prepare yourself then."

"For what?"

He gripped my arm tighter, then flung his free arm out and tried to grasp the jagged rocks. They sliced into his forearm and hand like a hot knife through butter. Blood wept down his flesh.

"Stop," I cried out. "They are as smooth as silk and sharp as steel. You'll never get a grip on them."

"Designed by who?"

"The Devil, Principal, we are literally on the road to Hell."

I can save you both, my beast whispered in my mind. *Let me.*

My heart thrummed in my chest like a hummingbird. Hudson's intelligent gaze surveyed me with interest, like he knew there was an internal struggle taking place. Damn him. I could have fallen to Hell, but I can't take him with me.

"Let me go," I yelled.

He frowned and gripped me tighter. "No."

I refrained from rolling my eyes. He was picking a hell of a time to be chivalrous.

"Do you trust me?" he asked.

Deep deep down—yes, I trusted him. Maybe not with my heart, but ironically with my life. "Yes," I shouted. He smiled like I'd made his day.

"Then don't fight it," he instructed.

"Fight what?"

My vision tunneled to a narrow point. Hudson's eyes turned vertical, and I was sucked into their depths. My body trembled, then the sense of falling reversed and it felt like being suctioned into a tight, confined space. My breath left my body, and the world went dark.

"Cora?" Hudson's voice was loud in my mind, like he was inside it.

"What's happening?"

A roar tore through the air, the sound vibrated in my chest like it was coming from me. "Don't panic, I'll separate us in a moment. Once it's safe."

"Separate us?"

My vision lightened, and I found myself the passenger in a fast moving ride skirting the edges of my property. Wait, not a ride—a cat. "You dragged us into your cat?"

Said cat growled, and I felt his annoyance filter through me.

"Better than a ride to Hell."

Hudson's animal huffed in agreement. "Don't get pissy with me. Only a few minutes ago you were chomping your fangs threatening to make mincemeat of my face."

Regret and shame washed over me. I felt bad for pointing out a situation he had no control over.

"You're about to feel weird," Hudson declared.

"About to?"

The suction feeling began again, like I was being vacuumed out of the cat's body.

"Just go with it," Hudson advised. I glanced around. Hudson stood before me, scowling face-to-face with his cat. I pushed to follow the suction. The cat popped a plug in and stopped me from leaving.

"Umm, you can let me go now," I tried.

"No." The word was a low animalistic rumble. "Not safe."

Hudson folded his arms. "Let her go."

"Mate," the cat stated. My beast peered out at the cat with interest. She was weighing up his suitability. Oh boy, that's the last thing we needed.

"No," I said.

"Yes," Hudson agreed with his cat. "No more running. She is our mate. I will never let her go ever again."

"That's what you think," I mumbled.

Hudson raised a brow. "Whatever you are saying is making him bury you deeper in there, Cora. Try reassuring him rather than challenging him."

"He's an arrogant dimwit," I told the cat, and he huffed in amusement.

"Keverin."

"That's your name?" I asked.

"Yes."

"What's going on?" Hudson asked.

Huh, interesting. Keverin was keeping him out. "Mate," Keverin reaffirmed to me.

"He hurt me," I explained.

"Dimwit."

"Agreed."

"Mistake," Keverin said.

I sighed. "Maybe."

"Stay."

"I have to go. I have to save as many people as I can."

"Mistake."

"How about this? After this is over, I'll allow him a chance to plead his case."

Keverin's indecision rippled through me as he weighed up my offer.

"If I believe he truly wants a future with me, I'll give him one more shot," I offered.

The plug popped open, and my molecules rearranged themselves before reforming in front of Hudson. I shook my head. Wow, that made me dizzy.

Hudson clung to my arms and held me steady. "You okay?" he asked.

"On a scale of one to ten, that registered as a twelve on my freaky shit barometer. Do you often absorb people into your animal?"

His eyes narrowed. "No, never. If he didn't consider you his mate, it wouldn't have worked."

I fist pumped the air weakly. "Go me. Wait, you weren't sure it would work?"

He smirked. "I was one hundred percent sure."

I released his arms, feeling the solid ground beneath my feet and trusting my legs would hold me up. His hands hovered around me for a few seconds, ready to catch me should I fall. He would catch me, I realized. Always.

We were standing behind the main house, near the Mississippi River. The portal had breached my roof and was a glowing dome peeking out. I swallowed as the call of Heaven's army thundered in my mind. They were close.

"What's the plan?" Hudson asked. "I got the shifters off the property, but Stephen is still doing his mojo."

"He's opening a gateway to Hell."

"For what reason?"

My instinct was to lie, because admitting I was responsible for an expanding portal to Heaven would give him further fuel to conclude I was too dangerous. I pressed my lips together and swallowed. Lying is easy. The truth might hurt, but it was the right thing to do.

"The shiny ball that's expanding is a portal to Heaven." I folded my arms and refused to look at Hudson. "Lucifer wants to use it to get access."

Silence stretched like a taut elastic band. I glanced at him. His face was doing an excellent impression of granite. "How do we stop him?" he finally asked.

"I think we are about to receive backup."

He blinked, and I started toward the front of the house, Hudson and Keverin flanking my sides. It was too late to run.

I'd made my bed and now I had to lie in it, even though it may become a grave rather than a bed.

We rounded the building, and I struggled with the violent scene before us. Shifter bodies littered my lawn like carelessly thrown rubbish. I narrowed my eyes on Stephen. He would die. As we closed the distance, a figure emerged through the gates behind Stephen. Oh goody, Lucifer was here—now we had a party. Lucifer stared at the portal with barely contained glee.

"We have to stop him from reaching Heaven," I told Hudson.

Hudson gave me a look reserved for idiots.

"Cora," Lucifer shouted across the chasm. "Don't stand in our way. I don't want to kill you. It would be such a waste."

"You have the sympathy of the Devil," Hudson mused.

"Life goals," I muttered with a roll of my eyes.

"Leave now," I shouted to Lucifer. "And I might allow you to live."

Lucifer shook his head and shoved his hands in his trouser pockets. Only the Devil would turn up to battle in a three-piece suit. "So be it," he answered.

A flood of beasts erupted from the chasm. Things that fueled your worst nightmares, monsters with too many heads, teeth, and eyes. Limbs that arched at odd angles. I leaned back, avoiding the talons of one of the creatures.

"Could you have maybe tried to negotiate?" Hudson asked.

"With the Devil? There is no negotiating, trust me."

We took several steps back, Keverin angling his body in front of mine. Oh boy, he wanted to protect me. This would end badly.

"Keverin," I commanded. "Do not get in my way."

"He told you his name?" Hudson asked with wide eyes.

"Yes. And we can discuss the fact that your animal isn't an extension of you later. He's something entirely separate."

"Sure, at the same time let's talk about why you can open portals to Heaven, and are on a first-name basis with the Devil."

"Touché."

A ten-foot-long creature similar to a dragon turned high in the air and dropped toward us. Its eyes narrowed into vertical slits and his jaw sprang open.

"Tell me it doesn't breathe fire," Hudson muttered.

"I could, but I avoid lies where possible."

We turned and began running toward the house. Heat licked at my flesh as it released the first fiery breath. I didn't have access to my element, so I couldn't douse the creature with river water. But I was far from powerless. I needed somewhere I could defend.

"Head to the stables," I shouted. We changed directions and began sprinting to the stables.

Keverin was in front of us. Suddenly, he turned and leapt between me and Hudson. He roared and my teeth jittered with the awesome power. The dragon returned the roar, but it was pain filled. I spun and found it shaking its head before it crashed into the ground and tore a path into my lawn. What on earth?

A creature on four legs, resembling a wolf on steroids, shot out from between the trees and made a beeline for Keverin. Several serpents slithered from the cavern and across the earth in pursuit. I ran to the front door before pulling on my magic and throwing a pale gold net around the house. Similar to a ward, but much stronger. It would keep out almost anything.

Hudson crashed into me and sent me sprawling to the floor. I landed with an oof, the big oaf knocking the air out of my lungs. I tilted my head and watched as a beastie smashed into my glowing net. It let out a pain-filled howl that made me wince. Hudson glanced over his shoulder.

"Will it hold?"

"Yes. Now, can you get off me?"

"Keverin is out there."

He jumped to his feet and offered me his hand. I took it and hauled myself up before walking to the open front door and looking at the chaos. "Where is he?"

Hudson scanned the encroaching horde with a frown. "I don't know."

A clatter of metal echoed from the kitchen. We spun and ran the short distance, finding Keverin snarling in pain as he struggled in my net at the back door. Hudson reached out, but I grabbed his arm and yanked back.

"Don't go being a hero. You'd be in an equal amount of pain and just as stuck."

I stepped forward and reached out to hold Keverin's cheek. "Shush, you'll be free in a moment." The tiger calmed and stared into my eyes. I concentrated on the shining net and pulled the magic inside myself, only from where Keverin was tangled. It ebbed into me, creating a hole in the mesh. Keverin tumbled through, and Hudson grabbed me and pulled me out of the way. *Squashed by a prehistoric beast* wasn't what I wanted written on my gravestone.

"Thank you," I told him as I let the magic leave me and reinforce the net. It was the only thing standing between us and Hell's army of nasties. Keverin stood and nuzzled my side.

"I'm glad you're okay too, buddy," I said, giving him a scratch behind one of his enormous ears. A rumble echoed deep within him. Was that a purr?

"Hate to break up your snuggle fest, but we still have an apocalypse to avert," Hudson stated.

I rolled my eyes as I stalked to the living room and glanced out of the window. "Don't be so dramatic, it's not the end of the world." The real villains hadn't shown up yet—then it would be an apocalypse. The horde had set up a perimeter around the main house, and Lucifer was making his way up the steps. Oh no. That couldn't happen. I ran back to the front door. Hudson's arm wrapped about my waist and halted me. "Let me go."

"What is the plan, Cora?"

"To prevent Lucifer from entering Heaven."

A pulse of power ricocheted through the atmosphere. Hudson fell back with me on top of him. The horde dug their claws into the ground to avoid being pushed back into the crater, while Lucifer held on to the porch railing and rode out the storm.

"What was that?" Hudson asked as I scrambled to my feet. I swept my hand through the net and created a hole before diving through and closing it behind me. Hudson rushed forward and slammed his hands against it. He hissed but didn't retreat. Idiot man.

"Cora," he growled. "Don't you dare go sacrificing yourself for this fight."

I smiled. "I'll be lucky if there is a fight."

His eyes tightened. "Let me out."

I shook my head and ghosted my hand over his. "You are exceptional."

I turned and stalked toward the house. Hudson's protests remained loud and appealing. I could hide with him, but I wasn't a coward.

Lucifer cast a glance my way. "Let her through," he commanded the horde. They parted and allowed me entry.

"You've garnered the attention of Heaven's army, now what?" I asked as I joined him on the porch.

"Now I fight," he answered. "The question is, which side are you on?"

In truth, I was on my side. I fought for my family, for my friends. I cast a glance at the stables. I was on the side of my heart and neither Hell nor Heaven held it.

"Certainly not Heaven's," I answered honestly. The Devil dealt in lies, deceit, and sin and was clever enough to see through any untruths, so I avoided them.

"Good enough," he answered.

The floorboards beneath our feet trembled with pressure, and I glanced up. The swell of light and power expanded. I backed off the porch onto the lawn, Lucifer following. My roof gave up trying to contain anything and collapsed as the portal expanded. Tiles scattered to the floor and the rumble of Heaven's army droned in my head.

"Here they come," Lucifer muttered as we sunk behind the horde of demons.

The orb pulsed and spat out the first angel. Both terrifying and awe inspiring, angels weren't the peaceful creatures that humans prayed to. They were ruthless, cutthroat, and while they had the moral high ground of the pope, they used it to fuel their agenda. I didn't recognize her, but her golden wings shone with the light of the divine, and her armor glowed despite the shroud of night. Her blonde hair flowed in an unseen breeze and she brandished a heavy sword at the horde. *Yes, yes, you are very pretty.* The next angel came through, and the portal hummed and seemed to press against an invisible barrier.

I stepped even further back. "It's going to blow," I muttered.

Lucifer scowled. "Not before I gain entry."

I shrugged. "If I could control it, I'd have shut it down already."

The orb shivered, and the glow became unbearable. I shielded my eyes with my arm and sank to my knees. The air became charged and my gut clenched. He was here.

The final blast lifted my hair. They'd shut the portal. Was it too much to hope that everyone returned to their respective realms and left me in peace?

"Cora," a masculine voice rang out. I guess it was a long shot.

I dropped my arm and climbed to my feet. I raised my head and zeroed in on the angel closest to me. Familiar green eyes shone with recognition from a face made in the heavens and chiseled by the divine. His shoulder-length, thick flaming hair lifted as his wings swooped to keep him high above me. He didn't hold any weapons; he didn't need to. His touch was deadly and his power unrivaled amongst his kind. He wasn't even dressed in armor, he'd shown up in black pants and nothing else.

"Oh goodie, a family reunion," Lucifer drawled.

"Father," I acknowledged.

My father's eyes narrowed as he angled himself so he sank to the ground. His feet landed on the lawn and he stalked toward me. I didn't bow my head or sink to my knees, but I trembled with the effort to keep upright. He circled me, causing the hairs on my nape to rise. He finally stopped in front of me and tilted his head. I gritted my teeth and swallowed. If I was to be executed, I would do it with my head held high.

"You have defied the natural order," my father stated.

"Yes." Ignorance was not a defense, and he would only see it as more fuel to crush me like an ant.

"Why?"

The angels created a circle in the air, ready for the encroaching battle. The horde pulsed with their need for violence.

"The beings that aren't afforded the correct rituals to garner access to their afterlife are left in the cold, bitter world of purgatory. It is not okay."

"So you would have an open gate policy to anyone regardless of how they had lived their life?"

"No. That was my error."

He hummed under his breath.

Just kill me and get it over with. The adrenaline was making me twitchy and my beast pushed against her chains.

"Show your true self," my father commanded.

I shook my head even as prickles of awareness erupted on my flesh. "No."

"Now," he commanded. The word reverberated through my mind. My beast clawed at my insides, fighting to be released into the world. Bile burned the back of my throat as I kept her on lockdown.

He sighed, and I held his eyes with my hard-assed Roberts' stare. I wasn't a pure angel—which made me an abomination—but it also made me stronger when it came to resisting the call of the angelic overlords.

"Can we get on with it?" Lucifer grumbled. "I have places to be."

My father's eyes tightened with frustration. "Which side do you fight on?" he asked.

"My own. I fight for my family, friends, and for those I love." I glanced at the stables. Hudson was standing dumbstruck at the scene before him, but he was still safely behind my net.

"Family?" my father checked as he followed my gaze.

Shit. "Those I love," I clarified.

"Fine, then fight for those you love."

My father swung his arm out. His power tore a path in my lawn, the dirt flung high into the air, scattering far and wide. It made a beeline for the stables. Hudson took a step back and his pupils turned vertical as he tracked the encroaching threat. My body trembled, and I took off toward the stables and made a life-altering decision. I unwrapped the invisible chains. They disappeared in one fell swoop as my beast strained against my spine. I allowed the pain to ripple down my nerves, igniting my true form with power and intent. My father's power hit the stables, and the building exploded, brick and mortar expanding into the atmosphere. Hudson would survive a collapsed building, but not my father's intent. He would explode with the house. Nobody could survive that but an angel. I gasped as my wings tore free of my back. Blood glistened in the air, suspended. Almost there. I shot into the rubble and wrapped myself around Hudson, my wings arched and cocooned us. Pressure gripped my entire body. The world shrank to this one square foot of space. My beast leaked out a little more, and I lost my grip on reality.

"*Let me save us,*" my beast roared.

Shards of glass and rubble cut into the flesh of my wings, the sting bringing tears to my eyes. It was only pain. I sucked in a deep breath and let go of the final restraints. She tore free, and I took a back seat as my body doubled in size and my wings tripled in number.

"What are you?" Hudson asked. I glanced down at The Principal who was dwarfed by my true form. He was studying my new appendages with awe, horror, fascination, and trepidation. *Don't worry, Principal, knowing will make it much worse.*

My beast grinned, showing a double set of dangerous needle-sharp teeth. "I am your mate."

Oh boy.

He blinked at me, a frown settling on his face as he tried to put together everything he knew about me. Love was stupid. I stood to lose everything because my stupid heart demanded we save him. His gaze burned into my flesh as he picked me apart over and over.

"Who are you?" he asked.

An extra wave of power made my knees tremble, but I stayed upright. "You can call me Indigo."

Oh wonderful, my beast had named herself and was flirting with The Principal.

"Our mate," she corrected.

"Really? You want to argue the finer points of my relationship status with The Principal here and now?"

"No, I'm hungry." Our stomach rumbled. Hudson arched a brow and glanced at my stomach, which was near his eye line.

I froze. *"For what? Like chicken nuggets or gumbo?"*

"No. Souls. You've left me starved and bereft of my food source for too long."

"This is why I keep you locked up. You can't go around eating souls. It's not savory."

"Our father seeks to destroy us. We need all the strength we can garner."

"What's happening?" Hudson asked as Indigo and I fought an internal battle.

"Cora wishes to starve me," Indigo complained.

"That's not okay," Hudson agreed. I rolled my eyes—or at least I did in my mind. Idiot man.

"See, our mate agrees. I should be fed."

"Because he doesn't realize your version of food is soul sucking."

"It doesn't have to be a nice person."

"No."

"You aren't being fair."

I could practically feel her sulking. *"Okay, let's discuss this after we've survived the Heaven versus Hell showdown."*

"I won't be chained again."

"I understand." I already knew that releasing her would be the end of the restraints I'd placed on myself. The cat was out of the bag and I had to deal with it now.

"After this, we shall see to it that you are fed," Hudson said.

"You make an excellent mate," Indigo told him.

"Try telling Cora that."

"She can hear you."

He blinked. "Who is your father?"

Indigo opened her mouth.

"Wait," I shouted.

She ignored me. "My father is Abaddon." Hudson stared at her. "The Angel of Death," she clarified.

Hudson swallowed and eyeballed my many wings. I had over a thousand at my full height and breadth. My father beat me by a few thousand more. "I am Nephilim," Indigo explained. "Half angel, half elemental. They fear me because my strength outweighs many of their strongest fighters, and mixed with the power of an original elemental bloodline, I am almost unbeatable."

Here was the thing: the curse would have drained my father of his power and fed it into me. My mother had wanted to make me invulnerable. What she didn't count on was my father being strong enough to fight that curse. I'd siphoned enough power to make me viable, to develop into a dreaded Nephilim. Then my father had yanked the power source away, protecting himself.

The world went silent. My muscles were a tightly coiled spring, ready to defend Hudson.

"Cora," my father's voice echoed around us. Indigo sighed and unfolded our wings from around Hudson. She turned and surveyed the damage. The stables were flattened. Not a speck of furniture or wall was standing. It looked like a tornado had torn through my land. Death might be my father's first name, but destruction was his middle one. The horde was now thinned out, half of the creatures were dead or missing. The remaining creatures were quickly disappearing into the crater. Lucifer was long gone. Now his portal was closed, he was no longer interested. Thanks, Uncle. That still left me with Stephen Proctor.

"Can I eat him?" Indigo asked as she narrowed her gaze on the Satanic priest who was making a beeline for the property gates.

"Later," I assured her.

She snapped her fingers and Stephen froze in his tracks.

The angels still circled our position with various weapons at the ready. They weren't here for the Devil, they were here for me.

My father stretched his arms wide. "Welcome, my daughter, to your trial."

Indigo paused, and Hudson froze at her side. "This is between you and I," she said. "Let the shifters go."

My father pointed at Hudson. "That is no ordinary shifter. Is he your mate?"

No. "Yes." For fuc…

"Then this is pertinent to him."

"So I am to be on trial before you murder me?"

"Don't be so dramatic, daughter. If you had done anything too heinous, I would have already put you down. This is merely a trial to weigh your intentions and your divinity."

"Still hungry," Indigo reminded me with a glance at Stephen.

We were fucked. The angels lifted their left hands, silver strands of power flowed from them and joined to form a circle around us. Now we were trapped.

Chairs appeared out of thin air—more like mini thrones. The angels settled into them because their precious asses couldn't stand for ten minutes.

"Sit," my father commanded.

I glanced behind us, finding two smaller versions of the thrones. I folded myself into one, Hudson followed.

"I want to be clear. This is a trial to determine how you have lived your life up to date. This will inform our next decision."

"You mean whether or not you kill her?" Hudson checked.

"Indeed," my father agreed.

"How does it work?" Hudson asked. "Do you call on witnesses?"

My father threw his head back and laughed. "No," he finally said. "I will weigh her heart."

"Get on with it," Indigo muttered. "I have to eat."

"Let me out," I told her. *"You dreaming of sucking someone's soul will not win over the hearts of the angels."*

"Fine."

My vision went dark, then I was back in charge of my body, albeit in my Nephilim form.

My father moved toward me, and I braced myself. This was bound to hurt. His fingertips touched my temples, and Hudson twitched at my side.

"Calm down, Principal," my father muttered. "The pain is temporary and not damaging."

Sure, psychic pain wasn't damaging in the slightest. Damn emotionless angels.

My father's power flooded my mind as he searched my memories, my actions, my decisions. He lingered over the more painful memories of Neil's betrayal, losing Hudson to political idiotness, of my grandmother directing me for her own gain. He examined the moments I'd relived the deaths of individuals to help catch their killers, the fight with Ric Nichols and my strong ties to my aunts. He tested my strength of resolve to keep my beast under lock and key for years. He picked apart my life like it was a bug under a microscope and made me relive multiple episodes of pain and terror. Eventually, he stepped back. I slumped in the chair like a noodle.

"Are you okay?" Hudson whispered.

I side-eyed him and nodded. The silver ring surrounding us pulsed with power. It was oppressive and squeezed my lungs.

My father observed us with a scowl as he placed his hands behind his back. "On balance, you have done more good than harm, daughter." He looked pained to be saying this. "We," he opened his arms and encompassed the circle of angels, "want you to be our weapon."

I straightened in my chair and blinked. "No."

"You haven't heard me out."

I stood and faced my father. "I don't need to. I will not be used as a pawn any longer. Not for friends and not for family."

He gazed down at me with a patient expression. "There's a war coming."

I tensed. "I know."

"Perpetrated by your own grandmother."

"I'm aware."

"We can't interfere with the disputes of humanity."

I rolled my eyes. "Of course not. It's totally beneath you."

My father sighed. "No, Cora, it's against the rules. But that doesn't mean we can't stack the deck."

I shook my head. "No."

He narrowed his eyes. "Fine, then you will answer for your crimes against Heaven."

I scoffed. "You are blackmailing me with my life?"

His lips twitched. "If that's how you want to see it."

"Whose side?"

"What?"

"Whose side do you expect me to fight on? The supernatural community or the human one?"

"Neither and both. I want you to prevent it. Failing that, you will minimize loss of life on both sides."

"Humans are no match for us," Hudson inserted.

I glanced at him. *Don't make yourself part of this.* "True, but their numbers outweigh ours ten to one. We have magic and strength. They have technology and weapons."

"It will be a bloodbath," my father agreed. "Unless there's a voice of reason, someone to span the divide and conquer the fear of the unknown."

I squeezed my eyes closed. I was a bed-and-breakfast owner with a supernatural medical side business. I was not a political hotshot with talent for calming the masses.

"I will help you," Hudson stated, standing beside me.

I took a step away from him and held my hand out. He needed to distance himself from me. With everyone pulling my strings, I had a short lifespan and I wouldn't be taking him down with me. "You ran at the first sign of political heat. What makes this any different?"

He pressed his lips into a tight line, and his eyebrows knitted together. "I made a mistake."

Anger flared from deep within me. "As did I."

Hudson's fists tightened at his sides. "You've never done anything you regret? Something you think is right, that is protecting everyone—but in hindsight is wrong? Are you that self-righteous?"

"Enough," my father boomed. The earth shook beneath our feet. "You will work alongside the Principal, *your mate*, to avoid exposure, and if that fails you will preserve life at all costs."

"Fine."

My father nodded with a smirk. "We will be watching your progress, daughter. Fail and you will forfeit your life." The chairs disappeared, and the angels swooped up into the air. They cast one last judgmental look at Hudson and I before soaring into the sky and blinking out of existence.

I was being backed into a corner - again.

Chapter Thirty One

Tasty mortals.

Hudson and I surveyed the damage in silence while we picked our way through the wreckage and debris. Furry limbs were scattered amongst the carnage, their lives taken in a brutal sacrifice that in the end served no purpose. My pulse pounded in my ears and my body trembled. Stephen Proctor would pay.

"Now can I eat him?" Indigo asked.

I sucked in a steady breath and my vision narrowed on Stephen's frozen form. The darkness in me stirred in anticipation. It was time to stop hiding, no more suppressing my true nature out of fear of rejection. If I was looking down a loaded barrel, I would do so with my eyes wide open. I stalked closer to Stephen.

"Yes, this one you can eat," I answered Indigo.

Hudson's head swiveled toward me. "What?"

I side-eyed him as I prowled closer. "You want to know how far my darkness goes? Buckle up, buttercup, this is about to get Hitchcock scary."

My footsteps were steady and my shoulders relaxed as I reached Stephen. His form was frozen, only his eyes moved, because when death marked you, there was no running, no hiding, no reprieve.

Indigo pushed forward. I let her out and sank into the back seat to watch. She tilted her head and studied Stephen. A slow grin crept across her face, displaying her razor-sharp teeth as Stephen's fear scented the air. She inhaled like it was a sweet smell. The atmosphere was taut with anticipation. Hudson stayed close but silent. Part of me wanted him to look away, another wanted him to watch so he could grasp the horror I held inside me.

Indigo's right hand twisted and curled, her six-inch claws growing. "Don't overdramatize it," I muttered to her alone.

"I have been starving for so long, I am going to savor it. I will make us stronger, Cora, invincible. Hudson will worship at our feet because no other can match what we offer."

"Or he will run screaming because you look like you are enjoying it too much."

"Enough, he will accept us or not. If he doesn't, he's not worthy."

Her hand whipped out, and she dug her claws into Stephen's chest. She twisted her hand, reveling in the pain he couldn't vocalize. That was poetic justice. She squeezed her fist around Stephen's heart and constricted the blood flow while tears leaked from his eyes. Indigo leaned forward and licked one. "That was unsanitary."

She smiled as she tugged on Stephen's blackened soul, drawing it into his heart. It was an oily, slick sensation that made me grimace. Indigo tipped her head back and tore Stephen's heart out of his chest. Blood poured from the wound as the life left his eyes. Indigo spun to face Hudson and devoured the heart in three bites. He didn't move an inch, transfixed by the warmth that spread down my chin and coated my chest.

Indigo shrank in size so we were back to my human height and her teeth retracted. Our wings trailed on the floor as we prowled closer to Hudson. He tracked her movements with his vertical cat eyes. His head tilted down toward us as she stopped a few inches from him and then retreated, allowing me to come forward.

My stomach roiled, and I swallowed the lump in my throat. His eyes trailed from my face down my blood-soaked clothing to my feet. I raised a brow and waited. I would not retreat, it was too late. I laid my soul bare for him to judge.

His hands flew out and clasped my face, his mouth descending onto mine in acceptance as he kissed me. I sank against his body and clung to him. He was my lifeline, my anchor to the world of the living and light. Without him I would drown in the oblivion. That was a terrifying thought.

He pulled back and gazed at me. "I am in love with you, Cora Roberts." I blinked. "I don't care that you eat the hearts of our enemies. You are my mate, my equal, my soul."

My chest tightened. "I am in love with you, too. But there's a darkness in me I can't escape. To be with me means you must accept the horror."

"I accept all of you."

Movement caught my eye. I spun as Maggie came wandering through the gate in a dazed, naked state, two young boys stumbling behind her.

I launched myself toward her and wrapped her in my arms, the relief making my knees wobble. She hugged me back. "Thank God you made it," I mumbled into her hair.

She clung to me tighter. "You too. I thought for sure the satanic guy got you when you disappeared down that hole."

I released her and stepped back to examine the hole. I sighed. "That's going to take some serious landscaping."

Hudson nodded at someone behind me. I glanced over my shoulder, finding a small army of naked shifters spilling onto my land. They wordlessly began picking up the dead animals and carrying them away. How many had we lost because of my enemies? How many more would we lose?

Hudson scowled and stalked toward me. "Your enemies are now mine. Stop blaming yourself for the acts of evil perpetrated by another."

It took less than fifteen minutes for the shifters to clear out their dead and leave me with the rubble of destruction. I pushed Maggie into the house to find some clothes. She poked her head out a little while later.

"Um, Cora?"

"Yes?"

"Rebecca is caught under a net with Bella. Is that something you can help with?"

Hudson and I shared a look and then ran toward the house. I beat him up the stairs, finding a pissed looking vampire princess and White Furry Menace eyeballing me with fury.

"You left me out of the fight?" Rebecca snapped.

"Actually, you got yourself knocked out courtesy of The Principal," I said as I drew the power back into my body. The net shimmered, then shattered, leaving a cloud of gold dust behind. The White Furry Menace meowed her displeasure.

"We can discuss your alter ego later," I told her. She stuck her tail in the air, then shot down the stairs.

Hudson helped Rebecca up. "Sorry I knocked you out," he muttered with a flush of red on his cheeks.

"What did I miss?" Rebecca said, disappearing down the stairs. We followed her outside. "Fuck me."

"Stephen Proctor opened a Hell mouth, then we fought him and Lucifer," I explained, leaving some fundamental elements out.

She walked into the garden, studied the flattened stables, then spun and looked at the house. "Why is part of the roof missing?"

"There were dragons," I answered. Hudson shot me a look. I shrugged. It was the truth— there *were* dragons.

Rebecca raised a brow. Yup, I'd failed at that lie.

A car engine rumbled down the road. The sheriff's vehicle pulled in through the gates and then paused. The engine cut out and Robert got out of the driver's side. Ray the coroner climbed out the passenger side with a slack jaw.

"Bad time?" Robert asked.

I waved a hand. "We are having some work done on the property. Follow me, I'll show you the body."

The men edged around the gaping hole. "I told you there was something fucking off about her," Ray muttered.

"Can I eat him?" Indigo asked.

I weighed up her request. "No, Indigo, he's more trouble than he's worth."

She huffed in my mind. "Spoilsport."

Cora Roberts—tamer of death and destruction.

Chapter Thirty Two

Outmaneuvered once again...

Hammering echoed in my mind, like an ice pick seeking my weak spots. I rolled over in bed. Ugh, it couldn't be time to get up yet. I peeked my eyes open. Sun was up, glorious. The hammering took up again. I sat straight up and frowned. What the hell was going on? It had been three days since Lucifer had scurried away with his tail between his legs and my secrets had been exposed to Hudson. He'd been busy burying his dead and smoothing over the agitation in the pack, whilst Dave was trying to weasel out who the traitor was amongst them. I hoped they were dead, so it was one less problem for Hudson to deal with.

My aunts had returned and Anita had replaced the earth, closing over the crater like it never existed. My grandmother had flown back to The Order's headquarters after replacing the wards on Dayna's house so she wasn't witness to my destruction.

In the wake of the destruction and Stephen's demise, my elemental power had returned with a flourish, wrapping around my beast like a comfy blanket.

The thumping sound became more insistent. I eyeballed the White Furry Menace who'd made herself comfy on my chair in the corner. She gazed back at me, all innocence and light, like she didn't turn into a beast when provoked.

"Best go see what that's about," I told her.

She blinked. Good enough. I pulled on some shorts and twisted my hair into a messy bun before swinging open my bedroom door.

I paused on the threshold. What on earth? Two pairs of jean-clad legs dangled through the gaping hole in my roof, which had gained a new timber structure. I walked underneath the hole, folded my arms, and gazed up. Hudson's smiling face greeted me alongside Dangerous Dave's scowling one.

"What are you doing?" I asked.

"Repairing your roof," Hudson answered as he passed Dave a tile. Dave hammered it into place.

I sighed. "I was doing it," I explained. "You don't need to do that."

Hudson smirked, then jumped down and landed in front of me. He backed me up against the kitchen worktop before grabbing my hips and lifting me onto it. I kept my arms folded and lasered him with my Roberts' hard-assed stare. "I'm a capable woman. I won't suddenly become the helpless damsel in distress for you to tend to."

He grinned. "I'm doing something nice for my mate. I am not trying to control you." He drew me closer as he pried my arms apart. "It's okay to depend on someone," he said as he dropped a kiss on my forehead. "It doesn't make you weak. Together, it makes us stronger."

"Fine, you can repair the roof," I conceded.

"Of course, your lack of a roof could be resolved if you moved into the pack house with me."

I pushed against his chest and slid off the kitchen counter. "No, this is my home, my livelihood."

"Mates don't live apart," he stated as I backed away. I couldn't think straight when he surrounded me with his delicious scent and feverish body.

I shook my head. "Your mate, if it is me, is an independent woman with a business and a job. I will not hang around your house barefoot and pregnant."

"Of course not. Shoes are important for foot protection."

I rolled my eyes. "We just got this show on the road. We can take this slow, a step at a time."

He narrowed his gaze, and the hammering stopped from above us as Dave eavesdropped on our conversation.

"Fine," Hudson drawled. I released the breath I'd been holding and relaxed my shoulders.

"I'm glad you're being agreeable."

A knock sounded on my door. I turned, swung it open and found Rebecca hanging out with my ghost. Harry pressed his lips together like he was holding in a laugh.

"What's up?" I asked her.

She glanced over my shoulder at Hudson. Oh, she needed The Principal's attention. I stepped to the side. Rebecca extended her hand. In it was a bright shiny key.

My gaze snapped to it. Then Hudson, then Rebecca. I shook my head. "No, nope, not happening."

"Paid in full for six months," Rebecca confirmed.

Hudson plucked the key out of her hand. "If you won't come to me, I will damn well come to you. Like I said, my mate lives with me."

Outwitted again by The Terror of Tennessee. What an idiot.

Chapter Thirty Three

Hudson

Fear and shame coat the walls of the room, thick and sticky like the humid Louisiana atmosphere. The concrete room was bare of anything but two chairs. Travis stared at the floor from his position on the central chair, not daring to meet my gaze as Dave stalked around him, a wolf circling his prey. He'd confessed to his sins, to being a pawn in Stephen Proctor's plans. He'd dosed the supplies, various items over weeks to avoid suspicion. What I needed to know was, why?

"Travis," I growled. His head hung lower. "Tell me why. We lost so many of our kind because of you."

Dave vibrated with violence. He was seconds from tearing his head from his shoulders and bathing in his blood like my mate had done to Stephen. He probably drew a line at eating his heart.

"Why?" Travis murmured. His head snapped up, and he met my eyes. "Because of your mate," he spat, like the word disgusted him. "Do you know what's coming?" he asked.

"Why don't you enlighten us?" Dave drawled.

Travis blinked a slow purposeful motion. Power whipped out from him, a wild unnatural energy. My beast rose to the surface and snarled. Dave paused. If he'd been in wolf form, his hackles would be raised.

The world dropped away, and we stood on a battlefield. Shouts of agony and terror cascaded around us. The sky was tarnished an apocalyptic black and red. Thunder rumbled the heavens, and Hell answered the call with a deafening roar.

Dave turned to me, his eyes wide. I spun and found a woman with obsidian wings amongst the carnage. Copper hair flowed in the breeze as she held in each hand a beating heart.

With a growl, she stretched her jaw, revealing two rows of needle-sharp teeth, and tore into one heart.

"What the actual fuck?" Dave said. The ground shook and a malevolent presence exploded behind the woman. She turned and its mouth lurched open. She flung her hands out and welcomed it as it swallowed her whole. My muscles twitched. I knew it wasn't real, but my mind was taking a hot second to catch up.

Travis let loose a howl. He staggered forward towards Dave. Dave snapped his neck and Travis crumpled to the floor. In human terms, it was death by forced suicide. Travis knew the consequences and forced our hand. The vision flickered in and out before returning to the room.

"Was that your mate eating beating hearts?" Dave checked.

I sighed and sat in the chair. "Sit down, Dave. I have some things to tell you."

The tale from start to finish took less than ten minutes, but the implications would last a lifetime. Neither of us in our research and understanding had thought for a second Cora would be part angel. I knew she was hiding a creature, and I hadn't concealed that fact.

Dave stayed silent long after I'd recounted the events.

"You are sure you want to mate with her?" Dave checked.

"I've never been more sure of anything in my entire life."

He sighed like the weight of the world was on his shoulders. "So we protect her, like one of our own."

"She is one of our own."

He grinned. "Who knew Cora Roberts was a wee beastie with a bloody appetite?"

She was my monster, and I loved her all the more for it. *Whatever was coming for Cora, I would be right by her side.*

The End

Thank you for beginning Cora and Hudson's journey…

If you want to stalk me you can find me here –

Facebook reader's group – Adaline's Warriors (where you will find a group of the most awesome, like-minded people who are currently sharpening their knives).

Instagram - @adalinewinterswriter (my main hangout because of all the amazing, supportive people there).

Email – adalinewinterswriter@gmail.com

Acknowledgments

Liberty and Zoe. The best decision I made was to be part of Team Voodoo. You have become so much more than my PA's. You are my best friends, my world is a brighter place because of you.

Michaella, thank you for your friendship and alpha reading my raw story. Words can't describe how kind and invaluable you are.

My betas – Tanya, Shawna, and Stephanie – thank you for being the best team. Your input has helped to shape the story and bring the characters to life.

To all the above, a reminder that you are stuck with my ass. Congrats.

To my daughter, you are strong and an inspiration. I love your sense of humor and the unique way you see the world. Don't ever change.

Most importantly to *my* Dangerous Dave. You have believed in me and given me guidance through the struggles, doubts and worries. You are my light when I can only see dark. I love you.

Adaline x

P.S. Liberty continues to claim Hudson. Sorry ladies, I'll let you know if he's ever on the market.

Shadows of the Soul: **The Playlist**

Secret Love Song - Little Mix

Blow - Ed Sheeran

Shivers - Ed Sheeran

World on Fire - Daughtry

Great Wide Open - Thirty Seconds to Mars

Dark Side - Cece and the Hearts & Ag

Who Are You - Raign

How Far Does The Dark Go? - Anya Marina

Silent Killer - Alexina

Buried - UNSECRET (Feat. Katie Herzig)

Raise the Dead - Rachel Rabin

Printed in Dunstable, United Kingdom